THE MALEFICENT FAERIE

FOR THE LOVE OF THE VILLAIN

BOOK TWO

REBECCA F. KENNEY

First Edition: May 2023

Kenney, Rebecca F.
The Maleficent Faerie / by Rebecca F. Kenney—First edition.

Cover art by Ann Fleur

PLAYLIST

"Centuries" Fall Out Boy
"Once Upon a Dream" Lana Del Rey
"Be Mean" DNCE
"Heavy" Powers
"Once Upon a Dream" VoicePlay
"Witch Image" Ghost
"Hollow" Daria Zawialow
"Do You Really Wanna Hurt Me?" Adam Lambert
"Lucifer" Elle Lexxa
"Girl Like Me" Dove Cameron
"Nothing Else Matters" VoicePlay, J.None
"Can't Tame Her" Zara Larsson
"Cold As Ice" Ava Max
"Higher" Reinaeiry
"Trustfall" P!nk
"Bad Idea" Dove Cameron
"Teeth" 5 Seconds of Summer
"Be A Witness" UNSECRET, Fleurie
"Dirty Magic" The Haxans
"Holding Out for a Hero" Adam Lambert
"You Can't Stop the Girl" Beba Rexha
"Titanium" Corvyx
"Moments Before the Storm" Poets of the Fall

TRIGGER WARNINGS

Age gap between fantasy characters

Attempted (unsuccessful) rape

Blood used in magical rituals

Gaslighting, light BDSM, light spanking

Suicide ideation, depression, mild PTSD

Negative self-talk, violence, death, war

Explicit intimate/spicy scenes

1

The Princess and I shouldn't be here.

As her bodyguard, I should know better than to indulge her, but—Eonnula help me—she's so damn persuasive.

When she looked into my eyes this morning, clasped her hands, and said fervently, "Aura, I want to go to the Lifegiving Festival," I couldn't tell her no.

Mostly because I wanted to go, too. I long to feel the Surge, when the adoration of the crowd reaches its height and our magic is refilled, when the presence of Eonnula Herself becomes a tangible thing.

Two high-spirited young women can only be kept in a castle for so long before they decide to indulge in a little rebellion. So the Princess and I are standing side by side, at the edge of the vast courtyard of the Annoran Temple, with the sweetish smoke from the incense burners filling our nostrils. The sunshine heats my skin, soaking into my leathers. Even here, with the incense so strong, I can discern the faraway fragrance of hot spun sugar, roasted bricklebones heavy with grease, and steaming fruit pies. After the Surge, most of the guests will scatter to eat, laugh, and exclaim over the experience. Others will find cool, quiet corners in which to fuck each other, purging the sexual arousal the Surge can incite.

But we won't stay for that part. We'll leave the minute it's over. It's a brief carriage ride back to the summer palace—shorter if we take the road through the woods. That path veers a little closer to the Daenallan border than the main road, but it's perfectly safe. None of the Daenalla have ventured into our lands for a couple of years now.

I've become a bit complacent, I suppose, but not totally careless. I insisted we bring along two of the best palace guards. They're flanking us now, a pair of grim-jawed mountains in bluesteel armor. Like the Princess, they're human, and the bluesteel offers them protection from magic. Not that they'll need such defenses here, among the joyful crowd of humans and Caennith Fae gathered for the Lifegiving Festival at the Annoran Temple.

Music shatters the air, the thunderous drumbeat resounding through my body, mingling with the jubilant blare of bright horns and the soaring melody of strings. The throng of worshipers has already been whipped into a frothy sea of adulation, and they're shouting along with the Priest who's leading the song. He stands on a platform under the blazing suns, naked to the waist, his lean body shining with sweat. He raises his jeweled staff and pumps his fist as he sways and sings. He doesn't have wings, but a pair of goat's horns mark him as one of the Caennith Fae. One of my kind.

Here in Caennith, our worship of Eonnula is boisterous, glorious. Every rite, every gathering like this one unites our minds, hearts, and energy, clearing the way for a fresh infusion of the magic we crave. When the worship reaches its peak, the Surge will come, refilling us all.

The humans in the crowd can't absorb and use the magic, but they will experience exhilaration and joy beyond anything they've ever felt. It will last for months, buoying them through their mundane lives.

I've been part of small Surges, minor adorations arranged by my three Fae mothers. Those gatherings did the trick, refilling my magic—but they didn't come anywhere near the reports I've heard about these huge celebrations. I crave the feeling I've been told about—the sensation of pure power and utter fullness, the delight of being blissfully united with a greater Being.

My stomach flutters with excitement as I lift one hand in praise, the other gripping the hilt of the sword at my hip. Even in a moment such as this, in a place so safe, so joyous, so full of our people, I can't afford to let my guard down. Our enemies haven't been seen in years, but that doesn't mean they've forgotten us.

It doesn't mean *he* has forgotten *her.*

I look to my left, at the bright, eager face of the Princess I'm sworn to protect. She left her coronet behind, and she's wearing a blue dress with a plunging back, a daring choice that blends with the bold fashions of the festival.

Princess Dawn is my age—twenty-five. Well... almost. Three months from now, on her twenty-fifth birthday, she'll come into her birthright. Like the other human royals before her, she will become a Conduit, a channel for Eonnula's power. She won't be able to perform magic herself, but her presence will bless gatherings like this one, opening the gates for an even greater Surge.

As the Crown Princess and future Conduit, Dawn is important to the kingdom. And she's important to me. My best friend, ever since we were introduced at age eight and I was given the job of protecting her.

My role as Fae guardian to the human Princess is more complicated than the average bodyguard assignment. Because this kind-hearted girl with the wide blue eyes and yellow hair— she's been cursed. Since birth. By no less than the King of the Daenalla himself.

I wish I could believe he has given up on her. Maybe he has, with her birthday so near and his curse about to expire. The assaults on the border have stopped, and there have been no attempted assassinations or kidnappings for over two years. I've been able to relax a little, and the Princess has been allowed some freedom—which might be revoked once her parents find out about this excursion.

Dawn has been shuttled from the primary royal residence to the summer palace, to the winter palace and back again, ever since I've known her. Kept inside castles, kept away from anything that might cause her harm—especially spinning wheels and spindles. She deserves to enjoy herself out in the world for once. To experience the glory of a Surge.

The Priest on the stage is practically screaming the lines now, urging the crowd to chant them after him. Every muscle in his torso stands out, hard and ridged. His mane of golden hair streams behind him, caught in the flow of wind across the great temple square. Magic is stirring already—building, swirling, rushing over him.

"He's beautiful, don't you think?" Dawn grips my wrist in a spasm of admiration.

"He is," I agree, while a different kind of thrill traces through my body.

As the Princess's bodyguard, I don't have much time for relationships. The most I ever get is a quick fuck in some alcove of the palace with a randy guard. They usually fumble over my delicate wings with a hoarse, "You like that? You like it when I stroke your wings?"

For many Fae, parts of the wings are erogenous zones. Not for me. I usually fake a breathy moan and redirect my partner's attention to more sensitive areas.

I'll bet that Fae priest knows how to tend to a woman's body…

Shaking my head, I clear away those thoughts and refocus my mind on Eonnula, our goddess, our protector. Giver of magic, by which our Priests and Priestesses hold back the Edge, the ever-encroaching darkness that surrounds our realm.

"Grant us your light, Goddess Magnificent!" cries the Priest.

"Grant us your light, Goddess Magnificent," Dawn echoes passionately, lifting both her hands.

"Push back the maleficent dark, the shadows of the Void!"

"Push back the maleficent dark, the shadows of the Void!" I repeat the words with Dawn, with the two guards, with the whole roaring crowd, with the shrieking music and the pounding beat. Everything is sleek bodies and lifted hands, shimmering fabric and bright faces, shining eyes and sun-soaked sweat, the glitter of wings and the flash of ivory horns, the quake of the ground as the crowd jumps in unison.

My heart is racing, my body thrilling, and I look up at the midday sky. Rings flash on my uplifted hand, and the light of the Triune Suns crashes into my eyes.

It's coming—I can feel it—the great wave rolling through everyone in the crowd, surging across the temple courtyard, racing up onto the platform.

A figure steps forward from a shaded bower on the stage—the King, Dawn's father, robed in white. As the royal Conduits, he or his wife always attend these gatherings. Two long strides bring him up beside the Priest, and they clasp hands, holding their joined fists high as the Surge crests—

It explodes through us all, a wave of quivering light, blasting from the clasped hands of the King and the Priest, rolling outward, reverberating through every human and Fae.

Dawn is gasping, shrieking—practically orgasmic with joy. The guard beside me groans in bliss, lifting his face to the suns. Not even bluesteel armor can divert the power of a Surge.

A tingle runs through my fingers, through the ten rings I've worn ever since I can remember. A faint pulse of joy quivers in my heart, and then it's gone.

All around me, Fae are visibly glowing, incandescent with the influx of magic, while the humans are crashing to their knees, weeping in ecstasy.

And I—

I feel nothing.

I want to cry.

Normally I wouldn't allow myself to weep in public, but the emotions around me are so violent, so enormous, I allow myself the luxury of a sob or two, and a few tears.

I wanted so badly to experience the Surge—but it's over, and I barely felt it. I was left out.

In this, as in everything else, I am different. I don't quite fit, not with the Fae or with the humans.

What is wrong with me? Have I been rejected by Eonnula for some sin I don't remember? Something I didn't realize was wrong?

Maybe the goddess is punishing me for bringing the Crown Princess here, when we were supposed to stay in the summer palace. Maybe I'm being condemned for my selfishness and stupidity. Cut off from the Surge, barred from the euphoria everyone else is feeling.

"We have to go." I seize Dawn's wrist and tug her backward. Reluctantly she yields, following me through the outer fringes of the crowd. The two guards accompany us, though one of them walks rather awkwardly thanks to the bulge in his pants. It's not unusual for a Surge to have a sexual effect as well as an emotional one. The temple chambers are wide open to the public after a Surge, to allow Fae and humans to release any sexual energy they want to expend.

Behind us, the rapture of the crowd swells in a new song, one of thanks to the goddess. Teeth gritted, I hurry the Princess along.

"Slow down, Aura," she complains. "What's wrong with you?"

"We shouldn't have come." I smack the side of the carriage to alert the driver, who wakes up with a start and snatches the reins. "We need to get back to the palace before the King does," I tell the driver. "Take the road through the forest."

A guard holds the carriage door open so Dawn and I can climb inside. He and his companion mount their horses, and we begin to work our way out of the maze of parked carriages and tethered horses surrounding the temple. On such days, the temple stables become full quickly, and the vehicles and mounts of the guests overflow into the surrounding streets and fields. We had to pay fifty tenets to a shop owner for our spot near the courtyard.

"What's wrong, Aura?" Dawn asks quietly. She sits across from me as usual, her cheeks stained bright pink from the Surge.

"Nothing." I adjust my gauzy wings as I take my place on the carriage seat. They're relaxed and limp at the moment, easy to manage, but I prefer not to sit on them if I can help it. "I just realized I shouldn't have let you do this. It's dangerous. Who knows what the King will do if he finds out we slipped away?"

"My parents love you, Aura. They wouldn't punish you. Especially since it was my idea." She sighs, tilting her head back against the seat cushions. "And it was worth it. I've never felt so alive."

"I'm glad." I force a smile.

"Was it good for you too?"

Men have asked me that question many times. Occasionally I've been able to respond with a wholehearted "yes." But I've also had practice faking a blissful expression and lying through my teeth, like I do now, to Dawn. "Oh yes, it was wonderful."

"Good." She gives a little wriggle of delight. "I'm so glad we did this."

She drifts off to sleep within minutes, her head propped against the cushioned side of the carriage. When we travel from one palace to another, she usually sleeps through most of it. I envy her, feeling so relaxed, so safe. So sure of who she is.

For my part, I have to stay awake. I need to be alert at all times, even when there's no sign of danger. I've foiled more than one attempt to kill or capture Dawn—the first time when we were both ten and I stabbed a kidnapper in the knee before he could carry her off. He'd managed to finagle his way into palace service, where he watched for his opportunity to steal her and deliver her to the Maleficent One.

Dedicated though I've been, I've grown more restless lately. Maybe a little jealous. Slightly bitter, because I see no end to this role I was given. I've always been trained as a fighter, as a bodyguard. My mothers taught me magic, and I had teachers who drilled me in swordplay, archery, hand-to-hand combat, strategy, and stealth. I learned history, music, art, science, and math alongside the Princess, benefiting from the best tutors. I'm grateful for that, of course, and thankful to be such a favorite with the King and Queen. I shouldn't want anything else— anything more. This is my life. This will be my life forever.

My mothers—Genla, Sayrin, and Elsamel—are the Regents of the Caennith Fae, subordinate to the human King and Queen, but working closely with them so our people can exist in harmony. My mothers are a triad, bonded by an affection so potent they conceived me during one night of especially passionate lovemaking. A miracle of Eonnula, or so they claim. Sayrin has tried to tell me the details a few times, but like most people, I'm not keen to hear about my parents' sex lives. It's enough for me that they remain happy together, hundreds of years after their first meeting.

15

I crave a love like theirs. But for some reason they've discouraged me from forming any relationships.

Every time I bring it up, Sayrin says, "Plenty of time for that later."

"Fuck 'em and leave 'em," Genla advises.

And Elsamel says, "Don't give your heart away to some stranger. Get to know them inside and out first."

I won't ever have time for that—not with my life threaded so tightly with Dawn's.

The carriage rattles over an obstacle and shudders so violently I have to brace my hand against the ceiling. "Goddess, what is going on?" I glance at Dawn, but she's still asleep. I brush aside the window curtain to peer out.

Darkness cloaks the window—a writhing, tenebrous smoke coiled against the glass.

It's mid-afternoon, and even in the deep forest, sunlight should be leaking through the canopy, dappling the road. Yet I see nothing but twisting, swirling shadows, like the darkness of the Edge, except the Edge is leagues away. Which can mean only one thing.

We're being attacked by the Daenalla. And not just any Daenalla, but the only Fae in this entire realm reckless and foolish enough to actually spin the Void into magic.

The Daenallan ruler, the Maleficent One, also known as the Void King.

Shit. What is the Void King doing here? It's too much of a coincidence that he's on this road, at this very moment. It reeks of spies and betrayal—maybe by one of the guards? The driver? Someone at the Festival? The last option is the most likely, but I don't have time to figure that out now. The fucking Void King is after us. And he's probably not alone. When he rides, his Edge-Knights usually ride with him.

My magic is not as powerful as my mothers'. I can perform simple glamours, shift air currents, make a spark for fire, and

16

create pulses of light-born energy that push back attackers. I can fly, of course, but not for long before my wings tire because, like Dawn, I've been kept indoors most of my life. My greatest strength lies in my combat skills.

I'm used to defending Dawn against single assassins or would-be kidnappers, not large groups of enemies. I protect her against the ones who slip through the castle defenses. But strong and skilled as I am, I haven't been tested in a battle against multiple assailants—especially not enemies this notoriously powerful.

From the teeth-shattering rattle of the carriage, I can tell the driver has already urged the horses to run. Pounding hooves shake the ground on either side of us—I can't tell if they are from the two guards' horses or from enemy mounts.

My mind races, cobbling together a likely scenario.

The Void King's shadows will overcome the horses and pull the carriage to a stop. The guards will fight on our behalf, possibly taking out a few of the Edge-Knights. I wish I knew how many there are. Four or five, we could handle, but no more than that, especially if there are Fae among them. And with the kind of magic the Void King wields, our chances are even worse.

I shouldn't have brought Dawn out here. Shouldn't have let her leave the palace, shouldn't have taken this shortcut. It's my fault, my own stupid fault. Our enemies left us alone for too long, and I became incautious, stupid, and self-focused. Fuck.

I should have insisted on bringing more guards—or at least Dawn's body double, Etha. Etha sometimes makes appearances on Dawn's behalf, acting as Crown Princess in situations where the King and Queen deem it too dangerous for Dawn herself to appear. Etha knows her role, and she's well-paid for the risk she takes. If she were here, she could switch clothes with Dawn—

But Etha isn't here.

I'm here.

Reaching over, I grip Dawn's shoulder and shake her awake. "We're under attack."

"What?" She rouses, staring at me blearily. "What are you talking about?"

"Switch clothes with me. Now."

"But—but your wings, and your hair—"

"I'll glamour them. Quickly, Your Highness."

"I can't let you—"

"Shut up and listen!" I hiss. "You are vital to the whole kingdom. I'm not. I don't think they'll kill me, they'll just carry me off somewhere. When they find out I'm not you, they'll let me go." I don't believe a word of what I'm saying, but lying has always come easier to me than it does to other Fae. I switch to a tone Dawn only lets me use when we're alone—the commanding voice of an older sister. "Do as I say, or I will kill Grayme when we get home."

Her eyes widen at the threat to her favorite dog. "You wouldn't."

"Then don't make me. Take off your clothes."

She should know I wouldn't kill her cantankerous pet—though I did yell at him once, when he snarled and lunged at me. I felt bad afterward and fed him a slab of beef, after which he and I secretly became friends. But perhaps that incident is fresh enough in Dawn's memory to convince her, because she begins to slide off her dress.

We swap clothing swiftly, clumsily. Dawn's gown has a plunging back that accommodates the telltale sign of my Fae nature—a pair of crystalline butterfly wings, veined with purple. They're flexible enough that I can sit or lie on them comfortably, but they stiffen when I'm ready to fly.

I screw up my forehead, casting a glamour to make my wings both invisible and intangible. The effect should last for at least an hour—I hope. I shift the color of my hair from blue to gold. Then I add Dawn's royal signet to the rings decorating my

18

fingers. My eyes are already blue, and a swift glamour hides the pointed tips of my ears. With my wings invisible and my hair matching hers, the resemblance should be close enough. Especially since no one from Daenalla has been granted a close look at the Caennith Crown Princess in years.

The Princess dons my tunic and leathers, and I color her hair a dull black. The glamour won't last long, but it might be long enough to give her a chance.

I'm breaking another rule by doing this—a promise I made to my mothers, that I would never trade places with the Princess. That I would let Etha do her job, and that I'd stick to my role: the defense of Dawn's life and my own.

But I don't have a choice. It's my fault Dawn is in danger now. My mistake—one I must rectify.

"I don't think you'll pass as a convincing bodyguard," I whisper to Dawn. "So I'll keep the sword. We'll pretend you're my maid. First chance you get, grab a guard's horse and ride. Or head into the forest and keep running until you lose them. If we're lucky, they'll focus on me."

"Aura, please don't do this."

"This is my duty. It's what I've been trained to do. With Eonnula's blessing, I'll be able to fight them off, and we'll continue the journey together. But you have to try to escape. Please."

She nods, her blue eyes wide. "Damn my father for not letting me learn to fight."

"I wish I could have taught you more. You remember the moves for breaking a chokehold?"

"Yes." The carriage jostles so horribly I can barely hear her answer. Something is happening outside—the guards are shouting, and there's a thread-thin whining sound, faint yet insistent, like wind through a crack in a wall.

"Goddess preserve us and help us, goddess be merciful and save us," whispers Dawn. She keeps chanting as I lean forward and peer between the carriage curtains.

Suddenly the entire front of the carriage lifts up. The floor slants dramatically, sending Dawn tumbling off her seat as our vehicle slowly shifts until it's perpendicular, balanced on its two back wheels, the front pointing straight up. The horses shriek wildly in terror.

The carriage slams down to the ground again, a bone-jarring crash. I hear at least one wheel splinter.

The door bangs open, and Dawn shrieks, clutching me. I hold onto her too, trying to maintain the mindset that I'm a coddled human princess, not a fighter. If our enemies think I'm helpless, they'll underestimate me; and then, once Dawn gets clear of this mess, I can turn the tables on them.

Tendrils of shadow undulate into the carriage like questing snakes.

"It's him, isn't it?" Dawn breathes. "It's the Maleficent One, the Void King. He wants—"

"Me," I say firmly, loudly. "He wants me. I am the Crown Princess, after all."

The smoky tendrils swerve, nosing toward me. Suddenly they whip out, lashing around my body while Dawn screams. They're cold and filmy, vibrating with latent power.

"Go," I snap at her. "Run."

And then the shadow-tentacles yank me through the open door of the carriage. I'm held aloft, halfway between the dirt road and the canopy of dark green leaves.

If I wasn't used to flying occasionally, this would be a lot more terrifying.

The Princess's two burly guards lie on the ground, unconscious or dead. Neither their mounts nor the carriage horses are anywhere to be seen—they must have fled.

Nearby are seven figures on horseback, wearing black armor shot through with veins of gold, emblazoned with the crest of the three suns. The Daenalla claim to worship Eonnula, too, but they do not know the true path. They are darkness, and we are light. We follow the God-Touched Royals, while they follow the black-winged monstrosity standing by the carriage, wielding the shadows that bind me.

I could break free, I think. But I'm pretending to be a helpless human. Best to keep my magic and my strength hidden, for now.

Out of the corner of my eye I see Dawn scrambling from the opposite side of the carriage, heading for the trees. I need to keep their focus on me so they don't notice her.

I turn my full attention on the Void King. "Unhand me at once!"

The Edge-Knights chuckle at my demand, but the Void King's mouth doesn't so much as twitch.

He's tall, and the arched peaks of his gigantic black wings make him look even more threatening. He has four horns, two on each side of his skull. Long black hair flows down to his waist, over a pauldron of dark metal. His muscled abdomen is bare, a foolish choice for a warrior in my opinion.

His face, upturned to mine, is pale, grim, and handsome, sharply carved as if someone cut him neatly from a block of white stone. Black brows slash over eyes as dark and deep as the Void itself, but with pupils of glowing green, like emerald stars. His hands are gloved in black from claw-tips to forearms, a telltale mark of the shadow magic he wields.

My gut churns, because even though I've never met the Maleficent One, I've seen him before, as clearly as I see him now. This creature has haunted my dreams ever since I met the Princess, ever since I knew that one day I might have to protect her from him. What scares me is the accuracy of those dreams, right down to the collar of raven feathers at the back of his neck and the black staff in his hand, with a glowing green stone at its tip.

"I know you." The words jerk out of me, like splinters being plucked from a wound. "I've seen you before. In my nightmares."

"Hair as gold as the Triune Suns." His voice is liquid darkness, a living threat. "Eyes blue as the sky. Beautiful as the dawn for which you are named. It is good to see you again, Princess."

2

I have her at last.

The Crown Princess of Caennith, the child of my two royal nemeses, protégé of the three fucking faeries who shamed me and foiled my plans nearly twenty-five years ago.

It's as if Eonnula wanted me to have my prize. Dropped her into my lap, so to speak. Thank the goddess one of my ravens saw the Princess at the Lifegiving Festival and told me the routes she might take back to the summer palace. I sent a contingent of Edge-Knights to watch the main road, too, but I suspected the Princess would use the forest road. She'd want to beat her father back home so her little excursion could go undiscovered.

But my raven was wrong about one thing. He claimed the Princess's bodyguard was with her at the Festival—a winged Fae woman with blue hair. There is no such woman here, only a frightened maid who crawled away into the trees when she thought I wasn't looking. Perhaps I should send someone after her, just in case—

"My lord." Fitzell, my second-in-command, speaks from her usual position on my right. "The passage we used will close soon. We should go."

"One moment." I press against the Princess's energy with my shadows, hunting for the edges of glamours, for signs of deceit. But I'm distracted by the dissonance of her aura—like a song that has been dismantled and put back together in jumbled phrases, out of order. Strange…

"Lord King, you told me to let you know when we were running out of time." Fitzell lifts her necklace, showing me the hourglass pendant. It's glowing red, which means we have mere minutes to return to the portal. My other group of knights must have already retreated through it by now.

By the blessing of Eonnula, we were near the border when I received word of the Princess's Festival appearance. Still, I feared we might not be able to take advantage of her unprotected state, since the window of opportunity was so narrow. Several of us worked together to create a temporary magical tunnel from Daenalla to Caennith so we could reach this area in time and avoid the border defenses. But now we need to get back through the tunnel before it closes, or we'll be stuck in enemy territory.

No time to pry for glamours or analyze the Princess's aura. I'll explore it further once we're back at camp.

"We ride." I nod to Fitzell.

"Ride!" she cries to the others, and they take off through the forest, back the way we came.

I lift my staff and harden my will, forcing the Void magic under my command to take the shape of a tall, spindly steed whose body streams long ribbons of darkness. I swing astride the creature, slinging my staff onto my back, where leather loops hold it in place between my wings. After draping my wings on either side of my mount's flanks, I tug on the shadows that hold the Princess.

She gasps as she's yanked from her spot in midair and pulled back to my side. I seize her by the waist, plant her in front of me, and send our steed forward with a firm nudge of my will.

The Princess's hand darts down and whips a short sword from the sheath at her hip. She's almost quick enough to stab me, but I catch her wrist, squeezing hard enough to make her yelp and drop the weapon.

So easy. Poor little human—she's not a challenge in the least—

Her head knocks back and smashes me in the face with a crunch of skull on bone.

"Fuck!" I spit, blood dribbling over my lips.

She's already moving, leaping upright, her boot smashing into my groin as she launches herself off my steed.

"Godshit!" I croak, holding my crotch with one hand while I snag the Princess with a coil of Void magic. I jerk her back to me, flinging her across my mount on her belly this time, her golden hair spilling down one side and her legs dangling on the other. I lash her in place with shadows, then reset my broken nose with an unsettling click. Another minute, and it would have healed out of joint. I'd have had to break it again to fix my face.

The pain in my dick is abating, slowly. I shift on my steed, ignoring the backward glances of my knights as we continue through the forest at a swift gallop.

Later tonight, my knights will joke about how I nearly let the Princess escape. In fact I'll probably hear about it for the next few decades—if our realm survives that long.

Keeping my voice low, I say, "That was a pointless effort, Princess. Someone should teach you better manners." I eye her rounded bottom, clad in blue silk, temptingly presented to me in this new position. Her dress is backless, giving me a full view of her sharp shoulder blades and the valley of her spine, all the way down to that smooth, plump ass.

She's writhing, fighting her shadow-bonds with surprising strength.

"Be still," I command.

"Fuck you."

Before I can think better of it, I smack her rump soundly.

She inhales a startled breath and stops thrashing.

"Good girl," I murmur. "Treat me with respect, and I'll give you the same courtesy."

The Princess responds with a flood of words so loud and filthy that Fitzell turns around in her saddle to stare, quirking an eyebrow. "I wouldn't have thought the Caennith Crown Princess so foul of tongue," she calls.

Nor would I. From the scanty reports we had of her, I expected a frail, mousy, soft thing, incapable of defending herself. Perhaps our information was wrong, and she has been secretly training as a warrior. A clever move on her parents' part, if so.

But no matter how skilled she is at combat, this girl is only human. She is no match for me.

3

AURA

I can't use my magic. Not yet. They have to think I'm human until we've gone through this portal they spoke of. If I show my hand too soon, they might decide to turn back and hunt for Dawn.

My rear stings from the impact of the Void King's palm. I've always been slower to heal than most Fae, but the pain should pass soon. My shock and humiliation, on the other hand—I suspect they will linger awhile.

Lying across the Void King's abomination of a steed, between his muscled thighs, is the last thing I expected to be doing today. His scent floods my nostrils—leather, rain-washed grass, and something darkly, enticingly bitter, like the blackthorn tea Elsamel makes me when I'm sick.

I'm told that in the old times, the Fae rarely sickened. But ages ago, when the godstars ruled, some of their great workings went awry. Chunks of land were torn from the human realm, Temerra, and the faerie realm of Faienna.

Instead of letting those pieces whirl away into space and be lost, our goddess, the godstar Eonnula, took the fragments and crafted a new pocket realm, a remnant of worlds, which we now call Midunell. She saved all the Fae and humans who might otherwise have perished, and gave them a place to start over.

Midunell is a single, oval-shaped plane of land with mountains, lakes, rivers, and hills, surrounded on all sides by the Void. The border where the Void begins is called the Edge, and it is forever pressing inward, eager to swallow up our little scrap of a realm, like flesh closing around a foreign object, inflamed and seeping along the borders of the invading element.

The Fae of this realm do not live for thousands of years as faeries once did in the home realm. We live perhaps five hundred years, and we can sicken like humans do, though we recover more quickly. By contrast, humans in this realm live longer than those in Temerra—up to three hundred years or so. Humans married to a Fae spouse live longer, but such unions are not permitted in Caennith.

The pace of the King's steed increases, and I turn my head in time to see an oval of whirling green magic up ahead, between two trees. The Edge-Knights are already riding through it.

The Void King plants one clawed hand on my back as we charge through. His palm is strangely hot.

As we enter the portal, magic blasts over me like a breathtaking wind. For several long moments we ride through a mad chaos of green light and twisting smoke—and then we break through on the other side, into a forest of tall pines with bare branches below and upswept green boughs high above our heads.

We are now in Daenalla.

Mentally I review what I know of this place, its landmarks and history. There's a spine of black mountains, some deep, cold lakes, towns with metalworks and mills, and a great spiked castle called Ru Gallamet, where the Void King reigns.

I've heard that Ru Gallamet sits among the mountains, near the Edge itself. Only someone deeply insane would place his residence so close to the Void. My people say the Maleficent

One built his castle there so he could access the Void and Spin his foul magic.

Years ago, one of Dawn's tutors explained how the rift between our peoples began. It all started with a prophecy, that one day a savior sent by Eonnula would arise and save our realm from the encroachment of the Void, stabilizing it forever. A group of humans and Fae, who later became the Caennith, decided to devote their lives to joy, worship, and the magic of light while they waited for the salvation of Eonnula. Another group, the Daenalla, rejected the prophecy and the promise of a savior. They decided they must save themselves. They abhor the "frivolity" of the Caennith, and they believe in the crafting of machines and the harnessing of the Dark for shadow-magic. They are a cruel, somber, wicked, faithless race.

And I am now at their mercy.

But at least Dawn is safe. If she can't make it back to the palace herself, my mothers can find her and bring her home,.

My mothers will worry about me, though. I suppose I have some worth as a hostage, when my disguise eventually fails. After all, I'm the daughter of the Three Faeries, the Regents of the Caennith Fae.

Perhaps I will get out of this alive, though I hate to think what price the Void King might demand for my safe return, once he discovers I'm not the Princess.

I should keep up the ruse as long as possible. Once we arrive at our destination, perhaps I can ask to use the privy and take a moment to lay my glamour afresh so it will last longer. Glamouring myself requires several stanzas of chanting and intense mental concentration. Whenever I practiced laying a glamour at home, Genla used to say I looked as if I was pushing out a week's worth of shit. Not particularly encouraging, and yet another sign that I'm nowhere near as powerful as my three parents.

Now that I've begun thinking about bodily needs, I have to piss. Which is an uncomfortable sensation at the best of times—worse since I'm lying on my stomach over the shoulders of the King's steed. Fortunately the creature seems to mostly float along the ground, so there's not as much jostling and bumping as there would be on a normal horse.

"Where are you taking me?" I ask.

The Void King's hand still rests on the small of my back, against my bare skin. I pray to the goddess that my wings remain intangible as well as invisible. When the spell begins to wear off, he will be able to feel the wings before he can see them.

"We're heading to my camp," he says. "We'll spend the night there, then continue toward Ru Gallamet tomorrow."

"And what are you going to do to me?"

A low chuckle rolls from him. His fingers skate along my spine, the claws scratching my skin lightly and raising goosebumps all over my body. "I believe you already know the answer to that question, Princess."

We've been riding for over an hour, judging by the angle of the sunlight filtering through the pine trees. I'm strangely cold; it's all I can do not to shiver as I lie on my belly, draped over the Void King's steed.

My need to relieve myself is becoming more urgent the longer I'm in this position. I haven't emptied my bladder since we left the summer palace this morning. We arrived at the Lifegiving Festival in a hurry and we left in a hurry, so there was no time.

Strange how, in spite of the greater peril, the immediate need of my body blazes at the forefront of my mind, driving everything else into the background. I'm going to have to ask the Void King to stop and let me piss. My other option is to soil myself, which I absolutely refuse to do.

"Can we stop for a moment?" He doesn't answer, so I say it again, louder. "Stop for a moment."

"Why?"

"Because I need to—relieve myself."

He scoffs. "You think I'm falling for that? Think again, Princess."

"Do you want me to piss on your—what is this thing you're riding, anyway?"

"A type of Endling."

An Endling—oh goddess, I've heard dreadful tales of those. They are demons of darkness the Maleficent One pulls straight out of the Void—hideous creatures of ash and smoke and teeth. In the years immediately after he cast the curse, the Endlings terrorized villages all along the border, until Dawn's father built the walls higher with the help of my mothers and other Caennith Fae. They'd add to the walls, and the Endlings would swarm up higher, crawling over the top, until finally the Caennith Fae placed spikes of charmed crystal that must stay forever lit, forever glowing, to ward off the denizens of the dark.

And now I'm lying on an Endling. Which explains the cold that's been seeping into my limbs since the ride began.

Fear and cold spike the need in my gut, and I bite my lip to keep from whimpering. "If you don't stop, I really will piss on your Endling."

"Go ahead."

"I'd rather not soil my dress."

He ignores me. After a few minutes I try again, desperation searing my voice. "Please—I won't try to run. You offered me courtesy if I respect you."

"I've seen no signs of respect."

"I happen to be ungracefully bound to this monster. There aren't many signs of respect I can perform in this position."

"So in a different position, you'd be willing to perform a sign of respect?" There's a darkly suggestive twist in his tone.

Is he—is he flirting with me? Or mocking me?

"I'll do anything if you'll pause and let me have a little privacy," I reply.

"Fitzell," he bellows to the female knight just ahead of us. "Ride on, and we'll catch up in a moment. The Princess needs to piss!"

A guffaw bursts from the riders ahead, and my cheeks flush scarlet. The things I'm going to do to him once I don't have to hide my magic anymore—

The Void King's steed jerks to a halt, and the shadows binding me loosen and slither away, evanescing. I slide off the mount and scan the forest for some bushes—anything to hide behind.

But there's nothing. Tall leafless trunks stretch high above earth littered with decomposing pine needles. No undergrowth at all.

The Void King dismounts. His steed remains motionless, ribbons of translucent shadow trailing from its ebony coat and fading into the air like smoke.

"Take care of it," he orders.

Shooting him a glare, I step behind one of the trees, keeping my back to him while I pee. Relief washes over me afterward, but I stay in the same position for a few minutes, muttering a chant to reinforce the glamour over my wings.

"Did you drink an entire pond before the Festival?" he says. "Hurry up."

I dab myself dry with a bit of moss and straighten, adjusting my clothes. Head held high, in my best imitation of Dawn's most regal posture, I walk toward the beast, with a distant nod and a cool "Thank you."

But as I pass close to him, I fly into motion.

A jab to his nose with the heel of my right hand, followed by a punch to his jaw with my left. My right knee rams into his crotch, and I hook my right foot around his leg at the same moment. I throw my body sideways, giving the back of his knee a sharp jerk.

It almost works. He staggers, off-balance, but he doesn't fall. His wings snap out, expanding like a giant black cloud behind him, keeping him upright.

I expect him to snare me with shadows again, but instead he blocks my next punch with his forearm. His eyes aren't glowing green at the center anymore. Perhaps they only do that when he is actively using Void magic.

I catch the wrist he blocked me with and duck, twisting his arm as I step into his space. The side of my hand chops at his wing joint, and he snarls, curling the wings forward, engulfing me in black feathers. No, not entirely black—near the roots and the arch, some of his feathers are iridescent blue, tinted with purple.

I snatch a handful and tug savagely, managing to pull a few feathers out. He grips the nape of my neck, hauls me in front of him again—but with another dive and twist, I'm free to land a hard punch to his abdomen.

It's like punching rocks. Pain blazes through my fingers, my knuckles, and I cry out. He gives me a tight smile, seizes my anguished hand, and begins to crush my fingers in his own.

"Do you yield?" His skin is blazing hot, and sweat beads across his pale forehead. His pupils are dilated.

Something is wrong with him. Is he sick? I hope so. Might give me an advantage—my knee pops up, aiming for his crotch, but he swerves his hips aside.

"I'm rather fond of that part of my anatomy." He twists my arm and whirls me around, my back to his chest. "If you would kindly stop trying to damage it."

I try smashing my skull backward into his face again, but he avoids that too.

"You have a limited number of tricks, Princess," he says.

His arm is locked around my throat now, his skin scorching my neck. His other arm bands my body, pinning my arms to my sides.

I buck and squirm, but it's no use. He's stronger.

So I twist my head down and sink my teeth into his arm, right below the pauldron.

"Little viper!" His grip loosens slightly, and with a wrench and a slither, I'm out of his grasp and several steps away, facing him head-on.

He grits his teeth, inspecting the twin half-circles my teeth left on his arm. When he looks up, I smile at him, my lips wet with his blood.

I could run. He'd catch up to me easily on his steed, or with his shadows. Unless—

I glance at his Endling, standing between two trees, heedless of the fight. Is it my imagination, or does the creature look a bit more translucent than before?

Realization flares in my mind. His magic has limits. He must have used a vast amount of it to pass through the border wall undetected, and now he's weakening. The feverish heat of his skin must be a side effect of magic overuse. It's rare among my people, but it still happens. It should have been obvious to me at once, but I wasn't expecting the Maleficent One to have a weakness.

Maybe my captivity can be more useful than a temporary distraction from the real Princess.

Maybe I can kill the Void King and end his dark magic forever.

4

MALEC

The Princess smiles at me savagely, her teeth and lips glittering with my blood. She watches me with a keen calculation I didn't expect from her. More like a warrior than a coddled royal. Her skirt must have ripped up the side when she was fighting me, and the new gap reveals a shapely, toned leg, ending in a boot that looks rather rustic for a princess.

"You promised me respect, and you promised not to run," I remind her. "You're a rutting liar."

"There's your sign of respect." She vents a breathless laugh, nodding to the bite mark on my arm. "And you're a fool to trust the word of a desperate captive."

I am a fool, in more ways than she knows. I'm too reactive, too impulsive, despite decades of trying to teach myself to take time before I act.

Perhaps I will pay the ultimate price for my foolishness today.

I advance, and the Princess tenses, knees slightly bent, fists ready. She's wearing rings on all ten fingers—thick rings marked with the ancient symbols of the home realm, Faienna. Few texts and artifacts from that realm remain with us, but I recognize the markings. Why is she wearing so many Fae-marked rings? Perhaps they give her additional strength and skill for fighting.

I haven't explored her aura again, or checked her for latent spells, glamours, and enhancements. That will have to wait until I've rested—or perhaps I can have one of my guards do it. I was responsible for probably three-quarters of the magic that went into making that passage into Caennith, and my powers were already low before that. I crafted an Endling to ride through the portal, then dissolved it to attack the Princess's carriage, which drained my magic still more. Creating another Endling to ride on the way back was a bridge too far; I should have taken one of the Princess's carriage horses instead.

As a result, I'm suffering the effects of magic overuse—and at the worst possible time. The fever is raging in my body, sending chills along my bones and soaking me in a cold sweat. I can't hold the Endling steed's form any longer, so I release it, and the smoke winnows away into nothing.

I need time to recover and replenish my magic.

Reaching over my shoulder, I seize my staff and pull it from its leather loops. With my hand cupped over the smooth green globe at its tip, I summon a raven.

I have a select group of ravens I've trained and gifted with higher consciousness, like the spies that I sometimes send into Caennith. But I can also use wild ravens anytime I like. I can summon the birds without my staff, but its unique magical signature lets my trained pets find me faster and serves as a beacon for wild birds, helping me link with them more quickly.

Within seconds a raven flies to me, perching atop the staff. With my knuckle, I stroke the glossy black feathers on its breast. "Go to Fitzell. Tell her to return here with an extra mount."

The raven bobs its head and flies away, while the Princess stares open-mouthed. "Ravens can talk?" she asks.

"Of course not. It will communicate my message into Fitzell's mind."

She stares at me, wide-eyed. "That's no less impressive."

I keep the staff in my hand, both as a weapon and for something to lean on. Fuck, I'm a fool. I should not have attempted a kidnapping like this with my powers so low. But there was no time to refill them. She would have escaped my grasp, and this was too perfect an opportunity to miss.

The Princess bends swiftly, snatching a long branch from the ground. She hefts it and approaches me, placing her feet carefully. A fighter's cautious advance.

"You're not going to run?" I ask.

"I don't think so." Her lips curve in a half-smile. "I believe I'll try to kill you instead."

I force a caustic laugh. "Lofty goals, Princess. I am the Void King, the Maleficent One. You are no match for me."

"Maybe not at your full strength." She prowls nearer, still with that half-smile. "But you're not at your full strength, are you? And I'm not keen on having my blood spilled on your gods-damned Spindle and then losing a hundred years of my life to a cursed sleep, so…"

"Like it or not, that is your fate." I lift my staff, gripping it in both hands, ready to block her first blow. "A fate your parents sealed when they humiliated me before all Midunnel on the day of your birth."

"And your humiliation justifies stealing a century of my life?"

I blink rapidly, trying to clear the fog that's crawling across my vision. "The King and Queen had to be taught a lesson. They put their foolish religion and their inane fears above the good of this entire realm. They endangered both our peoples, the Caennith and the Daenalla."

"Lies." She darts in, her branch whistling through the air. I block the attack easily, but she rains more blows down upon me, and I can't stop them all, not with this feverish furnace roaring through my body and this blur over my eyes.

The Princess lands a strike on my forearm, then my shoulder—then a hearty slam to my ribs, accompanied by a crack of bone. I suck in a hissing breath, backing away from her, curving my wings to shield myself.

Where is Fitzell? Why did I let her ride ahead? I should have told her I was feverish, asked her to stay behind—but I didn't want to admit that I couldn't handle a little human princess. Gods fuck me—

Another blow, this time to the arch-bone of my wing, then a sharp jab through the gap between my wings. The end of the branch rams into my gut.

"Enough!" It's meant to be a threatening bellow, but it comes out as a cry of pain. I lift my staff, ready to hail vengeance on this absurdly well-trained girl—

But pain spikes through my head, and my vision turns black.

I'm pitching forward, crashing to the ground.

I can't summon the energy to move.

Something pokes me tentatively—the Princess, jabbing my shoulder to see if I'm unconscious.

I'm burning, burning—the padding of my armor is drenched with my sweat, and I'm desperate to shred the leather pants I'm wearing, to tear them clean off. I need wind, a breeze, a breath, a drink of water—anything. I need magic.

With a violent surge of effort, I roll over onto my back, lying between my outspread wings. Where is my staff? I need it—I can call ravens to fan me, bring me water—

But the Princess has discarded her branch and kicked my staff out of my reach. She drags a knife from my boot, flips it expertly with one hand, then sinks down at my side, her knees crushing my feathers.

She sets the edge of the blade against my throat.

5

AURA

The goddess has smiled upon me today.

I have the Void King himself at my mercy. He's on his back, arms lying limp against the ebony-and-purple sheen of his wings. His skin is filmed with glistening sweat, and his abdomen contracts desperately with each quick, shallow breath. His eyes are closed, black lashes fringing his cheekbones. Behind his head swirls his long black hair, dark as his shadows.

Steadily I hold the knife against his neck, watching a bead of sweat travel the shining slope of his throat and slip into the notch between his collarbones.

He's panting, his lips parted and his black brows bent slightly inward, as if he's struggling to fight the sickness gripping his body.

Why haven't I already finished him?

I can do this. I've killed three people in my lifetime and wounded several more. Not all the attackers were sent by the Void King; he has always wanted to *capture* Dawn, not kill her. According to the terms of the curse, pricking her finger on any spindle would send Dawn into a hundred-year sleep; but the Void King plans to prick her finger on his particular Spindle and use her blood for his foul magic. She would fall asleep immediately afterward.

When her birthday passes, Dawn will become the new Conduit, sleeping or not. When a new Conduit comes of age, the previous ones begin to wane. The King and Queen will lose the ability to conduct Eonnula's power at all. And Dawn can't be part of a Surge while she's unconscious.

Without the help of a Conduit to enhance the Surge during our worship gatherings, the Fae of Caennith won't have the power they need to hold back the Edge. Our kingdom will begin to collapse. Not to mention that without the Surge, the humans of Caennith will lose their joy and hope.

For that reason, some of Dawn's attackers have been Caennith—zealots who believed that by ending her life, they could preserve the Royals as the Conduits and keep our kingdom safe.

Twenty-five years of keeping Dawn away from spindles and assassins, away from the Void King and his servants. And now I have the chance to end it all.

Perhaps this act would not end the conflict entirely—after all, the Daenalla and the Caennith have been at war for centuries. There was a short time of peace when the Void King first took the Daenallan throne, but since Dawn's birth and the reescalation of the conflict, more people have died on both sides. And I hold him responsible—this malignant monster who insists that we should embrace the Void and corrupt ourselves with its dark magic.

Without him, this realm would be a better, safer place.

I need to kill him.

Protect Dawn, protect my people.

The Fae can heal, but not from everything, and not in this weakened state. A good deep slash of the throat should do it. I need to act quickly, before his knights answer his call and return to this spot. They will be here any moment.

But as I begin to press the knife in, I glance at the Void King's mouth.

There's something charmingly sensual about the arch of his narrow upper lip and the soft curve of the lower one. Something lovely about the sharp angle of his jaw, the vulnerable hollow of his throat. Something about the quiver of the dark lashes against his cheeks.

He's beautiful.

My mothers would tell me I'm being insufferably silly right now. They would tell me to kill him.

Do it, Aura. Do it now, Sayrin would urge.

Kill him, kill him, you foolish child, you idiot, you imbecile... Genla can be cruel when she's angry.

Elsamel wouldn't yell at me for my hesitation, but she would be sorrowful. Disappointed that I'm not strong enough for this. *How could you show mercy to our greatest enemy? Don't you know what he has done—what he will do?*

My hand trembles.

The Void King's head tilts aside a little, his brow furrowing. "Fucking...do it..." he whispers. "If you must."

"Will it break the curse?" I ask.

He winces. "No."

So Dawn could still prick her finger before her twenty-fifth birthday and sink into sleep. But at least *he* would be gone—this curse-casting, shadow-spinning, heretical creature who claims to follow Eonnula but does so in the most twisted way.

A thought wakes in my mind—perhaps it's not my place to kill him. Perhaps I should let Eonnula judge him in her own time.

Perhaps I should flee instead. I can't use my wings while they're glamoured to be intangible, and I can't change this glamour until it wears off; but I could hide somewhere until then. Once the glamour is gone, I can fly back to the border in my usual form. Or perhaps *sneak* back to the border—I don't want to be shot down by the Daenallan guards.

Yes, fleeing is better than murder. I should do that right now.

I withdraw the blade, scooting back, my boot soles ruffling the Void King's feathers.

My boots—I didn't change my boots. I should be wearing Dawn's delicate leather shoes. These are the boots of a servant or a soldier, not a princess.

I wonder if the Void King noticed.

I'm about to turn and run off into the forest when a shout catches my attention, and hoofbeats thump against the carpet of pine needles. A rider is approaching—the one the King called Fitzell—and a raven flies in front of her, threading its way between tree trunks.

I bolt, but the raven is faster. It releases a loud *caw* and swoops at me, talons extended. I duck, swiping at it with the knife I stole off the King.

"Drop the weapon," shouts Fitzell. She's holding a crossbow, with a dart trained on me. Her horse skids to a stop near the Void King's prostrate body. "Drop it, Princess. I won't ask again. We don't need you in perfect health to accomplish the King's plan."

Gritting my teeth, I let the knife fall.

Behind Fitzell is another mounted knight, leading a third horse, presumably for the Void King. His skin is tinted lightly blue, though otherwise he looks human.

"Shit," says the blue-skinned knight. "Did she kill him?"

"No." Fitzell swings off her horse. "He's sick from using too much magic. I told him, didn't I? I said he needed to be careful." She shakes her head, stalking over to him, while still keeping the crossbow pointed at my heart. "Bastard doesn't listen to me. And now look at him. You'll have to help me get him onto the horse, Andras. Him and those huge rutting wings of his."

"What about her?" Andras gestures in my direction.

"She'll ride with me," says Fitzell, pulling off her helmet to reveal tightly curled hair, bright brown eyes, and coppery skin dotted with dark freckles. "And if she tries anything, she'll regret it."

It takes another hour to reach the Void King's camp, which places it a brisk two-hour ride from the border. The location makes sense, because someone as high-ranking as him wouldn't want to stay in one of the Daenallan garrisons near the wall; he'd want some distance, in case my people attack.

It also makes sense that the Maleficent One would be lingering here, close to the border, since Dawn's birthday is only three months away. He's been waiting for an opportunity to get to her.

And by helping Dawn slip out of the palace, allowing her to go to the Festival, I gave him that chance.

I could lay some blame on the King and Queen, I suppose. They're the ones who gave Dawn permission to join them at the summer palace for a week, even though it's close to the border— even though her twenty-fifth birthday is coming up so soon. But the summer palace is heavily fortified, with multiple thick walls and countless magical defenses surrounding its pools, fountains, and game lawns. Dawn has visited many times. They expected her to be safe inside such a fortress.

And she was, until someone intimately familiar with all those defenses helped her get out. I flirted with the stable-boy so he'd prepare the horses. I bribed the carriage driver and the keeper of the west gate. I convinced the two guards to accompany us. I smuggled Dawn to the gatehouse, avoiding the house-mistress and the maids charged with tending to us.

All the defenses of the summer palace are designed to keep intruders out. They weren't designed to keep Dawn from leaving. Her parents aren't cruel—they don't want her to grow sad and sallow, locked within some tower for her safety. They allow her some free time outdoors, even though she must remain within the confines of the castle walls. They let her move from palace to palace, despite the occasional attempts on her life and freedom. They love her, and they want her to have a pleasant existence in spite of the curse.

By association, I've had a fairly pleasant existence as well. Despite having to stay constantly alert for danger, I've enjoyed all the perks of royal life. I eat the same food as the Princess, read the same books, play the same games, swim in the same pools, and benefit from the same tutors. I'm even dressed by the same tailors. There are times when other guards take over for me so I can train, sleep, or spend time with my mothers—but otherwise, Dawn's life and mine are nearly identical. And I like to think her parents regard me as one of the family... almost.

They'll be sorry to hear I've been captured. But I think they will be proud of me, too, and grateful that I saved their daughter from falling into the Void King's hands.

Not that the Void King's hands are a particularly dangerous place to be right now. He's slumped in the saddle of the horse his knights put him on, held in place with a few loops of rope. His wingtips droop perilously close to the ground.

As we ride into camp, the other knights gather, concern etching their faces at the state of their king.

"Nothing to worry about," calls Fitzell. She pulls her horse to a stop and dismounts. "The King has expended too much magic, that's all. Just like he did at the Battle of Fargonnath.

He'll be all right. Alert the physik, one of you, and tell her to prepare a restorative. The rest of you—rejoice, because we have taken the prize of this quarter-century—the Princess of Caennith!"

A low rumble of approval rolls through the group, and several of them pound their chests or slap each other's armored shoulders. Some of the knights in the camp wear bluesteel armor, which marks them as human. The Fae do not wear that kind of metal, since it impedes their magic.

I'm surprised that Fitzell, who appears human, wasn't wearing bluesteel during the foray into Caennith. Perhaps the black armor is fortified in another way, by some fell magic of the Void King.

The interaction of both races feels familiar, at least. No animosity between Daenallan Fae and humans, as far as I can tell. I'm a little disappointed; I could have used such feelings to play them against each other.

"The King will rest tonight," Fitzell continues. "Tomorrow we make for Ru Gallamet and the Spindle, where our Lord will do his great work."

This time the cheer is slightly louder, but not by much. In Caennith, there would already be songs and dancing, people screaming their joy and leaping for sheer delight at such a victory. I've heard that the Daenalla are a sour, somber nation. I suppose I'm witnessing that sobriety first-hand.

Fitzell beckons to Andras. "I'm going to set a triple watch around the camp," she tells him in a low voice. "We have stolen their princess, and it will not go unanswered for long. I will escort the King to the physik. Get someone to help you with the Princess, and take her to the King's tent. Shackle her—hand, foot, and throat. Take no chances."

"Yes, sir," he replies.

"I mean it, Andras. Do not underestimate her." Fitzell looks up at me, where I sit quietly on the horse. The keen appraisal in her eyes unsettles me.

Any moment now, my glamour will begin to fade. First my wings will become perceptible to touch, and then they'll be fully visible. My ear-tips will reappear, and my hair will revert from gold to blue.

Once the Daenalla realize I'm not the Princess—if they don't kill me immediately—the bargaining can begin. I'll tell them who I really am, and they can send a ransom demand to my mothers.

Or, if I get some time alone in the King's tent, perhaps I can reinforce the glamour and keep up the ruse a little longer.

Andras and a powerfully-built female knight escort me to the King's enormous black tent. It's propped up by at least two dozen posts, and gold flags fly from its peaks. But despite its size, the interior is sparsely furnished.

The two knights chain me by the neck to one of the thick supporting posts of the tent. My wrists are shackled in front of me, and my feet are shackled too, with a bit more chain between them. Another chain runs from the shackle on my right ankle back to a metal band around the post.

I'm not sure what metal my shackles are made of, but they're worn smooth along the inside, not rough or sharp. Something to be thankful for, I suppose. Midunnel is a realm of limited resources, in which mines are scarce and metal is precious. Fortunately, the allergy to iron that seems to have plagued my Fae ancestors in the home realm did not travel with us to Midunnel. Perhaps Eonnula saw fit to cure us of it when she crafted this new world.

The knights give me a little water, then leave me alone in the tent. I try to sit down; but the metal collar around my neck stops me. The chain is too short for rest—I must remain standing.

Sighing, I close my eyes and focus on my magic.

When I was very young, my mothers told me that my power is centered in my palms. Unusual for a Fae, perhaps, but then again, I was an unusual child, born of three women.

I press my hands together, palms and fingers aligned, just as they taught me, while I form the intent in my mind—the goal of the magic I want to perform. Power flows from my hands, up through my arms, solidifying in my heart before rising into my brain, the center of thought and purpose.

Once I feel the magic in my mind, I can work with it.

Murmuring the stanzas of the incantation, I lay another glamour over my wings first, ensuring they'll stay invisible and intangible. Then I focus on my hair color—a much easier glamour, and it lasts longer. Next I shift my attention to my ears, planning to conceal the sharp tips—but a violent pinching sensation in my chest stops me. My fingers twitch as I strain, seeking my magic—but I barely feel the flow of power. There's only a trickle left.

Shit.

My mothers were supposed to arrive at the summer palace for a visit tomorrow, and we had planned to do a gathering then. They would have helped me refill my power. When I went to the Festival, I expected to enjoy the benefits of the Surge; but that didn't happen, and now I'm nearly empty. If I keep pushing, if I force it, I'll end up like the Void King—feverish and helpless. I've never let my magic drain that low before, and I'm not about to over-exert myself now, in the camp of my enemies.

With my magic this low, I can't use it to fight back against the Daenalla. And I won't be able to place any more glamours. When this one wears off, I'll be discovered.

Experimentally I pull on my chains for a while, but they're secure—no weaknesses anywhere that I can detect. My strength won't help me here. All I can do is wait.

Sometime later, voices sound at the entrance to the tent. Fitzell and a slim Fae with tiny antlers wrestle the Void King and his wings through the tent flap and propel him toward the bed. He's still wearing his dark pants, but they've taken off the pauldron and the leather chestpiece, as well as his boots. Fitzell is carrying the staff with the green stone, which she props against a post. I left the staff in the clearing near the Void King's body, when I decided to run instead of slitting his throat. Perhaps I should have tried to use its magic, but I could sense nothing from it. Maybe it only responds to him.

The Void King's cheeks bear a hectic flush, and his long black hair, damp with sweat, clings to his shoulders and back. I have the strangest urge to gather up that ebony hair and bundle it into a knot, so it's off his neck.

He's reeling, frowning, dizzily pushing away Fitzell and his other knight.

"You need to lie down, Your Majesty," Fitzell persists. "The restorative tonic should take effect soon. Once the fever breaks and you've gotten some sleep, we can ride to the Hellevan Chapel and conduct worship to refill your power."

Thank the goddess. Maybe I'll be able to refill my magic there, too. Not that it will do me much good at that point— they'll know I'm Fae by then, and they'll probably place a binding collar around my neck to prevent me from casting spells or glamours.

The tent flap bursts open, and an ebony-skinned man with broad features and glassy green wings strides in. "It has begun," he says tersely to Fitzell. "We just received word that a squadron of Caennith soldiers has moved out beyond the wall. They're attacking one of our garrisons."

"Fuck." Fitzell presses her fingertips to her brow. "I thought we'd have a little more time. They haven't sent a message? Asked for a ransom?"

"No." The green-winged man shakes his head. "They know he won't give her back. No use asking. They'll try to take her by force."

Fitzell nods. "This is a warning, a show of strength. Once the King mobilizes more of his army, their attacks will begin in earnest. No doubt they already have runners searching the woods. Our garrisons are well-fortified, but reinforcements couldn't hurt. I'll send the orders at once. As soon as the King's fever breaks and he takes a few hours' sleep, he can take a few knights and ride for the Chapel, and from there to Ru Gallamet. Come, Della."

Della, the slim antlered Fae, has just succeeded in making the Void King lie down on the bed. She arranges his wings on either side of him and tucks a thick pillow behind his neck, propping him up to allow space for his curved horns. She looks at him doubtfully, then glances at me. "Captain, is it all right to leave the prisoner in here with him?"

Fitzell walks over to me and checks each lock on my chains. "She is human, and with these bonds in place, she's no threat to the King. Now come, Della—we have messages to send. You're the swiftest, and I need you as one of my runners."

"Yes, Captain." Della heads for the tent flap, and I notice something I missed before. Her legs are unusually thin, jointed and furred like those of a doe. She must be a pureblooded descendant of the original Fae from the home realm.

Such dramatic physical differences used to be more common among the Fae, but over millennia, humans and Fae have grown more similar in appearance. I've heard that in Daenalla, Fae and humans actually interbreed. My mothers frown on interracial breeding between humans and Fae, since the offspring are sometimes born with weak magic or none at all. The Priests and Priestesses of Eonnula preach the same thing: that humans and Fae may fuck, but they may not have children together or bind themselves in marriage before the goddess. They say it is best for our two races to remain "partners, yet apart."

Something about that doctrine has never settled well with me.

Fitzell holds the tent flap for the other two knights, still eyeing me. "Have they given you water, Princess?"

"Yes."

"The chains are a necessity. You're more skilled at combat than we expected. I'll send someone in shortly to check on you both." With a curt nod, Fitzell leaves.

It almost sounded as if she was apologizing for chaining me up. Strange.

My attention swerves to the Void King, who is making a low, growly noise in his chest—a persistent discontented rumble. His horned head rocks from side to side on the pillow. Then he sits up suddenly, his wings shuddering. The feathers bristle into a fluffy black stormcloud.

This is why his tent is so huge, and why the furniture is so spread out. It's to allow space for his wings.

I'm lucky my wings are smaller, more pliant, easier to manage. I can't imagine having to deal with those enormous feathered appendages every day. And the four horns—they must make it difficult to sleep comfortably. Perhaps he's used to them, or perhaps he glamours them away at night—which he can't do now, since his magic is drained.

"It's so hot," he mutters. "So fucking hot."

As bodyguard and friend to the Princess, I often end up playing the role of nurse or maid as well, even though she has servants. It's easier and quicker, sometimes, for me to spot a need and take care of it, rather than calling a maid. The familiar compulsion rises in me as I watch the Void King scraping his sweaty hair back from his forehead with his claws. He's miserable. He needs cool, damp cloths, and something to drink, and someone to fan him. Surely one of the Fae here could provide some air flow in this tent.

Not that I give a damn about my enemy's comfort. It's just that his fidgeting and restlessness annoy me.

"Don't you have servants?" I ask.

He startles as if he'd forgotten my presence. "Shit. It's you."

"That's right. I'm the helpless infant you cursed."

"Helpless infant my rosy ass."

My eyebrows rise. "*Rosy* ass?"

"You heard me." He stands up unsteadily, blinking as if his vision isn't entirely clear. "By the Void, I'm burning alive." He fumbles with the buckle of his belt for a moment before managing to unlatch it. Swearing under his breath, he drags the belt out of its loops.

Wait, is he—

Is he getting naked?

He unbuttons the leather pants—or rather, he tries to, and then with a ferocious series of muttered *fucks,* he slashes off the buttons with his claws and forces the pants down. Thank the goddess he's wearing undershorts.

"And good riddance to you," he snarls at the pants, flinging them aside with such gusto he nearly knocks off one of the lanterns hanging from a tent post.

Then he grabs the waistband of the shorts and begins to slide them off his hips.

"Oh—oh no," I protest. "I don't think you want to do that. Why don't you leave those on?"

He looks at me vaguely. "Why?"

"Because—um—" I survey his body—stone-white, exquisitely muscled, almost luminous with the sheen of sweat filming his skin. The mortal enemy of my people is fucking beautiful.

"Too hot for clothes," he mutters, and the undershorts fall to the ground.

Long, muscular legs, pale as the rest of him—lean hips, swaying a little thanks to his delirium. And between his thighs hangs a thick, smooth column of flesh, tinged faintly pink. I've seen a number of decent dicks, but this one is impressive even in its flaccid state.

I did not expect to be staring at the Void King's penis today.

My captor, the man I have dreaded and dreamed about for years, is standing before me, utterly nude and dizzily feverish.

"That's better." A sigh of relief gusts from him, and he flutters his wings, creating a soft current of air. "I thought I might combust on the spot."

"Too bad you didn't," I mutter.

His brows pull together as if he's concentrating, extracting a memory from his addled mind. "You tried to kill me."

"No," I snap. "If I'd tried, you'd be dead."

"But you almost killed me, didn't you? I remember…" He touches his throat, his eyes going distant. "I thought it would be such a relief—not to have the fate of a whole realm hanging on my shoulders. To be done with the worrying and the striving and the scheming. To finally *rest*, and have it all out of my hands at last." He exhales, his lips parting the way they did in the forest, when he lay helpless under my knife.

"You don't mean that."

His dark eyes meet mine, an aching sadness shimmering in their depths. "Ah, but I do. I've plotted it before, you know. I've planned my own end. But too many people depend on me. I can't bring myself to do it."

Another thing I did not anticipate today—the Maleficent One confiding that he wants to die.

"Should you be telling me this?" I vent a breathless laugh. "We're enemies, remember?"

"You know how it is, being a royal," he says, with an airy wave of his hand. "You're always trying to portray your best self for your subjects, your warriors, your friends. If you can't talk to your enemies, who *can* you talk to?"

"You're not yourself. If you're so eager to rest, why don't you lie down and do it? And—cover *that* up." I nod at his privates.

He casts the bed an annoyed look. "Not *that* kind of rest. With that kind of rest, my mind whirls, round and round—" He twirls a finger in the air. "I can't stop it, except by drinking or taking a sleep tonic, and that's irresponsible. I can't soak my brain in spirits or herbs, because a king must always be ready."

That, I can understand. I barely allow myself to drink, since a bodyguard's duties never end.

The Void King takes a few unsteady steps toward me. "I've been trying to get to you for so long. Tried everything, short of all-out war. Didn't want that bloodshed, but now I'm fucking desperate, Princess." He braces one hand on the post above my head and leans in, biting out the words, manic intensity in his fever-stricken eyes. "The Edge crawls inward every day, eating houses and fields, sucking them into the Void. Have they told you about that? Or do they keep you ignorant, locked away in your castles, watched by a hundred guards, shielded by stone and magic, guarded by your blue-haired butterfly?"

Blue-haired butterfly—he's talking about me, the *real* me. The bodyguard to the Princess.

"She has done her job well, your butterfly," he mutters, his breath hot against my face. "She has foiled so many of my attempts to capture you. That's why we pulled back, you see. To prepare for a final battle, and also because I suspected that after so many years of guarding you, she must be as weary as I am. She must be longing for peace, for amusement, for a breath of freedom. I am not a patient man, Princess. But I knew if I could manage to be patient, that your bodyguard would make a mistake. After two years of patience, she finally did. And here you are. Do you know, I was actually disappointed she wasn't with you in that carriage? I'd hoped to meet her. I rather admire the woman, and I wanted to see her face, just once."

He sways and almost falls over. His wings spring out, helping him keep his balance, but he leans more heavily on the post, which brings his naked body nearly flush with mine. He stares at me, his warm breath on my cheek. Heated tension thrums through my body.

He admires me? He wanted to meet me?

Frantically I claw up my hatred for him, my ingrained animosity for his people, my revulsion toward the kind of magic he wields—and I build it up, a wall between us, a guard against the wicked thrill that rolls through my stomach when his gaze flicks down to my mouth.

"You're out of your mind," I whisper. "Go rest."

He blinks at me slowly. Wets his lips.

"I liked fighting you without magic," he murmurs. "I haven't sparred like that in a long time."

"I'll happily break your nose again. Just let me out of these chains, and we'll have a sparring match right here."

He grins, sudden and bright, a flash of white teeth. "You want me to set you free?"

A thread of hope twines with another thrill in my chest. Maybe he's feverish enough to release me. "If you'll let me out of these chains, I can help you feel better."

"And how would you do that?"

"Well…" I draw a deep breath. "Have you ever had a princess on her knees for you?"

His eyes burn into mine. "Go on."

"If you release me," I murmur, trying to appear calm even though my heart is racing, "I will fall to my knees, and I'll take your dick in my mouth. I'll let you come on my tongue. But you have to unchain me first—I can't kneel unless I'm free."

"Women always assume I want them subservient, kneeling before me." He traces a claw down my cheek. "They don't understand what I truly crave."

"And what is that? I have an open mind—I'll do anything."

"If I unchain you?"

"Yes."

He inhales slowly, as if he's savoring my scent. Then he pushes himself away from the post and turns toward the bed. "I think I should lie down, after all."

Shit, I'm losing him. "What about a little pleasure? Wouldn't you like to shove yourself down my throat, make me gag on the cock of the man who cursed me?"

He throws me an incredulous look. "Why in the Void would I do that to you?"

"Because you hate me. You hate the Royals, and my people, and our religion."

"I dislike the Royals, I pity your people, and I think your religion is foolish. Shoving my cock down your throat wouldn't fix any of that." He flings himself face-down on the bed, wings outspread. His ass does indeed have a faintly pinkish tint, like his dick. I have the strangest urge to smack those bare cheeks, like he spanked me earlier.

"I want this to be over." His voice is so muffled by the pillow I can barely hear him. "I want it done."

For a moment, I allow myself to think about life after Dawn's twenty-fifth birthday. Life beyond the ever-present threat of her capture or death.

The people who have tried to assassinate her, to prevent the curse and the resulting loss of the Conduit—they won't have a reason to kill her anymore. And the Daenalla won't keep trying to steal her away. At least—I don't think they will. For some reason, the Void King seems to want access to her blood *before* she takes her place as the Conduit. I've never heard any theories about why. Perhaps I should ask him.

What would a post-curse realm look like? Midunnel would still be torn by conflict, still under threat from the Edge, but it would be so much less stressful for *me*.

I can barely imagine the relief of a world like that.

"I want it done, too," I whisper.

But the Void King doesn't answer. I believe he has fallen asleep.

6

Groggily my mind resurfaces from a restless sleep. The fever has broken; I'm no longer blazing with virulent heat. Now all I need is a fresh surge of magic. For that, we can pause at the Hellevan Chapel on our way to Ru Gallamet. And then, once we reach my castle, I will bind the Princess to my Spindle, place her finger on its tip, and craft the magic I've been working on for decades—the spell that might be able to save our entire realm.

Her parents wouldn't give her to me when she was born. Wouldn't even let me try the spell, no matter how many times I promised them she would be safe, that the magic wouldn't kill her.

So I cast the curse.

The curse was supposed to force them to give her to me. If she pricked her finger on any spindle, she would pass into a century of sleep—which would deprive Caennith of their next Conduit and prevent their Fae from having the power they need to hold back the Edge with light magic.

If Dawn pricked her finger on *my* Spindle, the same fate would befall her—but with her blood, applied to my machine, I could Spin the magic to save us all. A much better outcome.

I'd tried the spell before her birth, with a vial of her father's blood, reluctantly given. It did not work, and I theorized that the blood needed to be younger, purer—applied prior to the subject's ascension as the Conduit. When I heard news of Dawn's impending birth, I was thrilled to have another chance.

But the King and Queen wouldn't see reason, wouldn't listen to logic—not even after I cast the curse, when I explained how they could save her from the enchanted sleep. It was a sacrifice one of them should have been willing to make. But perhaps love has waned in this realm, along with the shrinking borders of our world.

To wake the cursed Princess, the one who loves her best must kiss her, and thereby take her place, sleeping for one hundred years. During that time, they would age normally. Since both Dawn's parents are around two hundred years old, the one who took her place would likely not wake again.

Ideally, they would have given her to me as an infant, and the curse would never have been cast.

But even after our falling out, when I laid the curse, the Royals could have mended things. They could have sent the Princess to me, so I could try the spell. And then one of them could have gone to sleep in her place, restoring her as the Conduit, the heir to the Caennith throne. If my spell worked, our realm would be saved and the Caennith Fae wouldn't need their precious Conduit. If it didn't work, we would all be doomed anyway, Conduit or not.

Their stubbornness does not matter anymore, because I have her—the God-Touched heir, the Crown Princess. At last I can perform the great work of my lifetime, the spell to end the crushing pressure of the Void upon this realm.

I roll over and sit up, flaring my wings to straighten any bent feathers. I should preen them later, but right now I want to admire my prize. My gaze locks on the Princess—

But my heartbeat stutters, then begins pounding, pounding—thundering my shock through my chest.

My brain revolts, refusing to comprehend what I'm seeing.

The girl chained to the post of my tent is not the one I captured.

This girl has the same lovely features, the same pink lips, the same peach-colored skin—but her hair is a smoky blue, her ears are pointed at the tips, and a pair of gauzy, purple-veined butterfly wings wave softly at her back, on either side of the post to which she is chained.

This girl is Fae, not human. Blue hair and butterfly wings—

"The fuck," I say in a strangled voice.

She smiles, and I'm reminded of her grinning at me in the forest, my blood gleaming between her teeth.

I should have known it then. I should have seen that the woman with the bladed smile and the ferocity of a fighter wasn't the mild-mannered daughter of the Caennith Royals.

This isn't Princess Dawn. It's her bodyguard, the woman who has stood between me and the Princess for years. The dark-haired maid who crawled away from the wreck of the carriage—that must have been the real Princess, under a glamour.

"Fuck," I spit.

"Take your time," the girl says wryly. "Sort it all out. When you're ready, we can talk business."

"Business?"

"Yes. I'm the daughter of—"

"You are Aura, daughter of the Three Faeries. You serve as bodyguard to Princess Dawn," I growl. "I may not have met you, but I do know you."

"Of course. I'm the one you've always dreamed of meeting." Her lips curve in a sly smirk.

"Fuck you." I rise from the bed in a towering rage, my wings lifting and spreading. I stalk toward her—and then a breeze travels across parts of me where no breeze should be.

62

What in the Void? I'm naked. I don't remember taking off my pants. Eonnula's tits, what did I do last night? I vaguely recall speaking to my prisoner—what did I *say* to her?

Snatching a blanket off the bed, I hold it in front of myself. Then I say a quick prayer in my mind, asking Eonnula's forgiveness for swearing by her tits.

Before I can question Aura any further, the tent flap opens, and Fitzell enters, along with Andras.

"You should get an early start, my Lord," Fitzell says. "I apologize for not checking on you sooner, but the enemy's attacks have grown—" She breaks off abruptly, staring at our captive's altered appearance.

Andras's jaw drops.

I watch realization, anger, and despair travel the features of my second-in-command, until she reins in her expression, her face hardening. "We were fooled, then," she says stonily.

"So it would seem."

"I sent Nejire to check on you during the night, and he didn't report any such thing. He said you were asleep and the captive was secure."

"Her glamour must still have been intact at that point. Don't blame yourself, Fitzell—this was my mistake, my idiocy. I acted rashly, hastily—I didn't take the time to confirm her identity, or to sort out the confusion I sensed in her aura. Fuck me into the damn Void—" I punctuate each word with a blow to one of my tent posts. The post quakes at the impact, and the ebony fabric shivers overhead.

Andras is still gaping at the prisoner, but he manages to form a question. "If this isn't the right girl, then why are they attacking us like we've taken their princess?"

"Because this woman is the daughter of the Three Faeries," I tell him. "They are regents, not royalty—they operate under the rulership of the human King and Queen. Still, they are highly respected in Caennith, and they are great personal friends of the

63

Royals. Which is no doubt why they arranged for their Fae daughter to grow up alongside the Princess and serve as her bodyguard."

"So we could ransom her back to them." Fitzell presses a hand to her forehead. "But we don't have the Princess. And that means—" She gnaws her lip. "Shit."

"The very worst shit." Darkness presses on my heart, a crushing weight with which I'm all too familiar.

Failure. Again. Because that is what I do—I fail. I fuck things up with my impatience and my rash decisions. This realm would be better off without me. I make things worse for everyone.

I am the curse.

Goddess, I can't bear this weight, not again, not anymore, not when I thought I was so close. I have ruined it all with my eagerness and recklessness—I didn't check her thoroughly for glamours. I overspent my magic like a mewling babe fashioning his first spell. I am stupid, worthless—

I glance up at the prisoner, and our eyes lock. She's looking at me with a kind of sharp awareness, as if she knows what I'm thinking. Her cocky smile is gone.

"Ransom me," she says quietly. "And this won't be a total loss for you."

7

AURA

For a moment, when the Void King looks at me, I see the naked despair and raw self-loathing of the man who confided in me last night. But he shutters the expression immediately, gives his knights a few terse orders, and then dismisses them. Another Fae brings in his armor and fresh clothes, then beats a hasty retreat.

Lucky for me, the Void King is still empty of dark magic, even though his fever has passed. Otherwise I'm fairly sure he'd wreak some dire punishment upon me. His fury burns in every movement of his lean body as he pulls on a pair of undershorts, then bathes his chest and armpits at the washstand. His wings arch high, rigid with rage, feathers standing out at rakish angles. Once he's done washing up, he preens his wings swiftly, mercilessly, combing the bent vanes with his ebony claws.

He spends longer on his hair, running a bone-handled brush through it until it shines like a black river. Then he oils his horns—all four of them. When he dabs white cream on his throat and wrists, the scent of oleander and honeywood fills the tent.

I can't help a tiny scoff and a smirk.

"Something funny, viper?" His tone is a blade, a challenge.

"Not at all. It's crucial to look and smell your best when the Realm is in crisis," I tell him soberly.

He stalks over to me. "I suppose I should be like you." He plucks at my tangled blue tresses. "With this—elegant coiffure." Then he leans down, his nose nearly touching my breastbone.

I suck in a startled inhale at the proximity, but he only sniffs delicately, then wrinkles his nose and says, "You smell rather ripe, for a Fae. But by all means, sneer at my penchant for cleanliness and beauty. Those who can't achieve a standard are free to mock it, if it makes them feel better."

Turning away, he picks up his pants—black leather, just like the other pair—slides his legs in, and hitches them up over his hips. I watch his Void-stained fingers deftly manipulate the buttons and the belt.

He glances up again, meeting my eyes, and his mouth quirks at the corner.

Does he think I'm *admiring* him? Goddess… I need to say something, to provide some reason for why I'm watching him so closely. "You didn't order Fitzell to send a message to my people, to let them know you've discovered my ruse. Why not? Don't you want to put a stop to the attacks and enter negotiations?"

"No negotiations until I've refilled my magic." His gaze drops to my shackled hands. "Those rings you wear—what are they?"

"Gifts from my mothers. Heirlooms, for luck. A sign of family unity."

He snorts. "You're lying to me. Ah, if only we lived in the old times when our kind could not lie outright! Never mind—I'll figure it out."

I'm not lying. But it's no use trying to convince him of that.

Moving directly in front of me, the Void King reaches over my head to unlock my neck chain from the post. His chin is tipped up, his pale throat exposed, right in front of my face.

Damn, he smells good. The fragrance wafting from his skin sends a shiver of delighted arousal through my body, turning my sex slippery with need.

The awareness of that need floods me with horrified panic.

I react with the instinct of a trapped animal—without thinking. I lunge forward and clamp my teeth on the flesh of the Void King's throat. And then I rip free.

Blood spurts from his neck.

He yells, stumbling back, clamping his hand over the spouting artery. "You fucking animal!"

Two Edge-Knights rush into the tent, but he waves them out with an angry, "Begone! I have her under control."

Exchanging nervous grimaces, the knights duck back outside.

The Void King takes his hand away from the wound. It's already closing—fuck.

He stares at his hand, then slides those slippery, bloody fingers around my throat and jerks me forward. With my chain unhooked, nothing stops him from yanking me right against his chest. "What was the point of that barbaric violence, viper?"

"I thought maybe you wouldn't heal, with your magic so low," I mutter.

"Normally you'd be right... except the tonic I took last night restored my natural healing power. I may be lacking magic, but I'm not helpless. Nor am I easy to kill." He cocks his head, eyeing me. "You want me dead that badly?"

"You're a menace to my Princess and my entire kingdom."

He exhales, his blood-wet fingers flexing against my skin. "You think I am their destruction, little viper. But what if I am their salvation instead?"

"Now who's lying?"

His lips tighten, and he lets out a slow breath through his teeth. His gaze travels down my body, to the ruined skirts of my gown. The dress ripped when he set me astride his Endling, then ripped more when I fought him. The bodice is limp and sagging, and since I'm larger-chested than Dawn, the neckline reveals more of my breasts than I'd like.

Carefully the Void King wipes his bloody hand on the front of my dress, his palm sweeping from my right breast to my left hip, then across my stomach. My flesh tingles with heat where he touched me.

He gathers a handful of my torn skirt and lifts it, bending so he can use it to wipe the blood from his newly-healed throat.

As he turns away, he gives a quick tug to the crotch of his pants, so quick I almost miss it. As if they have suddenly become too tight.

The next second one of his wings hits me in the face as he flares them casually. I cough, spitting out a loose feather that got in my mouth.

He did that on purpose. But as revenge goes, it was surprisingly mild.

He puts on his pauldron and leather chestpiece again, then circles me cautiously before unchaining my feet. I breathe a sigh of relief as the shackles fall away from my ankles.

The Void King's talons trace the bare skin above my boot. "This footwear did strike me as an interesting choice for a princess. I should have guessed your identity from the moment you fought back."

"So a princess can't be a warrior?"

"Of course she can. It's less likely when she's the future Conduit, though." He straightens, and I tense, preparing to deliver a roundhouse kick—but he grips the chain that's still attached to the metal collar around my neck, and he yanks my head back at an awkward angle. "Think twice before you attack, viper."

"Stop calling me that," I spit.

"Shall I have you muzzled, Aura? Or can you promise not to bite me again?" His other hand curls over the top of one of my wings. If he expects me to be sensitive there, to fall prey to his touch, he's a fool. My wings have never been sensitive to pain or pleasure.

"I can't promise not to bite you," I retort.

"If you had other resources besides your teeth and your fighting skills, you'd use them against me," he murmurs. "Which means your magic is low, if not completely empty." He chuckles, jerking at my neck chain. "How unfortunate for you. Come, trickster."

On the way out of the tent he picks up his staff. I have to admit, he looks rather magnificent striding into the chilly pre-dawn gloom, with his four sharp horns, his billowing wings, and the tall staff in his hand. Two ravens flutter off a branch and fly to him instantly, one perching on his shoulder and the other on the green globe of his staff. My chain is wrapped once around his hand, and he tugs me along with an insolent triumph I find extremely aggravating. In contrast to his cool elegance, I must look feral, with my tangled hair, my bloodstained mouth, and my torn, ruined dress.

The Edge-Knights rise as we emerge from the tent. Judging by the wretched disappointment and fury on their faces, the news of my deception has already traveled through the whole camp. Hisses of "bitch," "liar," and "shit-eater" fill my ears.

When one of the human knights makes a foul comment about what he'd like to do to my lying mouth, with a vivid accompanying gesture, something in me snaps. I refuse to endure this quietly. I've had to prove myself to more than a few vulgar, arrogant men, and I know their language.

"I'll gladly take your cock in my mouth," I tell the knight sweetly. "And I'll bite it off and swallow it too. I hear the Daenallan men like girls who swallow, yes? If you're lucky, maybe a bigger one will grow in its place."

A moment's stunned silence—and then a few of the knights chuckle.

The one who made the gesture turns nearly as red as his hair. "You would choke on my dick," he says defensively. "It's big."

"Show me." I halt, and the Void King doesn't pull on my chain. He waits.

"Go ahead, Vandel, show her." One of the redhaired knight's companions elbows him.

I blink my lashes and purr, "Yes, Vandel, show the Caennith bitch what she's missing. Come on. Don't be shy."

The redhaired knight mutters an unintelligible excuse and retreats.

"Too bad." I fake a pout and follow the Void King as he moves on through the camp.

He glances back at me once, and I could swear there's a faint smirk curving his lips.

Some of the Edge-Knights are dismantling tents, but the camp isn't anywhere near being completely packed up. It seems the Void King and I are riding ahead to the Chapel in the company of a few soldiers. The smaller the group, the greater the speed, I suppose.

The Void King takes me to a foul-smelling shack that apparently serves as the outhouse for the camp. I manage to relieve myself with a decent degree of cleanliness, even though my hands are manacled. Then I'm placed on a gigantic black horse and tied to the saddle by a rope around my waist.

For several minutes I sit there, watching the King and his knights make final preparations. Fitzell will be in charge of the camp, while Andras and others will accompany the King. Among the Edge-Knights riding with us are Vandel, the redhaired knight I mocked, and a few of the men who were standing near him at the time. One of them, a blond Fae with bright purple eyes and a square jaw, gives me a wink and lets his tongue slither out between his lips. It's deeply forked, and its two halves writhe suggestively.

When I meet his gaze, he approaches my horse and pretends to check its bridle. "They say the Caennith Fae fuck each other during their glory rites and sun gatherings," he says, low. "Is that true? Is your worship just an excuse to have orgies?"

Holding back my anger, I smile at him. "Do you like orgies?"

"Never participated in one, but I wouldn't mind hearing stories." He sidles a little closer. "You're the Princess's bodyguard, right? Did you ever... play around with her at one of these orgies?"

Smiling wider, I lean down as if I'm about to confide something, and he moves forward eagerly.

My boot smashes into his chin with a crunch of bone.

The Fae staggers backward, howling, clutching his broken jaw.

"What happened?" Fitzell strides over. "Reehan, you idiot—keep your distance from her, you hear?"

"She's a maniac," slurs the knight through his crooked teeth.

"Hold still." Fitzell grips his jaw and reseats it with a pop, then forces his mouth open and straightens a few of the teeth I knocked sideways. "Go prepare your own mount, and stay clear of the prisoner."

As Reehan hurries off, still holding his chin, Fitzell plants both fists on her hips and looks up at me. She's thickly built under the black armor—a woman of strength and skill. I suspect she'd be a match for me in a fight.

"What did he say to you?" she asks.

The question surprises me. There's no judgment in her tone, no threat of retaliation.

"He disrespected my religion and the Princess," I reply.

"Reehan has much to learn about respecting those who aren't like him. He is an excellent fighter, but he's young and foolish."

In this realm, where we reach maturity around twenty and remain in that physical state for decades, youth is relative. And it's no excuse for being an asshole.

With a low scoff, I glance away from Fitzell.

"You hate us," she says. "You're angry because you were captured, angry that you're not going to be ransomed right away, angry because you believe we're ruthless monsters. I'm angry, too. I'm furious that I let my king risk himself and drain his magic to capture a princess who turned out to be *you*. I'm angry that I didn't check you for glamours myself."

"How can you check for glamours? You're human."

"I have a little Fae blood in me. Enough for that task." She vents a heavy sigh. "Most of all, I'm angry because for a few hours, I let myself hope that our realm could be saved. I should know better."

"Saved?" I frown at her.

She chuckles wryly, shaking her head. "You really don't understand why he needs the Princess, do you?"

"He wants her blood for evil magic."

"He wants her blood so he can stop the Void forever."

"But that's not possible. No human or Fae can stop the Void for good. Only Eonnula's prophesied savior can do that."

"And how will we know the savior when they arrive?"

"There will be signs," I say firmly. "The Priests will know, and the—"

Fitzell cuts me off. "And how long must we wait for the savior? Until the Edge has consumed mountains, crops, villages, and water sources? Until we are huddled on the last piece of shrinking ground? What is so wrong with trying to save ourselves?"

"Because we *cannot* save ourselves. Trying to do so is spitting in Eonnula's face."

Fitzell steps closer to the horse and grips my knee. It's a warm hold, almost compassionate, and her expression is both sad and earnest. "I wish I had time to help you see it. But maybe you'll listen to him."

"Him?"

"Malec," she says quietly. "The Void King. I suspect you could have killed him yesterday, but you chose not to. Thank you for that."

I'm stunned by her gratitude, and suspicious of it. "Do you and the King—are you two—"

"Goddess, no." She chuckles. "I'm married to a man who actually listens to me, thank the suns. He's home with the little ones. It's for them I fight." With a final squeeze, she releases my knee. "Perhaps there is still room for hope, after all."

She strides away, pausing to speak to Andras before passing beyond my line of sight.

What a strange woman. She reminds me a bit of my mothers—Genla's unflinching strength, tempered with Elsamel's gentleness and Sayrin's keen insight. I never really believed all of that could exist in one person, much less an enemy.

Not that I believe anything she said to me. Like all the other Daenalla, she has been deceived.

8

MALEC

My Edge-Knights are in good hands with Fitzell. She will oversee the breakdown of the camp and lead them to join the fight at the nearest garrison, while my party heads for Hellevan Chapel. Once there, I will have to make a choice about our next course of action. Ransoming the Regents' daughter seems the most obvious path, but the idea unsettles me.

I sent three ravens to Caennith this morning, to spy for me along the wall. The Caennith Royals and the Three Faeries know of my propensity for using raven spies, and they have shielded their castles magically against the birds; but those protective spells are limited in scope. My enemies can't conceal everything from me.

Unfortunately, ravens are also limited in their perception and communication abilities. They don't always understand what bits of information would be most useful to me. But they do their best. Without their advance warnings, Caennith would have succeeded in conquering my kingdom years ago.

I stroke the feathers of a fourth raven, imprinting her mind with an image of the commander at the Deforin garrison and an accompanying message to deliver. At my nod, the raven caws once and flaps away into the forest.

When I swing up behind the captive bodyguard, she stiffens and pulls herself forward. But it's no use—we're sharing a saddle, and she can't help touching me.

I check that my staff is secure on my back, and I arrange my wings on either side of the horse. Once I'm settled, I become conscious of the girl's shapely rear pressing against my crotch.

Her ripped gown is rucked up around her hips, leaving her long legs bare, except for the chunky leather ankle boots she wears. Her blue hair is pulled forward over both her shoulders, exposing the back of her neck to me. Between the parted locks of hair, her skin looks vulnerable, smooth, and soft—I have the irrational urge to plant a kiss there.

Her filmy wings extend from her spine, pliant as fabric. But as the horse we share begins to move, she stiffens the wings, creating a gauzy shield between her bare back and my chest.

I've slept with two Fae women who had similar wings, and both were very responsive when I caressed certain areas. But this morning, Aura had no reaction when I touched her wing. It's one of many odd things about her—things I intend to explore fully once my magic is refilled.

I hold the reins loosely in one hand, placing my other hand on Aura's hip. She tenses.

"Can't have you tumbling off the horse, Regents' daughter," I murmur. "The rope would stop you from flying or running away, but then you'd end up being dragged along. Very painful indeed."

When she doesn't respond, I lean in closer, between her wings, until I know she can feel my breath stirring her hair, warming the back of her neck. "I've been thinking about how I should punish you for tricking me."

"Isn't captivity punishment enough?" she mutters.

"Are you afraid of pain?"

"I didn't become a fighter by recoiling from pain," she retorts. "Pain is essential for excellence. I welcome pain."

"And you enjoy giving it, too."

Her spine straightens. "I deal pain to enemies who deserve it. I don't enjoy it."

"It's all right to admit it, little viper. You liked hurting me."

A moment's silence, and then she says quietly, "You liked being hurt."

My pulse quickens.

"Do you remember what you said to me last night?" she asks.

Fuck. How much did I confess about my secret needs and longings? "No," I grit out. "What did I tell you?"

When she speaks again, her voice is smug. "Let's just say I know more about you than you'd like me to know."

Heat flares through my body. "Once my magic is refilled, I will pry out all your secrets, viper. And I will enjoy making you writhe."

I say the last as a breathy growl, and she shivers. Her scent slithers into my nostrils—sweat and blood mingled with a faint sweetness, like fresh apples.

Before I can inhale more deeply, we break out of the forest onto a sloping hill that flows down into a wide plain.

The prisoner and I lead the gallop down the slope into the sprawling meadows below. Despite the wretched disappointment of this morning, the shimmering waves of green grass stir joy in my heart, while the fresh morning wind races over the plain and whispers through my wings, a temptation I can't resist.

I shift in the saddle, aching to take flight. The movement rubs my lower body against the girl's ass, and I wince at the answering twitch of my cock. Fuck these unforgivingly tight pants. I should have listened to Fitzell and brought different clothes with me.

I reach down between us and tug at the pants, hoping for a little relief. But Aura reacts with a hissed intake of breath as my knuckles graze her bottom.

"What are you doing?" she snaps.

"Adjusting things." But it's no use. I've made my arousal worse, not better.

I leap to my feet, balancing on the saddle just behind her. "Be a good little captive," I say, and then I flare my wings and let the wind carry me up into the sky.

The rush of flight thrills me. Here, far from the corroded Edge of the realm, it is easier to forget about the Void and its eventual triumph. When the wind is pouring over my body, I think less about my past mistakes and my future goals.

When I fly, death doesn't seem so alluring.

I soar high above my prisoner, my shadow gliding over her like a warning. The horse will continue running in a straight line unless I tell him otherwise, and if she tries to take control, I can swoop down and overcome her in a moment.

Ember and Kyan leap off their horses as well, sailing into the bright morning air with me. Their horses are also trained to stay with the group, and if one swerves aside, catching the steed is an easy matter for us.

We race a little ahead of our group, darting, dodging, weaving our flight-lines together. Kyan's silver feathers flash, while Ember's leathery wings glow translucent scarlet whenever he passes between us and one of the suns.

I glance back at my captive, still riding the horse. She hasn't tried to escape yet. Maybe she realizes it would be pointless. Her wings stand out rigid behind her, a clear sign that she would like to be flying with us. Her face is upturned—she's watching me.

With a mighty wingbeat I soar higher, into the arch of the clear sky. I tuck my wings and dive, flipping one, two, three, four times before I catch myself and lift out of the dive, banking upward again. Then I plunge once more, streaking far across the plain before turning and racing back toward the oncoming group of riders. I skim over my captive's head, so close she could reach up and touch me.

And then I spin around and drop into the saddle behind her.

"Impressive," she says dryly.

"It's more impressive when I have magic." I fold my wings again, relishing the clean flush of the fresh air in my lungs. "Sometimes I use the shadows to create patterns across the sky, or to write words."

"You use Void magic to draw on the sky?" She sounds incredulous. "Is this what you would do with the Princess's blood? Use it to show off and bolster your ego?"

"Of course not." Anger sparks in my chest. "Caennith Fae are the ones who waste precious magic on trivialities and parties."

"We use magic to hold back the Edge."

"Your Priests and Priestesses do, some of them. But the rest of the Fae—how do they use magic? Why do they not help with the reinforcement of the Edge?"

"Because only the most dedicated worshipers of Eonnula are holy enough to wage war against the Void," she says. "The rest of us have other tasks."

How does she not see the foolishness of that system? "Would it not be more effective if all the Fae joined forces against the Void?"

"To what purpose? We don't need to overcome it, just hold it at bay long enough for the savior to arrive."

"Ah, the prophecy." Disdain leaks into my tone despite my best efforts. "What about the villages being consumed by the Edge while you wait for this savior?"

She sighs. "What matters is Eonnula's will. If she allows the Edge to consume something, there must be a reason for it. A greater purpose."

"A greater purpose in pointless deaths?"

"Pointless deaths like those caused by your Endlings?"

It's a fair accusation. At times, in my desperation to save the whole realm, I convinced myself that certain attacks were necessary, certain losses justified.

"I cannot undo what I've done," I say quietly. "Nor can your people reverse the harm they have wrought."

"What harm?" Her voice shrills, incredulous and defiant. "All we have ever done is worship, rejoice, and live our lives in the light of Eonnula's grace."

Her ignorance, her willful blindness to the truth, stuns me for a moment.

She's intelligent, yet she will not allow herself to see the real nature of the Caennith system and its rulers. She speaks with a sturdy, innocent faith that silences me as I debate how to answer.

Perhaps I should not answer at all. The Priests, the Royals, and her own mothers have twisted their thorny vines so deeply into her consciousness that removing the invading ideology will cause her extreme pain, no matter how gentle I am.

Maybe I should let her drift in her delusion. After all, she will soon be gone, sent back to her mothers, another pawn in this unending game.

Aura gives a satisfied nod, as if she believes she has won the argument.

I dislike losing any fight, whether the battle is fought with words or weapons. Usually I would keep pressing my opponent until they had no choice but to yield.

But with her, I don't want a forced surrender. I want to watch her mind open, her heart swell, and her eyes brighten with the realization of the truth—that she, and all her people, are servants to a fool's hope, in bondage to those whose only purpose is control, and whose only goddess is power.

9

AURA

I did not think my enemy could be more beautiful. But when he flies, he takes my breath away.

And when he's in the saddle behind me, with his thighs pressed against mine and his heat warming my back, I can't help the trickles of arousal that circle through my lower belly.

He doesn't keep arguing with me. We ride in silence for a while, until we reach a valley shaded by willows. Violets grow thickly over the valley floor, carpeting it with their velvety purple blossoms and their broad, fresh leaves. Their delicate fragrance suffuses the air.

The Void King inhales deeply through his nose, then releases a satisfied sigh. "I love early summer. So much beauty."

His comment, like so many things he has said and done, clashes with the stories I've heard of him. In those tales, and in my nightmares, he was a thing of darkness and grace—a haunting, malevolent presence. He's recognizable from those dreams, as a person is recognizable by their shadow; but the reality of him, up close and personal, is vivid and compelling, terrifying and startling by turns.

Minutes ago, he threatened to punish me painfully. And now he is telling me about his favorite season.

In our scrap of a realm, the three suns hang in the sky all the time. When they are bright and near to us, we call it summer. But there is a period in which two of the suns recede far away from our lands, appearing as mere dots in the sky, and leaving Midunnel much colder and darker than usual. We call that period "winter"—though judging from our ancient history books, the seasons of Faienna and Temerra were somewhat different. Night in Midunnel is different from the old realms, too—it occurs when the rhythmic surge of the Void's darkness flows between us and the suns, temporarily cutting off their light. The number of stars we see at night depends on the thickness and distance of the Void's shadows on any given evening.

Night and day, winter and summer—it was all set in motion by the goddess, ages ago.

How can the Daenalla believe in the goddess and worship her while rejecting the prophecy of the savior?

"The chapel we're going to," I say. "What kind of worship do you perform there?"

"Can it be that you're curious about our heretical habits?" asks the Void King dryly.

"Just gathering information so I can plan my next escape attempt," I respond in an equally dry tone.

He laughs, a rich, dark sound, like the glimmer of starlight on a raven's wing. "Then I think I shall keep you in suspense, viper."

His hand shifts from my hip, until his thumb grazes the bare skin at the small of my back, below my wings, right above the edge of the backless gown. It seems like a casual adjustment on his part, but then he strokes that thumb across my skin, once, twice, and again.

The gentle touch sends tingling pleasure snaking down my spine to my tailbone, where it spreads over my sex in a warm flush of sensation. I fight the urge to roll my hips and rub myself against the saddle.

My elbow jabs backward, slamming into the King's ribs. He huffs out a startled grunt, and his hand disappears from my back.

Holding my breath, I wait for him to touch me again. I imagine how it would feel if he dragged one claw lazily up my spine—ah, the vengeance I will wreak if he dares to do something so wicked—

But with a gust of unfurled wings, he leaps off the saddle, soaring along the valley, high above our party. And he doesn't descend until we take a break for a quick noon meal in a meadow.

After that, he flies for most of the afternoon, until the trees close in once more, shading the narrow road. Then he sweeps back down in a gust of dark feathers.

Alighting near my horse's head, he takes the bridle and strokes its nose. I'm entranced by the angles of his elegant profile, the slant of his sharp cheekbones, the alluring curve of his lips.

If he were a guard or a courtier in Caennith—someone who caught my eye—I'd have him once and be done with it. But he's my enemy, my captor. I can't purge this attraction in that casual way. Can I?

Just picturing myself with him is treachery, heresy, betrayal of my parents and my people.

The Void King glances at me—the swiftest of looks, his dark eyes taking me in. My lower back tingles in the spot where he touched me.

"We're nearly there." He gives the horse's nose a final pat before leading it onward.

Minutes later, we emerge on the bank of a broad woodland stream, in yet another valley. Beyond a stone bridge lies a wide meadow, surrounded by thick forest, with trees piled upon themselves in mounds of leafy dark green, heaped all the way up to the pale blue of the afternoon sky.

In the center of the lush green, the chapel stands like a dark jewel, formed of smoke-colored stones and black marble veined with amethyst. Arched windows reflect the blue of the sky, but dimly, like shadowed mirrors. In front of the chapel lies a courtyard of neatly-placed paving stones, surrounded by several buildings.

"What are those?" I nod to the structures.

"Stables, a dining hall, and bath-houses," replies the Void King, tugging gently at the horse's bridle as we cross the bridge. "We'll bathe before entering the Chapel for worship. Yes, that includes you, little viper."

I cast an uncertain glance over my shoulder. Though there were women in the Void King's camp, none of them are in the group that traveled here. It's me, the Void King, and five knights—all male.

I swerve my gaze back to the King. He's looking at me, a mocking awareness in his eyes. "Don't tell me you're shy with your body. You certainly aren't shy with your words, or your teeth."

"This is the punishment you devised?" My voice is hoarse. "You'll make me bathe naked with you and your men? Because I pretended to be the Princess?"

"A complete revelation of the Regents' daughter." He raises his voice slightly. "Nothing held back, nothing hidden. Everything laid bare. Doesn't that sound fair, men?"

An appreciative murmur rises from the knights behind us.

This, I did not expect. I don't mind revealing my body in the right circumstances, with people of my choosing. Not like this. This is cruel. This is—I don't think I can bear it. If I refuse to undress, will the King tear the gown from my body himself?

This is the wickedness of the Daenalla. The Edge-Knights heckled and threatened me earlier, and now I'm to be naked before them. Will the King let them molest me? I'm only a hostage after all—my life is valuable, but they haven't promised to leave me untouched.

I've hunched my shoulders unconsciously—I straighten them again and lift my chin, trying to swallow my terror.

The Void King leads our horse into the courtyard before the Hellevan Chapel. Three women and two men, clad in dark, simple robes, descend the steps of the chapel and bow low before him.

"You and your knights honor us, Majesty," says one of the women. She wears a woven band across her forehead, gold and black braided together.

"High Priestess." The King bows to her. "The honor is mine. I have spent far too much power, and I need to replenish it. Is there worship this evening?"

"Yes, my lord. It will be a small gathering, but you are most welcome."

"Thank you. We will dine with you after the service if you have anything to spare. Please do not go to any trouble—a little soup and bread will be more than enough."

The High Priestess smiles warmly. "I think we can do better than that." Her gaze rests on me, confusion flickering over her face as she registers my manacled hands.

"This young woman will be joining us," says the King. "She is the daughter of the Three Faeries, the Regents of the Caennith Fae. We mistook her for a greater prize, but she may yet be of some use."

"Indeed." The High Priestess's eyes meet mine, their gray depths cold as frozen stone. "Lord King, would it please you and your men to bathe before the service?"

"Yes, thank you. And please prepare a private bathing chamber for our unwilling guest, if you would be so kind." He says it so smoothly I barely register the meaning of the words until I hear disappointed whispers from two of the knights to my right. The grumbling stops abruptly when the Void King's head turns in their direction.

A private bathing chamber for our unwilling guest.

He isn't going to force me to bathe naked in front of them all.

Gratitude and relief rush through my heart, and I have to bite my lips to keep from thanking him.

He terrified me with the idea, then removed the danger. I'm certain it wasn't done out of kindness. Is he trying to make me feel beholden to him? Trying to soften me up so he can steal my secrets? He said he wants to make me writhe—he wants to torment me, punish me.

If my mothers were here, Sayrin would warn me not to trust any gift from an enemy's hand. Genla would advise me to find some way to slay my captors. And Elsamel would tell me to look for potential allies, for people with soft hearts who might be willing to help me.

Difficult tasks to reconcile, since the only one in this group who has shown me any softness is the enemy I need to kill—the Void King himself.

Our horses are taken away to the stables, and our group moves toward the nearest bath-house. Inside the stone building, steam hangs in the air, warm and thick, cloying my lungs and filming my skin. Stone benches surround a large, square pool whose steaming waters glimmer in the light of candelabra affixed to the walls.

The knights begin to strip at once, removing armor and boots. A robed woman directs me around the communal bath to a curtained doorway in the far corner of the room. I'm not sure if she's a priestess or simply a servant at the Chapel, but I nod my thanks as she motions for me to proceed through the doorway.

"One moment." The King's rich voice arrests me, and I turn, trying not to think about the way my stomach dropped when he spoke to me.

Tentatively he reaches for my manacles, a humorous caution on his face. "Easy, viper. I only want to remove these so you can bathe."

I hold out my hands to him. "Aren't you afraid I'll try to escape?"

"The private bathing rooms are completely enclosed. Stone walls on all sides, no way out." He slips a tiny key from the pocket of his pants and inserts it into the lock on one of the manacles. With a click, it opens.

Judging by the splashes and shouts, I'll wager at least two of the knights are already naked in the pool. Thankfully, the Void King's great black wings block my view.

I've always wondered how Fae with feathered wings cope with water, but I've never questioned any of them. "How do you bathe with those?" I say impulsively, nodding to the wings.

The King finishes unlocking my second manacle and removes it, his fingers grazing my wrist. "The feathers shed water, mostly. They are cumbersome, to be sure. I don't go swimming often. But like everyone else, I enjoy indulging in a hot bath."

An image of him blazes in my mind—his lean, muscled body, gleaming wet and naked in the golden haze of steam and candlelight. Soapsuds sparkling on his pectorals as he washes himself, framed by the arches of his black wings.

Horrified by how attractive that vision is, I retreat hastily through the curtained doorway the robed woman indicated.

The room beyond is small compared to the communal chamber, but the deep bath is large enough to comfortably fit four people, if they were seated. The hot water bubbles invitingly—probably set in motion with a spell—and every part of my weary body aches to be in it. I haven't slept in far too long—I've been fighting, traveling, and worrying. I'm exhausted.

I tug off my boots and peel Dawn's gown from my body, along with the panties I was wearing. On a stone seat near the bath lies a fluffy towel, a folded linen shift, a plain set of undershorts, and a pair of woven slippers. Not what I'm used to wearing, but at least they're clean.

When I step into the bubbling bath, the heat stings at first, but I acclimate quickly. My wings yield to the water, going limp and lax. Filmy and lightweight, they've never deterred me from swimming. But they're definitely not as powerful as the wings of the Maleficent One. The height he achieved, the flips and dives and maneuvers—I've never been able to do anything like that, even during the short periods when I was allowed to fly, under the close supervision of one of my mothers.

Near the pool lies a stone basin with bars of soap, sprigs of fresh herbs, and heaps of dried flowers. I take a few handfuls and toss them over the water before lathering myself with the soap.

After washing my body and my hair, I seat myself on a low bench under the water. I can't relax fully, not with the male shouts and guffaws coming from the communal bath; but I can take a few moments to inhale the perfume of the dried flowers and let the firm pulse of the hot water beat away some of my tension. My head tips back against the edge of the bath, and I close my eyes.

I startle out of a drowse at the low hum of voices just beyond the curtain covering the doorway. There's a swish of fabric, then a soft slap of large, wet feet.

I open my eyes in time to see a half-nude male figure darting back out through the curtained doorway of my bathing chamber.

If he was trying to catch a glimpse of me naked, he couldn't have gotten a very good look through the bubbles and flower petals. Still, I'm too vulnerable here. I need to leave the bath and get dressed.

Climbing out of the bath, I twist my hair to squeeze out the excess water, and then I turn to the stone seat where the towel and clothes are waiting for me.

They're gone.

So is Dawn's gown, and so are the panties.

I'm alone and stark naked in a stone room—nothing with which to dry or cover myself.

One of the knights stole my towel and clothes so I would have to walk out naked before them all, despite the King's mercy in giving me a private bath.

Or maybe the King put one of them up to this. Maybe this was his plan all along—to put me off my guard and then humiliate me. And I fell for it. I let myself believe he could be kind.

Stupid, stupid. Don't be an idiot, Aura. Stop acting like a fool.

Whenever I chastise myself, it's always Genla's voice, echoing through my mind. She means well—she has only ever tried to keep me sharp, alert, cautious, and careful. She cares about me, even when her words hurt. *Pain is essential for excellence. Suspicion ensures safety.*

But her lessons primarily focused on avoiding foolish choices. She never advised me on how to fix them once they were made.

I could stay in here until someone comes to fetch me; I'm sure they won't leave me in here unattended much longer. But if I linger, the knights will know I'm hiding. And they will laugh.

The only scrap of cloth available to me is the thin curtain hanging across the doorway. It seems to be fastened into the very rock itself with large nails.

I reach up and tug on the fabric—lightly at first, then harder—and the fucking thing rips diagonally, leaving me holding a useless triangular piece of cloth, opening the communal bath to my view.

Hastily I duck out of the doorway and wrap the ragged cloth around my waist. But there isn't enough of it to make a knot. I can cover my privates, my ass, or my chest, but not more than one area.

A bell rings somewhere outside the bath-house—a melodious triple chime. Probably some sort of warning that the service will begin soon. I'm running out of time.

"Regents' daughter," someone calls in a singsong voice. "Bathtime is over. Come on out, or we'll have to fetch you."

That wasn't the Void King's voice. Is he even in the bath-house at all?

I peek around the edge of the doorway. Five knights lounge in the room beyond, some in the bath and some beside it. I'm fairly sure the one who called to me was Vandel, the red-haired knight whose dick I threatened to bite off. He has a towel wrapped around his waist. Maybe my quip about his size struck a nerve and he's out for revenge. Or maybe I shouldn't have kicked Reehan in the face—he's climbing out of the pool, stark naked, wearing a triumphant sneer.

"Don't be shy, little Caennith whore." His forked tongue flickers out between his lips. "Come here, or we'll drag you out."

The Void King is nowhere to be seen. He must have finished his bath quickly and left.

He's my enemy—so why do I feel as if some measure of safety departed with him?

"You should leave her alone." Andras speaks from the far end of the pool, where he's reclining with his elbows propped on the edge. His skin has a bluish tint, all the more striking in this light. "The King won't be pleased about how you're treating his prisoner."

"This isn't just any prisoner," retorts Vandel. "She has killed our people. Haven't you, girl?"

"When they tried to kidnap or kill the princess—yes," I reply stoutly.

"It's your kind that's bringing doom upon the realm," Vandel says. "Fighting against *us*—against the ones who are trying to save Midunnel."

Reehan nods, taking another step toward me. "Your kind prefer to dance and sing and fuck, while the Edge eats up families and farms."

"You claim to worship Eonnula," says another knight, one with leathery wings and umber skin. "Yet you make choices that put everyone in danger, not just your own kingdom."

An olive-skinned knight leaps from the bath, silver feathers flashing in the candlelight. "Where's your sharp tongue now, oh great defender of the Princess?"

"Take her clothes and weapons away, and she's nothing." Vandel spits on the stone floor.

If I don't go out there, they will come and get me. And I refuse to sidle shyly into that room, cringing and attempting to cover myself. If I must do this, I will do it like a warrior. Unashamed.

I crumple the piece of curtain in my hand and force myself to breathe more slowly.

One deep breath. Two. Three.

Then I let the cloth fall, and I step into the doorway, bare to them all.

Their eyes rove over my body, a grudging admiration mingling with the anger on their faces.

"Your people are not blameless, nor is your King," I tell them. "Who demands a baby's blood and then curses the infant when her parents refuse to yield their child to dark magic? Who would force a young human to give up a hundred years of her life? Your king dallies with the Void itself, pulling monsters from the very Edge that wants to devour us all. Why would he risk toying with such darkness?" I scan the group boldly, my chin up, shoulders back. "Some of my people say he fucks the

Endlings. Maybe all of you do. Void-fuckers and Edge-worshippers."

I shouldn't antagonize them. It's idiotic to taunt these powerful men, when I have no magic left and no weapons at my disposal. But my interactions with a certain type of warrior male have taught me to talk back with every ounce of boldness I possess. Fierce words and a strong right hook are the only things they respect.

My name-calling elicits a response from one of them, at least. The olive-skinned knight with the silver wings strides forward, fists clenched. Violence and pain swirl in his eyes.

"Kyan," Andras says warningly.

When Kyan lunges, I take to the air, my wings buoying me as I flit sideways. I perch on a stone bench and wait, my body tight and thrumming with dreadful anticipation as the winged Fae seethes at me.

Tension shines in the air, bright and brittle. The moment one of the knights touches me, that tension will crack—an unspoken barrier removed, a line crossed. Once the first dog bites, the whole pack will attack. They'll do what they want to me, because that's who they are—animals. Monsters. Wicked ones.

Part of me craves the brawl that's coming. I know I won't win, but at least I can tear a few of them up before they overcome me.

As Kyan's body tenses for another charge, Vandel speaks up. "When we planned this prank, we said no one would touch her."

"This bitch killed Forresh," Kyan seethes. His teeth are bared, and tears glitter in his eyes. "Or have you forgotten?"

"Forresh volunteered for that mission," says the knight with the leathery wings. "She knew the risks."

"So I'm to have no justice?" Kyan's feathers bristle, their edges shimmering with a keen, dangerous light. "I must permit

93

this arrogant girl to befoul the honor of our people? To sleep on the bones of my sister?"

"I don't sleep on anyone's bones," I say. "And your people have little honor, from what I can see. You've pursued my best friend since she was born, trying to capture her and use her for a heretical spell that won't even work—"

"But it will." Kyan grits out the words. "It will, because it has to. Because if it doesn't—" He runs shaking fingers through his wet hair, his big shoulders slumping.

My understanding shifts, like when Dawn's tutor adjusted the lenses on a star-glass we used one night. A blurry view at first—then one tiny alteration, and everything turned pristinely clear.

These men may have thrown coarse words at me in the camp, words born from their shock and their deep disappointment—and they may have punished me with this prank, against their king's will—but they haven't touched me in the way I feared. They'd like to kill me, perhaps, but they won't molest me. Their pain and grief prompted this, along with their terror of the Edge, their fear of the future.

Back in Caennith, talking about the encroaching Edge too loudly or dreading it too deeply is considered sacrilegious fearmongering. It's viewed as an affront to Eonnula, a lack of faith in the goddess. We are supposed to believe that everything will be all right—that Eonnula will rescue us, and that if any of us perish before that day of salvation, it must be her will.

By contrast, the Daenalla are open about their fear. They face it head-on. They express it clearly, without veiling their words or making hasty professions of faith afterward.

How liberating it must be to fully express such dark emotion, without having to rein it in, qualify it, or conceal it.

I almost envy them.

10

MALEC

I wash quickly and leave the bath-house before three-bells, eager to discuss a few things with the High Priestess. Her answers only confirm a suspicion I have—one I cannot allow myself to believe until I have proof, which will come after the service, when my magic is refilled. I won't have full access to Void magic again until I reach Ru Gallamet and my Spindle, but I will be able to use a little of it, as well as the powers I was born with. I only hope it's enough for the thing I must do to the girl.

I stride back to the bath-house, intent on fetching her out and hurrying my men along. The sooner we complete our worship, the better.

But as I burst through the bath-house doors into the hazy heat of the chamber, I'm paralyzed by the scene in front of me.

Aura is poised gracefully on a bench, her long legs damp and shining, her butterfly wings gleaming behind her. My startled mind latches onto parts of her bare body—her slender waist, her stomach faintly outlined with taut feminine muscle—her breasts, full and heavy, tipped with pink nipples—her blue hair, clinging wetly to her shoulders.

Utterly naked in front of all my men. And each one of their faces is turned to her, their eyes fixed on her pretty features, her lovely form.

I want to strike them all blind.

Rage boils in my gut—a twisted, hideous, red-hot monster I'm unprepared to fight.

"What the fuck?" I growl.

Aura's eyes widen as I stride forward. "They took my towel and clothes."

I snatch up a spare towel on my way to her. She steps down from the bench as I approach, her wings relaxing from their rigid state, draping loose against her bare back.

I wrap the towel around her whole body, including the wings. "Where are her clothes?" I snarl at my men.

With a shamefaced expression, Vandel picks up a pile of clothing and holds it out to me. I frown at the plain vestments, then glance at Aura. "This is what they gave you to wear?"

She nods.

"Fuck that. Andras, go tell the High Priestess I demand a gown worthy of Aura's station."

Andras scrambles out of the bath and hurries to dry himself. "I told them you wouldn't approve of the prank, my Lord," he says while pulling on his pants.

Reehan and Vandel shoot Andras bladed looks, but he only shrugs and hurries off half-dressed to do my bidding.

I wrap my hand around the back of Aura's neck and push her into the private bathing room. "Why would you walk out naked in front of them?"

She glares. "So their actions are *my* fault?"

"No, but you went out there. You could have waited for me to fetch you. I would have—"

"I didn't know where you were. At first I thought maybe you instigated the trick."

"If I wanted to see your body, I could. Without stealing your clothes."

"Oh, you think so?" Her blue eyes narrow. "You think I would strip for you upon command?"

"That's not what I said."

"Perhaps you should be rebuking your knights, not me." Fury and bitterness storms in her gaze, along with a flicker of shame, a hint of confusion. Her fair skin practically glows, damp and luminous in the candlelight. Moisture beads along her collarbones and the curves of her shoulders. A floral fragrance wafts from her body, slipping into my nostrils, trickling down my throat, warming my lungs. The scent of her—by the Void and the goddess, it makes me harder than I've been in weeks.

"Trust me, they will be punished," I manage.

"Don't punish Andras as harshly. He asked them to leave me alone." She surveys me, seeming to notice my clothing for the first time. "Do you always wear the same pauldron and pants? With no shirt?"

"I—no, not always. But I prefer this outfit. It suits me."

"You like to show off these." She lays her palm across my stomach, and I tense, remembering her teeth ravaging my throat. But she only presses her fingers over the ridges of muscle.

Her touch, just there—by the goddess, I think I might explode.

A living, hungry heat throbs between us, palpable through the steamy air. Thoughts blur into sounds and sensation... the ragged whisper of synchronized breath, the drumbeat of racing hearts. Her palm scorching my abdomen. Her face upturned to mine. My lips feel tender and sore, inflamed with the urgent need for her mouth.

I have not craved a woman this quickly or this fiercely in a long time. It's a fucking shame, because I must resist. I can't allow myself to falter or fail. Not again.

No more failure.

"I will speak to my men now." My voice sounds thick, heavy with lust. "When Andras brings your clothes, get dressed."

Back in the communal chamber, I assign Vandel and Reehan the job of washing every dish after dinner tonight, and mucking the stables tomorrow. Then I order Ember and Kyan to sweep all the rooms in the Chapel after the service, before they sharpen everyone's weapons and polish every piece of armor.

"The Chapel attendants deserve a break, so you'll give it to them," I say. "And you are forbidden from using magic to speed the tasks along."

"Yes, Lord King," they reply.

It's not enough to soothe my anger, but it will have to do. I have no time to deal with them the way I'd like to—by thrashing each one soundly with my fists. Perhaps tomorrow I can punish them as harshly as they deserve.

These men are a younger group of Edge-Knights; I left my older, stronger warriors with Fitzell. The numbers of seasoned Daenallan fighters have diminished lately, thanks to heavy raiding from the Caennith. As their farmlands disappear, the Caennith Royals have become more desperate, sending troops over the border to steal our crops. I've refused to retaliate with all-out war, instead focusing our efforts on defensive tactics as part of my two-year plan to lull our enemies into complacency. It wasn't a popular choice among my counselors, but I persisted.

And it worked, even if the results weren't what I envisioned.

None of this is going to plan. Not the attempted capture of the Princess, nor the response of the Caennith Royals. And certainly not my increasing desire to lie down in front of my beautiful prisoner and let her put her foot on my throat.

11

AURA

The dress Andras brings me is beautiful. The purple skirts are voluminous enough for kicking, running, and fighting, while the fitted, sleeveless bodice shimmers with purple silk and spirals of blue embroidery. Lace arches over my hips where the bodice meets the skirts, and more lace clusters along the neckline.

Andras cuts slits in the back for me and helps me get my wings through the openings. When he steps around to face me again, his bluish skin has flushed purple along his cheekbones.

"My apologies," he says, low. "For not stepping in and giving you something to cover up. I don't—I'm not—" He rubs the back of his neck. "Taking charge, leading, making choices—not my strength. Still, I should have done more. Caennith or not, you didn't deserve that."

"What were they saying about someone called Forresh?" I ask him.

He winces. "Kyan's sister. She went to Caennith with a few others to try and kidnap your friend the Princess. They were all killed. We heard from one of the King's ravens that Forresh nearly got her hands on Princess Dawn—but you stopped her."

I think back over the incidents—too many to count. Some were handled before they ever got to me and Dawn.

"Did she have purple hair?" I ask. "Silver scales along her jaw, neck, and collarbones?"

Sorrow fractures Andras's gaze. "Yes."

I killed her. I don't have to say it—the truth hangs heavy and somber in the air between us.

Killing kidnappers and assassins is my job. Easy enough, thanks to my training and the defenses placed around Dawn and me. I was always congratulated by the Royals afterward—pulled into fierce, grateful hugs. Once, after a particularly close call, the Queen stepped over a pool of blood, cupped my face, and kissed my cheek. She was so thankful I'd protected her daughter.

The people I killed or injured were enemies. Invaders. But in my mind, one of them has now transformed from an "enemy" into someone's sister. Forresh, friend and fellow warrior of the men I met today. A member of Kyan's family.

No wonder they hate me. I'm surprised they haven't done more than yell empty insults and briefly humiliate me. I suppose Kyan might have done more—maybe even tried to kill me, if the Maleficent One hadn't appeared when he did. Though it seemed as if Kyan's anger was waning, yielding to fear and sorrow, even before the Void King made his entrance.

"Come." Andras gestures for me to precede him out of the bathing room. "We should go to the service."

I walk into the big communal room, glancing back at Andras. "I'm permitted to attend the service?"

"Shackled, of course," says a velvety voice.

The Maleficent One is leaning against the wall right outside the private bathing chamber.

"How long have you been lurking there?" I narrow my eyes at him.

"The whole time. Had to be sure you didn't smash Andras's jaw, break his nose, or tear out his throat."

The thought of hurting Andras never entered my mind. Which is strange, considering the level of anger and violence I've felt toward the others. Though in the case of Vandel and Reehan, I merely repaid disrespect and rudeness with caustic words and one swift kick.

As for the King himself—his presence sparks a panicked desperation inside me—the conviction that I *should* kill him, clashing with the horrified awareness of how he affects me physically.

I stand speechless, unable to voice any of it aloud. Unable to meet his eyes.

"Go on," the King says to Andras. "We'll follow in a moment."

With a bow, Andras hurries out of the bath-house.

Something clinks in the King's hand as he moves toward me. A pair of manacles, and a bluesteel collar. His dark eyes trail from my face, down to my breasts, then lower.

"The dress suits you," he says quietly.

"I don't often wear dresses like this. Usually leathers. Simple fabrics, clothes I can move in easily. But I do like this gown." Why am I babbling?

He advances in a slow prowl that makes my heart pound. "I understand how you fooled me. You look like a princess. One with the heart and skill of a warrior." He lifts shadow-stained fingers and I recoil, my muscles hardening for an attack.

"Easy, Aura," he says softly. "I'm not going to hurt you."

"No," I breathe. "I'm going to hurt *you* if you touch me."

He laughs, and his immense wings flare suddenly, high and proud, spreading out and then curving forward until they partly encircle me. The act reveals those shimmering purple and blue feathers near the roots of his wings.

"I'll make you a deal, little viper. I won't put this bluesteel collar around your neck—if you'll give me the rings you're wearing. Every single one of them."

102

I splay my fingers, looking at my family rings. "Why do you want them? I told you they are heirlooms, worn for luck and the goddess's favor. They're useless to you."

"True." He smiles a little, offering no further explanation.

"So you're going to let me attend the service with you, where I could potentially refill my magic—and you won't collar me?" I hook an eyebrow at him.

"Precisely."

"Your people don't experience the Surge like mine do. Perhaps you think I won't be able to refill my powers through your ritual."

He shrugs. "We shall see. Do I get the rings or not?"

"Will you return them to me?"

"Tomorrow morning."

I don't understand what he's doing. Perhaps he has gone mad. If so, I should take full advantage of that.

"Very well." I tug at one of my rings, frowning when it doesn't want to budge. Gritting my teeth, I pull harder.

The Void King watches me with keen interest. "Having trouble?"

"I—fuck." I pull vainly at first one ring, then another.

"You haven't tried to remove them before?"

"No." My heart races, heat flushing over my skin. Why won't they come off? "They must be too tight."

He sets the collar and manacles down on a bench. "May I try?"

After yanking on the rings for a few more seconds, I give up and hold out my hand to him.

His fingers close around mine, claws grazing my skin. He tries to maneuver one of the rings, then another, but it's no use. They're stuck tight.

A bell begins to ring, deep and sonorous.

The Void King lifts his eyes to mine. "It seems we're out of time. Come with me." He grips my wrist and drags me along, out of the bathhouse, across the courtyard bathed in twilight, and up the steps of the chapel.

"Do not attempt to fight or flee," he orders me under his breath as we cross the threshold. "If you do, there will be severe consequences."

Two robed figures stand in the vestibule, holding silver bowls of incense which they wave before me and the King in a complex pattern. A dark, herbal smoke flows into my nostrils, unfamiliar and bitter at first, but the longer I inhale it, the more I crave another hit of the scent.

When the robed figures step back, the King leads me on, into a wide hall with soaring, arched ceilings. The windows are arched as well, each one divided into a thousand diamond-shaped panes. Candelabras stand between them, lighting the otherwise gloomy space. At the head of the sanctuary is an immense window of painted glass.

There are no benches, seats, or platforms. No place for a Priest or Priestess to stand. No instruments, no bursts of dazzling magic. The knights, clad in simple trousers and tunics, sit on thick rugs along with the Chapel's residents and some other guests. They form a circle around the High Priestess who sits cross-legged on a large cushion.

Instead of moving to the innermost part of the circle, near the High Priestess, the King seats himself near the outer edge, letting his wings drape on the floor. He gestures for me to sit as well.

I don't understand how worship can be conducted like this. How is one supposed to generate a Surge of magic without exciting the worshipers, ramping up their emotion to the necessary heights? Even in the small gatherings I've done with my mothers and their close friends, we've always had loud music and louder cries to the goddess—communal chants and dancing bodies swaying together.

In this blue-shadowed chapel, a delicate silence prevails.

Until one of the devotees begins to hum softly.

A few others join in, creating a layered harmony. No words, just quiet humming that echoes in the vast chamber.

"How can this produce a Surge?" I whisper.

"We do not scream for an external application of Eonnula's power," murmurs the King. "We believe that the goddess is already inside all of us, and we have only to link with other friends and worshipers to call Her forth and share Her power. Our worship is about an internal infusion of magic—the true magic we all possess. Sing if you like, or not at all. There is no compulsion to participate, no gaiety forced upon the sorrowful heart."

"And this must be done in a chapel?"

"It can happen anywhere, but the strongest power comes when we quiet ourselves in a sacred place, under the guidance of those fully devoted to the goddess. Now please… sit."

I gather the purple skirts of my gown in both hands and arrange them over my knees as I sit cross-legged beside him.

The singing swells gradually, phrases slipping from the lips of the worshipers, new harmonies introduced in layers of deep bass, rich alto, honeyed tenor, and faint, high soprano. A smooth baritone enters the song, gliding through the rising melody, following its own path in an exquisite flow of notes.

That beautiful voice is coming from the man beside me, who sits with his horned head bowed, his wings relaxed, and his eyes closed.

I could leap up now and run for the door. The robed figures in the vestibule could not stop me. I could take a horse and flee.

Or I could attack the King. I could seize the flaming sunburst medallion from his belt and slice his throat with its sharply pointed rays. I'd cut deeply this time—far deeper than I did with my teeth. If I wound him badly enough, he won't be able to heal.

But such an attack would be sacrilege. Because in this candlelit chapel, in this everchanging river of quiet song, I feel the presence of Eonnula, just as I felt her presence at the Lifegiving Festival... except instead of frenzied joy and impassioned glee, peace reigns here, flooding the sore, ravaged places of my heart.

The music enters me through the jagged seams of my inner self. Its soothing flow reveals all the parts of me that are wrong, more clearly than ever before—glowing along the seams of the anger that's been splitting my heart for more years than I've let myself acknowledge.

I am deeply, wretchedly angry. And I don't know why.

I have no reason to be this angry. I've had a good life, a better life than many. Loved by Dawn, by my mothers. Favorite of the King and Queen. I'm respected among the Caennith, or so my mothers tell me, even though Dawn and I rarely appear in public. I've had training, tutoring—a high-level education. I'm Fae, gifted with magic and wings.

And yet...

Something inside me is wrong. Disconnected, misshapen. The energy circulating through me sharpens that certainty so painfully that I gasp, tears pooling in my eyes.

Self-conscious, I keep my head bowed, but I look up through my lashes at some of the others in the room. At least three of them are crying quietly, and Kyan is kneeling with his forehead pressed to the rugs, sobbing openly while Andras grips his shoulder.

"The goddess is found in sorrow as well as joy," murmurs the King, his voice blending seamlessly with the song.

He turns his head, the candlelight gleaming on his four sharp horns. I meet his gaze, my breath hitching with a sob, tears escaping my eyes.

"Here you can be afraid," he says softly. "You can be angry, and wretched, and so discouraged you want to die. And still you are accepted, and still you are fed. And still you are loved."

I bite back a sob. I'm cracking open inside—I'm breaking—the pieces I've pushed together and held so firmly intact—they are unsealing, falling apart.

"Sometimes I need to be reminded," he murmurs.

"Reminded of what?" I whisper.

"That I am enough. Even when I'm not."

There is no Surge. No crashing wave of magic experienced all at once, no orgasmic blaze of power or delight. Each person in the room seems to be refilled at a different moment, to experience it in a different way. Some gasp audibly, others simply close their eyes, features softening with an expression of supreme peace. A number of the Fae begin to glow visibly, like the Caennith Fae after a surge. When Reehan's skin turns luminous, he rolls his neck and shoulders, nods to the others, and gets up, leaving the chapel with a bounce in his step. Andras and Kyan leave together, their fingers interlaced, one limned in blue light, the other in silver.

One after another, the worshipers slip out, leaving the song thinner, but no less beautiful.

When there are only a few people left in the chapel, the Void King begins to glow.

A haze of green light hovers over his skin and flickers along his horns, while green flames ignite among his black feathers.

Slowly he turns to me, his dark eyes transformed into pits of green fire.

My breath catches.

It's only for a moment, and then he's back to normal, as if he has reined in or absorbed the fresh power.

The green glow reminded me briefly of his staff. I haven't seen it since we went to the bath-house. Perhaps he left it in whatever chamber has been given to him for the night. No one brought weapons into the chapel, so perhaps there's a rule about such things.

The Void King doesn't move, not even when the last threads of the song fade and everyone else has left the chapel; and only I remain beside him, silent and contemplative.

The High Priestess is the last to go. As she passes by us, her eyes lock briefly with mine. They're no longer cold—instead, there's a flash of pity, of eagerness, of interest. The change in her demeanor confuses me. I haven't spoken to her or seen her since we first arrived. What could have changed her opinion of me so drastically?

"You didn't receive any magic?" The Void King's words pull me out of my speculation.

I search for the familiar threads of power, pulling gently. I'm still drained to the dregs. Eonnula did not refill me.

Tears spring to my eyes again. Why am I weeping so much today? I don't usually cry in front of others. It's a sign of weak faith.

I want to ask someone what this means, to express the wretchedness I feel over Eonnula's apparent disfavor.

The Void King's fevered words echo in my mind: *If you can't talk to your enemies, who can you talk to?*

"Eonnula hates me," I burst out. "I've done something to anger her."

"Why do you say that?"

"At the Lifegiving Festival, I didn't feel the Surge. Even in the gatherings my mothers have conducted, I experience the Surge differently than others. I always thought it was because the groups were small, but—it seems I'm the problem. I'm *wrong,* somehow. I think I've always been wrong."

Angrily I brush tears from my cheeks. When he doesn't speak, I continue. "No matter how many times I've saved Dawn from death or capture, I never feel quite confident in myself. And when I fail, when I make a foolish choice or a mistake, I can't bear it. It plagues me for days—weeks—longer."

"I know the feeling."

I cast him a disbelieving look. "What about everything you said just now? That you're enough?"

"I can know that, and not always feel it." He sighs. "As much as I tell others they can reveal themselves fully in these sessions, I have trouble allowing myself to be open. I have to maintain a certain level of control, even when I worship. If I let everything out—if I showed my true fear and rage and violence, my men would lose hope. I don't have the luxury of experiencing all my inner pain, or yielding all control. Not ever. Not with anyone."

He rises, stretching his wings. "But we're talking about you, little viper. You say you've always felt wrong. What do you mean?"

I cringe, knocking a fist against my forehead. "Why did I tell you that? I'm so fucking stupid—"

"Don't call yourself stupid," he says sharply.

Startled, I glance up.

His handsome face tightens with pained disapproval. "You're not stupid. You didn't have a choice about any of this."

I get to my feet, which brings me tantalizingly close to him. There's a hands-breadth of space between our bodies, and the proximity thrills through me, a heated compulsion.

"So you think it's true," I say hoarsely. "You think Eonnula has cut me off for some reason. I suppose that makes you happy. Keeping a powerless Fae prisoner is so much easier, after all, isn't it, Your Majesty?"

"Nothing about you is easy."

I spin away with a scoff, but he catches both my hands and whirls me back to face him.

"Call me Malec," he says.

I inhale sharply, trying to think of a taunt, a retort—but I can't speak as his fingers curl around mine, gentle, almost caressing. I stare at the two tiny dots of green shining deep, deep in his pupils. Those glowing spots seem to advance and recede as I watch them. It's a mesmerizing dance, and I can't look away.

"Do your wings respond to your emotions?" His low voice reverberates through my chest, quivering along my very heartstrings. "Anger, pain, fear, joy, arousal? Are they sensitive to touch?"

Why is he curious about that? Does he think it's related to my problem with Eonnula? I don't suppose it can hurt to tell him. I answer in a dazed, distant voice, still entranced by his eyes. "My wings respond when I think of flying. But no, they aren't sensitive."

"And why do you think that is?"

"The circumstances of my birth were unique. As I said, I'm different from other Fae."

"And that distresses you." His eyes are liquid sin flecked with emerald light, luring me in, compelling me to confess.

"I think my distress is fairly obvious." My words are barely a breath. Why can't I look away?

A delicate tug at my fingers, then another. Metal sliding over skin.

"What are you doing?" I whisper.

"Taking off your rings," he says soothingly. "A simple task, now that I've applied a little magic."

Something falls to the carpet beneath us—several small objects. My rings, all of them, gone.

Dread thrums in my bones, along my nerves. The sense of being lured and lulled, of being ensnared in a silken trap, grows stronger, quickening my heartbeat. I may only have dregs of magic left, leaving me at risk for overexertion—but I need to use the last of my power to get away from this monster, before he does something worse than stealing my family heirlooms.

I try to pull away from the Void King, but my movements are sluggish. My body is fixed in one spot, and my eyes are chained to his—unblinking, mesmerized. When I try to reach for the remaining bits of my magic, there's nothing. Not a drop. Not even an echo.

"What have you done to me?" I whisper.

The King's right hand slides around the back of my neck, and his thumb rests against my cheekbone. He places his other hand on my hip. "I am sorry, Aura, for the pain I must cause you. I promise it will be brief."

My heartbeat gallops in my chest, a frantic flight my body cannot follow. My breath quickens, my breast heaving against the Void King's forearm as he holds my neck and face, as he bends his head and furrows his brow in concentration.

A dot of exquisite pain sparks in my skull. It blooms wider, then fractures, snaking down my spine, coiling in the center of my back. Something is glowing behind me—glowing brighter and brighter—a white light tinged with pink, purple, and blue. The colors of my mothers' magic.

My voice won't work. I want to fight, to scream—but all I can do is slowly, slowly move my hands up to his arms—huge muscled arms, and my hands are too small, and my reflexes won't work. I grip the Maleficent One's shoulders, unable to do anything more.

A current of air swirls by our feet, surging and coiling upward, tearing at his wings. Feathers loosen and fly around us, and his long black hair swirls in the rising wind, but he doesn't stop whatever he's doing. His eyes are closed, his brows dented, his mouth tight. I stare at him, mute and frozen, seared by bone-splitting agony along my spine.

Pain screams in my ears, my brain, my veins, my very bones. It's as if the Void King has taken all the ill-fitting pieces of my heart and wrenched them forcibly apart. I am raw, broken, and bleeding inside, and still the excruciating pain spikes higher, and still the wind roars around us, and still the light burns. Whips of purple, pink, and blue lash from somewhere behind me—from my back, where my wings are rooted.

"Almost there," the Void King grits out. "Almost."

His wings are being torn apart—a cloud of black and indigo feathers racing through the churning wind. The colorful whips of light snake out from behind me and slice at his body, splitting his armor, carving deep grooves into his flesh. He grimaces, but he only clasps my neck and hip more firmly. His power drives into me, chasing out some other force—something that has always been part of me, and yet the harder he pushes, the more I realize he is carving out something alien, something *wrong*.

A shattering flash of agony, a high keening sound—did it come from me? He's covered in blood now, his wings ravaged and torn—but suddenly the stained-glass window of the chapel lights up, a fierce blaze of light tinged faintly green. That light rushes over the King and me, and with a final spine-cracking convulsion, all the broken pieces of me snap into place.

The whip-like colors of my mothers' magic loosen and flail. They fall to the floor and quiver there like severed tentacles, lurching and thrashing before they finally dissipate in the force of the new light. The wind dies, leaving a cracked stillness in its place.

With a cry of agony, the Void King lets me go and staggers backward. He falls to his knees, heaving great breaths.

I stand rigid where he left me, while the light from the window fades away.

The candles along the chapel walls are still burning. How did the wind not blow them out?

What happened?

Why do I feel—

I feel different. Like some disjointed thing inside me has been reset.

I lift my shaking hands, bare of rings. I brush them over my body—the dress is flecked with the Void King's blood, but otherwise everything seems fine. I am whole, I am—

Something gold lies over my shoulder, draping my breast.

Golden hair.

Dazed, I lift the lock of hair… and pull.

There's an answering tug on my scalp.

Did the King glamour my hair color?

I glance at him again. He's kneeling between his ragged wings, one fist planted on the floor. Blood drips from the gashes in his skin. Ruined leather and metal hangs from his broad shoulders.

"Why—" I begin, and then I catch sight of myself, reflected in the dark glass of the windows behind him.

My hair is golden, and my—

My wings—

A frantic sweat bursts across my skin.

I know what it feels like when my wings are glamoured invisible and intangible. Even under such a glamour, I can still feel them, rooted in my spine, connected to my brain.

This is different. My wings aren't just glamoured. They're gone.

"You—you took my wings." My voice cracks. "What did you do? Oh goddess, what have you done to me?"

He struggles heavily to his feet. "Destroying another Fae's wings is beyond my power. That's not something I can do, not even with Void magic. The wings were never yours, Aura. They were stolen from another Fae and fused to you. Those wings had been dead for years, animated only by a powerful spell. With the shattering of the spell, they disintegrated."

"What?" My legs are trembling, my stomach churning.

He casts aside the remnants of his armor and approaches me, his dark eyes soft with sympathy, no hint of green light in them now. "The wings were part of a visceral glamour. A physical alteration so pervasive, so convincing, it required three extremely powerful casters. The Three Faeries."

"I don't understand you."

"Touch your ears, Aura."

With shaking fingers, I feel my left ear. Instead of a sharply pointed tip, the top edge is rounded.

"Those are your true ears," he says quietly. "That is your real hair. Your false wings are gone. The charmed rings that gave you the ability to do magic have been stripped away. You are as you were meant to be—the human daughter of royal parents, Crown Princess of Caennith, and the future Conduit of Eonnula's power."

Bile shoots up the back of my throat, and I lurch forward, vomiting onto the carpet. I manage to claw back my hair just in time—my hair, my hair—my golden hair—

"What is happening?" I whimper. "This doesn't make any sense."

"Your parents must have given you to the Three Faeries for concealment and protection right after I cursed you. The Faeries transformed you with a visceral glamour—which, I might add, has been forbidden for centuries because of its unpredictable effect on the subject's mind. They taught you to fight, to defend yourself. And the Royals placed you right next to their fake daughter, so you would have all the advantages and protection afforded to the Princess. You were hidden from me in plain sight."

12

The Princess vomits again. This time I step forward and hold back her yellow locks while she heaves and sobs. I rather miss the blue hair. But her natural tresses are glorious.

Finally she straightens, and I fetch a cloth from an incense cabinet nearby so she can wipe her mouth.

"You're saying I've been human all along." Her voice is tight and raw.

"Yes. Your parents gave you to the Three Faeries and adopted a human girl to stand in your place. Dawn has been your double since you were both small."

"Yet they told me to guard her."

"They taught you to fight. They gave you magic and wings. You had all the benefits of being secured within castles, guarded as closely as the Princess, yet with the added protection of a secret identity."

"Don't try to make it sound clever. It was a stupid plan."

"It was a brilliant, sadistic plan. One that almost worked perfectly."

"Sadistic," she says slowly, frowning. "Do you think Dawn knew?"

"I'm fairly sure she didn't."

"They put her in the most dangerous position in the kingdom, but they didn't give her a choice. They raised her as their own, as if she was the true Princess, and she never knew—" Aura breaks off the sentence, biting her lip, furious tears sparkling in her eyes. "How did *you* know who I was?"

"I began to suspect some trickery because of your nonreactive wings, and the strange heirlooms you wore. But those things in themselves weren't conclusive—they could have been explained by other means. The strongest indication was the report Fitzell gave me right before we left camp. She was supposed to ride with me to Ru Gallamet—all the Edge-Knights were—but we received word of massive attacks at various points along the border. The sheer scale and intensity of those attacks— the King wouldn't have ordered them for the daughter of the Three Faeries. Nothing less than the kidnapping of his own child would warrant such an invasion. So I left Fitzell and most of my knights to help with the fight, and headed straight here. After I bathed, I told the High Priestess my suspicions, and she gave me more information about visceral glamours. She agreed to keep the others away from the Chapel after the service, so I could explore your mind and body and discover what lay concealed there. But I didn't truly know if I was right—not until your mothers' magic began to attack me."

"The Three Faeries are not my mothers." She speaks the words slowly, vaguely, as if she can't grasp them yet.

"Correct. The Royals are your parents."

"Fuck them," she snaps.

I raise my eyebrows, but I don't reply. She's going through a range of emotions I can't possibly fathom. Once she processes her new familial connections, she'll realize what else her identity means.

I *did* capture the cursed Princess. My triumph is real this time. At long last, I have the one girl who might be able to save us all.

But will she listen to me? Will she be able to hear what I have to tell her, about herself, about my plans? About the curse that will steal a hundred years of her life?

She's pacing the floor, hands fisted. "I couldn't experience the Surge. Why? If I'm to be the Conduit—why?"

"The Conduit comes of age at twenty-five, as you know. Until that time, the Surge would be experienced in the usual human way, as a flood of joy and hope. But you were blocked from feeling that, because of the rings the Three Faeries gave you, and because of the way the visceral glamour interfered, not only with your inner self, but with your aura. That was another hint that you were different—when I tried to check you for glamours, I encountered the clumsily-reassembled pieces of your aura. It confused and distracted me."

"And my parents allowed the Faeries to perform this visceral glamour on me, knowing it might fuck me up inside?"

I want to soften this for her. But half-truths and gentle lies will do her no good. She must know everything.

"I can't say for sure," I tell her. "It has been years since I spoke to either of your parents directly. I believe they love you in their way. But this was never about you—not entirely. It was always about religious prejudice, arrogance, and power. After the curse—even before it—this was about your parents and the Three Faeries triumphing over me. It was about them winning."

"Winning?" Her fingers go limp and her shoulders sag, her anger replaced by betrayal and grief, for the moment.

"To understand the antagonism between your parents and me, you would need to hear the whole story from the beginning, and I'm not sure you can take that right now."

"As if you care about my feelings at all." Her cheeks redden. "You—you cursed me. Not Dawn—*me*. Oh goddess— you're going to take me to your Spindle and use my blood for your magic! And then I'll lose a hundred years—you monster!"

Fire rages in her eyes, and she pulls herself up tall, her fingers balling into fists again. Her breasts heave against the lacy neckline of her blood-spattered dress.

I need to calm her, to soothe her somehow. And I need to rest—my wounds are healing more slowly than usual, and I've lost a lot of blood. The Three Faeries' magic, when combined, is nearly a match for mine, even when they're not physically present.

"We can't talk about this anymore tonight," I tell her. "I need to heal, and you need time to think. And you should eat something. You threw up what was left of your lunch."

"I don't want to eat," she snarls.

"Then drink something, at least. I swear no harm will befall you tonight."

"How magnanimous of you." Her lip curls in a sneer. "Are you going to chain me up again?"

"Not unless you deserve it. Before I rest, I will wreathe the Chapel grounds with magic. You won't be able to escape the boundary, but you may wander freely within it, if you swear not to harm my people."

"If they taunt me and torment me, I will hurt them."

"Fair enough." I soften my tone. "Just don't kill anyone. Remember, my men didn't do this to you."

She scoffs, turning away and wrapping her arms around herself. Her nails scratch restlessly at her skin.

"Does it itch?" I ask. "That can be a side effect of a forcibly broken glamour."

"It does itch," she admits. "But only a little."

"Any pain?"

The look she gives me—incredulity, accusation, agony. I wince at my own foolish question. "Stay here as long as you like. I'll let the others know not to disturb you. When you're ready, please join us for food and drinks." I dip into a low bow, though

I fear it's less impressive than it should be, what with the state of my body and my wings. "Your Highness."

When I glance over my shoulder on my way out of the chapel, she is standing alone in the candlelight, her hands clasped over her heart and her face transfixed with pain.

13

AURA

This human form—it must be a glamour. This is something the Maleficent One has done to me. He's trying to trick me...

But I can't convince myself of that, not when I feel *settled* for the first time in my life. I didn't realize how much dysfunction plagued my spirit until everything snapped back into place.

I once reseated a human guard's dislocated shoulder—popped it back into the socket. The joint was functional again, seated correctly, but the pain and inflammation remained for a while. That's how I feel right now. I am a human who has been operating under an invasive glamour for decades, my mind and body inhabited by the magic of three Fae. It makes sense that my restoration to my true self would leave me emotionally swollen and sore, even though my spirit is finally whole again.

I was always human. That's why my magic was never very strong, why it was centered in my hands—I was unconsciously siphoning it from the charmed rings. That's why my mothers had to teach me to channel magic from my palms, to my heart, and then to my head before I could use it.

I have to stop calling them "my mothers." They're not my mothers; they're liars.

They told me to never trade places with the Princess. They warned me about it, over and over. "Let Etha do her job as the Princess's double. Defend your own life, and Dawn's." Now I understand why they were so insistent about that point.

They subjected me to training, hours of it, endlessly building my strength. Making me into my own bodyguard. They hosted their own type of gathering to "refill" our magic. No doubt the Faeries infused more power into my rings during those sessions, so the energy in the charmed objects would not run out.

No wonder one of them was usually present when I flew any significant distance—probably to ensure that my borrowed wings functioned as they were meant to. Oh, I could fly on my own—short jaunts, a quick flutter here or there—but never very far or very high because my wings were *not mine*.

Where did my mothers get those beautiful butterfly wings? What Fae's body was mutilated so I could masquerade as Fae? How much of that Fae's spinal cord and nerves did they weave with mine? No wonder the Void King had to hold me still while he unraveled the spell. I might have been paralyzed if he'd done it while I was struggling against him.

Why would the King and Queen risk permanently scarring my mind and heart with forbidden magic? Why would they keep me at arm's length all my life, feigning love for another child?

And who is Dawn? Some orphan girl my mothers brought to the King and Queen as a substitute?

The Faeries aren't my parents, but Goddess help me, I still love them. I still want Elsamel to fold me into a warm hug. I want Sayrin to guess exactly what kind of tea I'm craving. I want Genla to storm around the room, threatening harm on whomever has made me sad.

But they're the problem. They have devastated me beyond words. And behind that devastation looms rage—the anger I've carried all my life, though I never knew why.

At last my fury has form and cause.

I'm angry for myself, and I'm angry for Dawn, too. What were my parents going to do when my twenty-fifth birthday arrived and the threat of the curse was past? Would they raise me up to my rightful place and toss Dawn into the streets?

There must be more to this story. The Void King said I need to hear the whole tale, from the beginning.

Normally I would never entertain the thought of believing him over the Regents and the Royals. But he's the one who broke the visceral glamour and reassembled me as I was meant to be. *They* are the ones who lied to me and Dawn for years.

Disguising their daughter as Fae—such an idiotic scheme. I can see a hundred holes in their plan—not the least of which is its cruelty to a pair of unsuspecting children.

I pace the floor for seconds, for minutes, for an hour—I'm not sure how long. My mind races, straining the lies I've learned, sifting for truth. Rearranging what I know. Realigning all my memories in light of this new identity.

Finally I step too close to the vomit on the rug, and its stench flares in my nostrils. I nearly gag again, but I manage to control the impulse.

I need to get out of here. I need to breathe fresh, cool night air. And damn me—I need a drink. Several drinks.

I've never allowed myself to overindulge in liquor. But tonight seems as good a night as any to get roaring drunk.

Before leaving the Chapel, I pick up my rings and put them all back on. I hunt for the threads of magic in them, but I can't feel anything. The rings were already weak, low on power, and the Maleficent One must have finished deactivating them. They are useless to me. Besides, wearing them stirs faint nausea in my stomach. They are symbols of betrayal, of deceit.

I scatter them on the rug and walk to the exit.

Placing my palms against the smooth wood of the chapel doors, I take a deep breath before pushing them open.

I half-expect there to be a joyful mob outside, ready to roar their delight at me, their long-awaited prey.

But the stone steps are empty, and so is the square beyond.

Briefly I think of running, before I recall what the Void King said—that he would weave a barrier along the border of the grounds. A border I can't break, now that I have no magic.

No magic.

The loss bites into my heart, an unexpectedly sharp pain. I will never be able to use magic again. Not without fully-charged magical tokens like my rings.

I've heard of such items—rare talismans and unique objects imbued with temporary magic that humans can use. But I'd never seen any, nor did I suspect my rings were like that.

In truth, I never had any power at all. I was tricked into thinking I did. Perhaps the Three Faeries laughed quietly behind my back as they trained their "child" to use her "magic."

Anger spouts inside me again—anger at myself this time, for being so thoroughly stupid. For not seeing the pieces that didn't fit. For accepting the lies and explanations. For not perceiving the truth.

Fuck me, and fuck everyone I've ever known.

A few lanterns and lighted windows dot the darkness of the square, shining from the outbuildings of the chapel complex. Beyond one of the long buildings, half-obstructed by its bulk, I can make out a brighter glow—a bonfire, and several torches on posts. I can see the ends of a few long wooden tables. That must be where the dinner is being held.

The clank of tankards, a lilting trickle of music, and the roll of merry male voices draws me in. Much as I dread facing anyone right now, I am desperate for a drink. I can't take the torture of my own thoughts any longer.

After crossing the square, I pause at the corner of the building, taking stock of what lies beyond. Tables covered in dishes, a platter with a half-eaten roast pig; bowls of cherries, stewed apples, and buttered potatoes; a plate of sliced bread. Some of the tables are empty, probably abandoned by locals who came to worship and then returned to their homes after the meal. A few of Hellevan Chapel's robed denizens sit at the end of one table, conversing quietly. A drummer, a piper, and a fiddler perch on stools nearby, nodding to one another as they play pleasant music.

At the nearest table sit the five Edge-Knights, either shirtless or with their tunic sleeves rolled up. Andras is popping grapes into his mouth. Kyan's silver feathers flash, his wings flaring as he arm-wrestles with Vandel. Vandel must be losing, judging by the way he's flushed right to the roots of his red hair. Blond Reehan seems to be in a drinking match with the bat-winged knight—I think he's called Ember.

No sign of the Void King. He must have gone to rest—he was in bad shape after smashing through the Three Faeries' spells.

I did not have close connections with any of the other guards and soldiers in the Caennith palaces I frequented. Some of them were jealous of my position and privileges, and they showed it. That's where I got my sharp tongue and vicious reactions—from fielding their envious barbed words, forcing their respect. If they'd known who I truly was, they would never have dared to attack me, verbally or otherwise. At best, my connection with the Royal Guard was a tenuous, grudging acceptance, and a temporary camaraderie on a few occasions, when I had some rare free time and I wanted someone to fuck.

These Edge-Knights have a ribald sense of humor like the Royal Guards, and they share the same penchant for mocking those they view as rivals or threats. But unlike the Royal Guards, they are more driven and desperate. Like me, they are tangled in a web whose weaving began long before any of us were born—caught in a neverending war of ideologies, prey to a realm that's collapsing in on itself.

Has the King already told them who I really am? I suspect he has—he seems like the type to share information with his men. I hate that I like that about him.

All I want is to drink. And the best way to get a drink quickly is to stride out there and face this head-on.

I straighten the blood-flecked skirts of my purple gown and hitch the bodice a little higher. My feet are still bare, soundless as I leave the shadows of the building and walk forward into the firelight.

I step up to Ember and Reehan and pluck the drinks out of both their hands, gulping first one, then the other.

Sighing, I set the cups down and wipe my lips with the back of my wrist.

The music screeches to a stop, and the murmurs of the chapel attendants cease.

The five knights stare at me. Vandel takes advantage of Kyan's distraction from their arm-wrestling match and slams his opponent's hand down to the table, a solid thump in the silence.

Reehan clears his throat, stands up, and grabs a bottle. All eyes lock on him as he lifts it high. Shaking back his blond hair, he looks around at the others and cries, in a triumphant voice, "The Princess of Caennith wants to drink!"

"And drink she shall!" Andras replies, and the others roar their approval. Ember holds out his cup for Reehan to fill, then hands it to me with a nod.

"We need some merry music!" Reehan calls to the musicians, and they begin playing again, a jauntier tune this time, while Ember quietly places a few slices of meat, cheese, and fruit on a plate and passes it to me.

While I drink and eat, Kyan begins growling at Vandel over the result of their little game. "That wasn't a fair match. I was distracted." His silver feathers bristle.

"Not my fault you can't keep your mind on the competition," Vandel says.

"No excuses from the loser," Ember interjects. "That's the rule. Accept defeat, and move on."

Kyan huffs out a breath. "Fine. We go again."

"I'd like to take Vandel on," I say through a mouthful of stewed apples.

Kyan looks at me, and for a second, all I can see is the enraged grief in his eyes as he charged at me in the bath-house.

I killed his sister. I killed her to protect Dawn; but really, I was protecting myself. I just didn't realize it.

Everything I knew is twisted now, distorted.

I let my expression crack a little—let some of the confusion and pain I feel leak through. Kyan's eyes soften in response.

Pulling my gaze from his, I drink again.

"Very well." Kyan moves to sit closer to Andras, yielding his place to me.

I walk around to his spot and hitch up my skirts so I can sit astride the bench. Then I prop my elbow on the table.

Vandel looks from his own freckled arm with its bulging bicep to my slim, toned arm. "Haven't you suffered enough embarrassment for one day, Your Highness?" The last two words carry a faintly mocking twist.

"Not nearly enough," I grit out, cupping the fingers of my right hand. "Come on, dicklet. Show me what you can do."

Two of the other knights snicker, and Vandel's face turns a shade redder. He clamps his right hand around mine. "On the count of three. Ember?"

Ember counts, and when he says "three," I tense my right arm, exerting pressure against Vandel's palm.

I may have lost everything else, but this body is still mine. I worked for this strength, this skill. It belongs to me.

Or at least, I hope it does. I do feel slightly weaker with my rings gone. Perhaps one of them enhanced the strength I already possessed, to augment the illusion of my Fae nature. All the more reason I should test myself, to discover the true limits of my body.

Vandel is human, which means I stand a better chance of beating him than I would with the Fae knights. But there's plenty of power in his grip; it's going to be close.

"Get him, Princess," Andras bursts out. "Take him down!"

"He'll save his best strength until you tire," Kyan warns me.

I'm not as strong as I was, that's for certain. But thankfully most of my strength is still there. Muscle and sinew, not magic.

"Pin her!" Reehan is leaning across the table, pounding on the wood in his eagerness. His blond hair tumbles around his face, and his eyes are brightly intense. "What's taking you so long, Van? Down with the Caennith!"

At his urging, Vandel presses me harder. I yield a little, and a bellow of delight breaks from Reehan and Ember.

But the yielding was a calculated move on my part. I watch Vandel's face, and when he grins at his friends, I strike.

I throw all my rage into my arm, my shoulder, my hand. Strong as Vandel is, the current of anger and violence inside me far outmatches him. With a cry of agonized fury I force his arm back until it's hovering just above the table.

He's groaning, trying to keep from giving me that last bit of space—but with another yell I slam his arm against the wood.

"Yes!" I shout, leaping up and wringing out my arm. "That's how it's fucking done!"

"I was tired from wrestling Kyan," Vandel complains, but Ember leans over the table, bat-wings flared, and smacks him on the back of the head. "No excuses, Van. Goddess, both you and Kyan are such poor losers."

"Maybe *you're* a better loser." I lower my lashes, a challenge in my hooded eyes as I meet his gaze. "Care to try me?"

His full lips curve in a grim smile. "I accept."

"But first, we drink again!" Reehan shouts.

129

Cups are refilled, and I throw back three burning swallows of the liquor before switching to Ember's side of the table. We agree to do left arms this time, and I'm grateful that my trainers insisted I practice with both sides of my body, no matter which hand I preferred.

Did any of them ever suspect who I was? I remember a few guards, tutors, and trainers disappearing suddenly from time to time. Dawn and I were told they'd been reassigned. I see those events in a different light now, and I can't help wondering...

Too much wondering. I need to drink more.

I put up a good effort against Ember in the arm-wrestling match, but he is Fae, and he conquers me after a few minutes of ferocious straining. We drink again, and somehow I end up seated on the table, nibbling almonds and cold roast pork, drinking whatever the knights pour for me.

Fire trickles along my veins, and my chest burns with the liquor. A buzzing heat soars into my head and softens the edges of all the thoughts that have lacerated my mind since the King broke my glamour.

I'm not sure what I've been drinking, but it hasn't all been wine. There's stronger stuff in some of these cups.

The musicians begin a soaring dance tune, deeper and wilder than the ones I've heard in Caennith. It twines with the strings of my heart, tugging on them unbearably. My body wants to bend with that melody, to curve and sway and shudder along with its crests and dives.

"Let's dance," I say, jumping up on the bench.

They stare, and I remember that the Daenalla are not as enthusiastic about dancing as the Caennith are.

Whether I am Fae or human, I remain a child of Caennith. And I want to lose myself in that glorious song. I'm fairly sure it's the best I've ever heard. Or perhaps the wine is flavoring the music.

"You can all sit there like big somber rocks," I say. "I'm going to dance."

The Edge-Knights exchange glances, and Reehan half-rises from his seat.

"You four should be doing as the King ordered—cleaning and polishing, not drinking and dancing," Andras interjects.

"We'll get it done." Reehan throws a grape at him. "Stuff some more fruit in your mouth, won't you, and stop nagging like a crotchety housewife."

I burst into laughter. Somewhere in my muddled mind, I know his comment wasn't particularly humorous, but in the moment it feels like the funniest thing I've ever heard.

Kyan jumps up, silver wings flaring, and pulls Andras to his feet. "Dance with me, housewife." Kyan's grin is half-mockery, half-seduction. Andras takes a swing at him, but Kyan catches his wrist and pulls him closer, their profiles aligned. There's a palpable tension between them, something beyond the camaraderie of soldiers. I smile as I watch them moving awkwardly together, clumsily swerving with the rhythm. Their connection makes me ache in a different way, and anything different feels like relief right now.

Still standing on the wooden bench, I touch Ember's shoulder. Lashes lowered, I sway my hips, let my waist bend and my shoulders roll with the music. His wings rise and stiffen as he watches me.

Then I turn to Reehan, at my other side. My fingers caress the jaw I broke back at camp. "Is your pretty face all right now?"

His purple eyes take on a richer glow, and his forked tongue flickers over his lips. "Perfectly all right, Princess."

"I'm glad." I smile at him, and then I laugh because I think I like being drunk, and I've never seduced two men at once but these knights are so beautiful I can't resist playing with them. They move closer, two tall, muscled bodies on either side of me, two gorgeous Fae who, in the liquid glow of music and drink, seem to have forgotten themselves just like I have. Reehan is shirtless, and I stroke my palm down his bare chest briefly before I step out from between them, up onto the table. There's already a clear space where we arm-wrestled, and I move into it, leaning down to the scowling Vandel.

"Come dance with us." The words ooze from my lips, slowed and slurred by the drink. "Come on. Forget who we all are and what we do—let's just *live*."

"I'll drink to that," Reehan exclaims, passing a goblet up to me.

I drink, one hand raised high above my head, the other tipping wine into my mouth while I bounce on my heels. When the goblet is empty I toss it away and I move to the music. My thighs slide against each other, my hips undulate, and my hands travel over my chest and my waist while I toss my head, flinging my new golden hair. I'm burning, tingling, thrilling—my dress is much too hot for my sensitive skin.

Dragging my fingers along my neckline, I peel down the bodice slowly, exposing my breasts. The cool night air feels marvelous against my scorched skin.

"Princess." Ember reaches up, trying to pull my clothing back into place, but I twist out of his reach.

"It's nothing you haven't seen," I tease. Reaching around to my back, I unfasten the dress hooks and let the whole thing slide into a silky pile on the table. With one bare foot I kick the gown away, and I keep dancing, wearing only the panties I was given along with the dress.

The music is slower now, honeyed and sensual. Maybe the musicians are enjoying the show. Maybe I don't mind that I'm mostly naked in front of strangers. Maybe that's the magic of wine.

Or maybe I simply don't care what happens to me anymore. I'm nothing but a pawn in the game, after all—a sacrifice, a curse—

I blink away that last thought and throw myself more fully into the dance, my body surging with the rhythm. Vandel gives a low whistle as I bob my thinly-clothed ass right in front of his face.

"Fuck yes, Princess!" crows Reehan, his cup upraised. He drinks, slams it down, then steps onto the bench, cocking his hips and swerving with me, mirroring my movements while I smile encouragement. Ember sways to the music too, growing bold enough to let his fingers trail down my thigh.

The touch feels good, so I let Ember keep stroking my leg while I dance for them on the table. The song kicks into a new, frenzied pace, and I seize Reehan's hands, placing them on my hips. When he looks up, his forked tongue lashes between his grinning teeth.

Fuck, I should let Reehan lick me. Him—or someone else— maybe someone taller, with pale, handsome features, and long black hair, and sharp horns, and wings...

I toss my head to shake away thoughts of the Void King. "Touch me," I say hoarsely to Reehan.

His palm brushes my breast, while Ember's hand slides up my thigh.

The shudder of massive wings, a whirlwind exploding out of the darkness. Black fingers clamp around Reehan's throat right before he's slammed flat on his back with earthshaking force. His attacker whips around and smashes a punch into Ember's cheekbone, sending him to the ground.

The music dies with a squawk. Kyan and Andras separate hastily, and Vandel retreats several steps.

We all stare at the Void King, who glares back, bare-chested and furious. His wings still look a bit ragged, but the rest of him is—well, it's succulent masculine perfection. I lick my lips.

"Enough of this," he growls. "To your chores, men. And you—" his gaze locks with mine— "What the fuck do you think you are doing?"

"Having fun." I tilt my hips and smile at him. "Want to dance with us?"

"No, I do not want to dance." He picks up my gown and throws it at me. "Put that back on."

I glance around at the knights—two still on the ground, three standing nearby, all of them watching me and the King. In their faces I read lust, admiration, shame, and interest. All things that give me a strange, heady kind of power. I like the feeling, especially after how powerless I felt in the Chapel.

I've been remade, the poorly-assembled chunks of me cracked apart and rebuilt. I've been peeled down to the bloody core of myself and seared with fiery truth. In light of that gargantuan change, the fear of physical exposure I felt in the bath-house seems ridiculous. In fact, I relish the nudity now. The power of it, the freedom. It's luscious, addictive. It's just what I need.

"Put on the gown," repeats the King.

"No," I say lazily, toying with one of my nipples. "I don't think I will."

"Oh for Eonnula's sake—" The Void King plants a booted foot on the bench, throws an arm around my waist, and sweeps me right off the table. I don't have time to react before he's stalking away from the bonfire area, carrying me under his arm.

I wriggle a little, but he's shirtless, and the sensation of his smooth, hard body against my heated flesh is wildly arousing. So instead of fighting, I relax, and I let him tote me along. His feathers brush my bare legs as he hauls me back toward the Chapel.

"You interrupted my fun," I tell him. "You said I could do whatever I wanted."

"I didn't expect you to get drunk and dance naked for my knights."

"Ah, but I didn't harm or kill anyone. I wasn't hurting your men, just playing with them."

"Were you going to fuck them?"

"Maybe. Normally I wouldn't fuck with Daenallan men, but your knights are so pretty and strong. And when in Daenalla—"

"You're out of your mind with anger and grief," he says firmly. "You don't know what you're doing. You'll regret this tomorrow, trust me."

"Trust *you*? That's rich, seeing as you're the reason for all this. If you hadn't cursed me, my parents wouldn't have needed to disguise me, and the Faeries wouldn't have glamoured me." I pause to think through what I just said and make sure it's logical. I think it is, but I can't be sure because *wine*. "Without you, none of this would be happening," I repeat. "So really, it's all—your—fault." I punctuate each word with a hard jab of my elbow to his ribs.

We've nearly reached a side entrance of the Chapel, a narrow wooden door in the deep shadow of a tower. The King drops me into the grass suddenly. I like the feel of the cool, ticklish blades against my naked skin, so I stay there, lying at his feet.

"*Part* of it is my fault," he snaps. "You think I don't know that? You think I haven't regretted the curse a thousand times? But I can't break it. In my rage and hubris I made it unbreakable, except by one method."

"And what is that?"

"Once your finger is pricked and you fall into the hundred-year sleep, you can be awakened if the person who loves you best kisses you. But that person must then take your place, and the clock restarts. They lose a hundred years of their lifetime to that charmed sleep."

I prop myself on my elbows amid the lush grass. My drunken mind can barely grasp what he's saying. "So—there's a way out of it? No one ever told me or Dawn about that."

He nods grimly. "After I prick your finger and you fall to the charmed sleep, I will allow the King or Queen to kiss you and rest in your place."

"You think they're the ones who love me best?" My voice cracks.

The King hesitates. It's too dark to read his expression perfectly, but I think he looks rather guilty, or maybe sorry for me.

"I honestly don't know who loves you best," he says quietly.

"Because no one does. Everyone loves themselves best." I flop back down on the grass, staring up at the night sky.

The pain is coming back, eating away at the edges of my wine-soaked glow. Soon the vast black hollow of my sadness and anger will swallow me again, like the Void swallows realms.

I need more to drink—or some other pleasant sensation to push back the great Nothing inside me.

14

MALEC

Aura lies in the deep grass, her pale body luminous with starlight. Her breasts are among the most perfect I've ever seen—pillowy and lush, with small, tight nipples.

Earlier today she cringed at the thought of being bared to me and my men. Since then she's been naked before us twice— once through a prank and now again, by her choice. A drunken choice, but hers nonetheless.

I should not have left her alone. I thought she needed some time to think, or perhaps a quiet walk around the grounds to contemplate her true identity, maybe some food in her belly. Never did I think I would find her prancing naked on a tabletop, letting my knights fondle her.

They will pay for it—by the goddess, they will bleed regret for every touch.

But right now, I need to handle this woman. I've been where she is, though for different reasons. I've descended to a dark place where I did not care what happened to me, where physical pain was welcome, if only as a distraction from massive mental and emotional torment.

"Get up," I tell her, as gently as I can manage. "Come with me. You need rest."

"I don't think I can walk."

"You were just dancing."

She moans and rolls onto her stomach in the grass. Her panties barely cover the twin mounds of her ass. Even now, when her body is mostly relaxed, I can see the strength in her long legs, the taut calves and strong thighs born from years of physical training.

Propping her elbows on the ground, she begins playing with her hair. "I never wanted to be blonde. Will you glamour my hair blue, like it was?"

"Haven't you had enough of glamours? Now come, or I shall have to pick you up again."

She gives me a sultry smile over her shoulder. "What a terrible threat. Where will you carry me?"

"To the room that has been prepared for you, where you can spend a peaceful and solitary night."

Fear shivers across her features, so quick I barely see it. I recognize that fear too—the horror of being left alone with my thoughts.

"I won't go," she says. "I'd rather stay here."

I bend down and scoop her up again. This time she struggles more fiercely, which is—goddess, it's torture, having a beautiful, nearly nude woman thrashing in my arms. I shoulder my way through the side door of the Chapel while Aura clings to the frame, digging in her nails.

I have little Void magic at the moment, but I send out a tendril of shadow and whip it across her fingers. She gasps and lets go of the doorway, and I forge on, carrying her inside and up the stairs.

No one stops us. I burst into the room next to mine, the one I requested for my prisoner. Attached to the upper bedposts are a pair of cuffs with accompanying chains.

Aura stiffens in my arms. "No," she moans, and her voice breaks. "No—please, no shackles. You said I couldn't get through the boundary you put around this place—"

I kick the door shut behind us and dump her onto the mattress. At first I expect her to fight back, but she only lies there, dazed and whimpering.

"Please," she whispers. "Please don't chain me. Lock me in, but don't chain me again."

"The boundary I set won't last all night, and I can't risk losing you." Fuck, those words sounded—I clear my throat. "I can't risk losing my prize, I mean."

Aura gazes at me, her red lips soft and parted, her lashes half-veiling her blue eyes, her beautiful body pliant and submissive. I could touch her now. Take her, right now. The way she's looking at me—I think she would allow it.

But she is suffering through a crisis, facing a terrible fate, bound by a curse I placed. And she is drunk. Placing my hand on her breast would be wrong. And it would also be wrong to grasp her panties and work them down her hips until I can see the soft triangle of flesh between her thighs, until I can probe between her tender folds and see how wet she is…

Shit. No.

She blinks at me, docile and innocent. Gently I take her right wrist and move it toward one of the manacles.

She reacts in a blink. A wrench of my arm, a twist of her body, and I'm thrown onto the bed, wings and all, while my wrist is the one being slammed into the cuff.

It snaps shut, the lock clicking in place.

No matter. I can easily get out of this with magic.

But when I call on my power, nothing happens—and I realize my mistake.

When I requested that chains be attached to the girl's bed, the High Priestess promptly asked, "Bluesteel?"

I hadn't expected the chapel to have bluesteel manacles available. But I didn't question it; I merely nodded.

At the time, I wasn't certain of Aura's true identity. Bluesteel seemed like a safer choice in case my investigation revealed her to be a true Fae after all.

The shackles on the bed are bluesteel. And my captive just snapped one into place around my wrist.

A single piece of flat bluesteel cannot block magic. Like a magnet, bluesteel has positive and negative poles, and must be connected end-to-end in circular form in order to work. Once connected, it creates an anti-magic barrier around the form to which it is attached—in this case, me. For complete protection against magic, humans require a large amount of bluesteel, like a suit of armor that encircles the body. But to hamper a Fae's magic, one needs only a small band of it, like a collar, anklet, or a bracelet. Something as small as a ring wouldn't disrupt all my power, but a cuff like this—it's enough to block everything.

Aura may not have realized the nature of the cuff at first, but she knows now—she can see the consternation on my face.

Triumph threads through her smile. "Oh," she says softly. "How unfortunate for you."

I lunge for her, jumping off the bed, but she scampers back, out of my reach. When I reach the end of the short chain, I yank on it, to no avail. It is well-secured. I keep straining—but the bed frame is a ponderous one, and the best I can manage is to drag it forward a little.

Aura taps her chin. "Such a useful material, bluesteel. Why didn't my parents simply build me a suit of bluestell armor and keep me in that for twenty-five years? Or they could have crafted a prison cell from bluesteel."

"Bluesteel is rare," I grit out, still straining at the chain. "Too rare and valuable to keep making new suits of armor as you grew, and too rare to build an entire dwelling from it. Besides, though it is excellent against magic, it's not so hardy against certain types of blades. And a shot from a powerful crossbow pierces it easily."

She cocks her head. "That's why not all your human knights wear it."

"That, and our bluesteel mines are nearly depleted. Yours too, in Caennith."

Her brows pinch together, distress twisting her pretty features. Ah, she didn't know about that. They have kept so many things from her, these guardians and parents of hers. She thought she was trusted above others—a warrior gifted with the duty of protecting the Princess. And now all of that is gone.

"It would be silly to keep a growing girl encased in bluesteel all her life," I say quietly. "There are many ways your parents could have tried to circumvent my curse, Aura. They chose one, and you have to admit it worked well, until now."

Rebellion flares in her gaze. "I do not 'have to' admit anything." She takes a step toward me, then sways a little. Definitely drunk. Although judging by the way she flipped me onto the bed, she's still dangerous.

This is ridiculous. There has to be a way out of my predicament; something I haven't thought of. I can't be magic-less, chained to a bed by the Princess I cursed.

We're in a quiet, mostly deserted part of the Chapel, but if I shout loudly enough, someone will come.

"I'm going to shout for help," I tell her. "But I'll wait until you put some clothes on. The chapel attendants should have laid out some nightclothes for you to wear."

"You want me to get dressed so you can call for help? The Maleficent One, bested by his captive yet again. The Void King, crying for his precious knights to come and save him." She changes her tone to a small weak voice. "'Help me, help me, the human Princess has chained me up.' I'm sure your men won't have a good laugh about that."

Teeth gritted, I pry at the latch on the manacles. But it needs a key. Which has probably been laid out in my room. "Fuck." I jerk at the bedpost again. I flare my wings while I pull, in case they can give me extra leverage. Useless. I only end up bruising the tapered bone of one wing against the dresser.

Finally I give up and pinion my wings tightly to my back, cursing the small size of the room.

I can figure this out on my own—maybe even convince her to let me go. No one else has to know she bested me yet again, like she's been doing from the moment I wrapped my shadows around her carriage.

Aura pads nearer on quiet bare feet, until she's within my range—but I don't reach for her yet. I let her come to me. Her golden hair pours over both shoulders, partly concealing her breasts. Her expression has shifted again, from mockery to misery.

"I need more wine, or ale, or whatever they had at dinner," she says. "It's wearing off."

"You've had more than enough."

"I need it, though."

"You need sleep. Did you eat anything?"

"Nibbles," she says. "Not much. I am tired, but you're chained to my bed, so… I'd rather not lie down."

"You could release me. The key is probably in my room, right next door. You gain nothing from keeping me bound like this, Princess. I still have my strength, even if I lack magic. You can't… you can't overpower me…"

My voice falters over the last few words, because she is standing so close to me now, with her beautiful blue eyes and her toned, silken body. My heart is galloping like a wild stallion, and my cock swells against the front of my pants.

Every worry and plan in my head blurs into smoky shadow, while she takes on vivid color and exquisite detail. She is golden strength and delicate pearly skin, fathomless blue eyes and rose-petal lips.

Her soft breasts are almost touching my chest. I take air in tiny sips, afraid to breathe too deeply lest she back away. Tension hardens my arms as I fight the urge to touch her.

"Do you remember what you said before— 'if you can't talk to your enemies, who can you talk to?'" she murmurs.

"Not exactly."

"You were feverish. You told me things—like how sometimes you want to die. You want to be done with it all, because it's too much. Is that true?"

One word scrapes through my throat. "Yes."

She eyes me appraisingly. "You really believe you can save this realm?"

"I trust in my magic."

"It's heretical, you know. This belief that you, a Spinner of forbidden Void magic, could be Eonnula's prophesied savior."

"I don't believe in the savior at all. So no, I don't think it's me."

She reaches up, tracing the curve of my shoulder with her fingertips. The delicate touch turns me weak, vibrates through me more powerfully than any blow dealt in battle. I want to sink to my knees before her. It's all I can do to remain standing.

The submissive impulse clashes with my knowledge of who she is—my prisoner, my prey, the Princess I cursed at birth. A torturous self-loathing writhes inside me, because I should not crave her. The age difference does not matter—in our realm of long lifetimes, all pairings are acceptable provided both parties are above twenty. But lusting for the woman I condemned, the one I've been hunting for years—it's despicable, perverted.

Worst and most twisted of all—I get the sense she wants me, too. Hates me, and craves me.

Her fingertips slide along my collarbone. "Why didn't you come for me yourself, oh Maleficent One?"

"I did, at first. But I failed twice, and after that the Three Faeries warded the castles with spells designed to detect me, specifically. My presence would have jeopardized any mission to retrieve you."

Her fingers arch, nails grating down my breastbone, leaving long scratches. "I dreamed of you sometimes. Nightmares of you dragging me into the dark, or snatching Dawn away. Yet I had never seen you."

"You saw me once. At your christening, when I leaned over your cradle and spoke the curse."

Her blue eyes flash up to mine, realization and disgust flooding her gaze. "Bastard," she hisses. "I should kill you."

A thrill skates through my abdomen at the words, at her threatening tone. My cock twitches.

"Do it then," I say.

"You think I won't?" She grabs my throat, a frenzied grip. I tip my head back, dragging in air through my constricted windpipe. My cock swells harder, and my nipples tighten to sensitive beads.

"Fuck," I choke. And then, another word slips out—a confession I didn't intend. "Harder."

15

AURA

My grasp on the Void King's throat almost loosens, I'm so shocked. "What?"

But I heard him very clearly. He said, "Fuck," and then "Harder."

Even though the pleasant blur of the liquor has receded a bit, I'm not sober, by any means. I'm hot all over, greedy for a new sensation to erase the thoughts swirling in my head. So I don't think too deeply about what I do next.

I sway my hips forward, pressing my lower body to his, and I renew my grip on his neck.

The thick ridge under his pants pulses against me in response—a heavy throb.

"You sick asshole," I whisper. But heat pools at my core, liquid and undeniable.

My enemy gets hard when I choke him, and choking him makes me wet. How perverse is that?

He's wheezing, barely able to breathe. He could fight back—could probably overpower me quickly with his physical strength. But he yields.

The memory of his fevered speech returns, sharp and clear. *Women always assume I want them subservient, kneeling before me. They don't understand what I truly crave.*

He wants the opposite of a woman's submission. This man who must stay strong, who must always maintain appearances before his people—he longs to lose control. To be broken down and ruled by someone else.

I release his throat and grip his jaw instead, forcing him to look down at me. "You're not the one in control anymore," I say softly. "Tell me who is."

The words change everything. They charge the air between us with lightning, with a scintillating awareness and a naked opportunity. He can resist... or he can yield. My whole body aches with the need for him to bend, to bow, to submit. I need this. I need to take back some measure of power and autonomy, any way I can get it. And I've wanted him—fuck, I've wanted his body since the minute he dragged me from the royal carriage.

The King releases a shuddering breath. "You're in control," he breathes.

Euphoria surges through me. He's going to play the game.

I've been with a couple of men who enjoyed it when I was rough with them verbally and physically during sex. I'm not entirely unused to this kind of thing.

But this isn't just any man. This is the fucking King of Daenalla, wielder of heretical dark magic, enemy of my people, nemesis of my family. Doing this with him is deeply transgressive. My mothers and my real parents would hate it.

They would hate it so much.

Which is perfect.

A savage, furious glee blazes through me, and I collar the King's throat again, squeezing until he chokes. His wings flare slightly, and his pupils dilate.

Goddess, he's beautiful.

Releasing him, I notch a finger in his belt and tug. "Take these off."

Despite the cuff around his wrist, he manages the task without too much difficulty, thanks to the length of the chain. He unbuckles his belt and slides it off, then shucks off his boots and pulls down the pants. His cock bobs free, a huge shaft, thick and veined. Kicking the pants aside, he stands before me, one wrist chained to the bedpost, dark wings half-extended, his entire lean, muscled body bared to my view.

Wine and wonder mingle in my head, blurring my thoughts in a moment of speechless admiration.

And then his mouth slants up at the corner.

He's smirking at me. Because I'm staring at his body like a virgin schoolgirl.

I react the way I always react to mockery—with a burst of violence.

I deliver a swift kick to his balls with my bare toes.

He cries out, cupping himself. "Fucking damn you!"

I throw myself at him, bowling him over onto the bed in a tangle of black wings and powerful limbs. His four horns grind along the headboard and shred the pillows as we wrestle on the mattress. My heart pounds like an earthquake, violent enough to rattle my bones.

He's bucking against me, but not fighting me as fiercely as I know he could. He wants to be ruled by force.

I manage to pin one of his sinewy forearms to the bed—the wrist that wasn't chained—but his hips buck upward, nearly dislodging me from my place astride his body. I'm not used to fighting like this, with my breasts hanging loose instead of secure in a corset. It's disconcerting.

"Be still," I bite out, struggling to pin him down.

"Is that a command, Highness?"

"Yes."

He stops fighting me. But despite his obedience, I vengefully twist one of his nipples until he gasps with pain.

"What was that for?" he seethes.

"That was for cursing me. Asshole."

"Bitch."

I slap him.

His cheek reddens from the blow, and because he looks so beautiful that way I smack his other cheek. He growls a protest, low in his throat. The power of his tense body beneath me sends a flood of frenzied arousal through my belly.

I stand up on the bed, careful not to step on any of his wing bones. He goes utterly still, staring at me with ravenous lust in his dark eyes.

I discard my last scrap of clothing and toss it away.

"Fuck, you're beautiful," he whispers.

A tiny thrill chases through my clit at the praise.

"Will you do something?" He speaks thickly, reluctantly, as if he wants something terribly but he hates himself for asking. "Put your foot on my neck."

"Gladly." Holding onto the bedpost and placing my left foot carefully so as not to hurt his wing, I plant my right foot on his throat.

"Shit, yes, little viper." His cock jerks and his eyes roll up; he's panting, his stomach flexing with each gasp. Relief and desperation churn in his gaze. "Tell me how much you hate me."

"I despise you," I grit out, pressing my toes more firmly against his warm skin. "I hate you for cursing me. I hate you for the twisted way you worship my goddess. I hate you for your demented attempt to control the Void and turn it into magic. I hate the way you think you know best for everyone in this realm, and the way you believe you're better than my people, my teachers and my rulers."

He gazes up at me, looking as pretty and pliant as he did in the forest. He's not truly helpless, of course; he's incredibly powerful. He could grab my ankle, throw me down, and snap my neck. He's letting me do this because he needs it, because he's in pain, like me. Pain, so much pain—

"I hate you for breaking the glamour and unveiling my real self," I say hoarsely. "I hate that you've stolen away everything I once believed. I hate that you've made me question my faith. I hate you for showing me the lies of the people I loved and trusted. I hate you for being the only one who has told me the truth."

The tender concern in his eyes—I can't bear it. I push his jaw with my foot, knocking his head aside so he can't look at me.

"Tell me you hate me, too," I order.

"I hate you for making me crave your admiration, your touch, your glance," he says, low. "I hate how my fucking body turns traitor in your presence. I hate the way I'm ravenous for your soft skin, your strength, your passion—I want it enveloping me, swallowing me whole. I hate you because you remind me of my own arrogance and idiocy, of the failings that drove me to speak the curse. I could have found another way, a better way. I was a fool." He turns his face back toward me. "And I hate you for not hating me enough. For not being merciless, for not killing me in the forest, when you set that blade to my throat."

I switch positions, settling astride his chest, riding the swell of his breath. My thumbnail strokes along his jugular vein. "I could fix that. I could kill you now."

His eyes darken. "I won't stop you."

Angrily I slap his cheek—a light smack this time. "Quit asking to die."

"Why does it upset you?"

"Because—I—" I blow out a frustrated breath. "Stop talking."

"Make me." He lowers his dark lashes, blinking at me slowly, insolently. Then he runs his tongue across his lips, a suggestive wet glide.

"If I sit on your face," I say, breathless, "you won't be able to talk."

"True." A spark of rabid excitement leaps into his eyes.

My stomach jumps and thrills, but I refuse to let him know what the idea does to me, how it terrifies and exhilarates me at the same time. Instead, I lift my chin in my most haughty, royal manner. "Ask me nicely."

"Please, Princess." His deep voice vibrates through his chest into my body. "Please sit on my face."

16

MALEC

I don't care that my wings are awkwardly pinned beneath me, or that my horns are tearing up the mattress, or that my magic is suppressed by the bluesteel shackle.

My entire body and brain are celebrating the fact that Aura is kneeling astride my face. That the shining lips of her sex are hovering over my mouth. That I can see her clit, a small bit of pink flesh, the part I'll need to tend with special care. Her inner thighs are glazed with the glistening evidence of how much I arouse her.

But she hesitates, murmuring breathlessly, "What am I doing?"

Oh goddess—is she reconsidering? If she doesn't let me taste her, I think I will die.

And yet, I don't want her to do this because of the wine. I want her to choose this act because she needs it as much as I do.

"Your choice, little viper," I murmur. "You can go sleep in my bed, or stay here and let me lick you until you come so hard you can't stand upright."

"Fuck," she whimpers, and lowers herself against my mouth.

She tastes like vanilla and roses, like the scented water in which she bathed, with a faint twist of lemon that lingers on my tongue. I lick deeper between the soft lips of her sex, finding the slick groove beyond, sliding my tongue through the inner parts of her. Then I tip my face up, closing my lips over her clit, sucking and tugging.

"Don't hover," I say raggedly. "Sit."

The Princess inhales sharply and presses closer. My tongue dances over her clit, flicking as fast as I can manage. Her thighs quiver, and when she whines aloud, I smile against her pussy. The sound is shrill and needy, threaded with earnest intensity, like everything else about her.

My world is wet and warm. Her smooth thighs press my cheeks, and her earthy, floral, human scent floods my nose. When I nuzzle deeper, her body jerks a little and she gives a tiny, adorable moan.

Snatching a quick breath, I go back to lapping her clit, whipping the bud back and forth with the tip of my tongue. She's breathing in short, sharp gasps now. Her hips tilt inward, and I growl my pleasure at the improved access. My tongue plunges into her, as far as I can go, straining at the root. I'm rewarded with a gush of renewed wetness.

She's close now. Her moans are nearly sobs.

When I open my eyes, I can see her lean stomach above me. Her body is bent over, shaking. She grips two of my horns tightly to anchor herself. My horns aren't sensitive, but the tugging sensation, the passion behind it—that makes my cock even harder.

I work my open mouth over her pussy, then shake my head back and forth slightly so my nose and lips jiggle against her in a new way. Another firm nuzzle, right into her clit, pushing it, suckling—Aura jerks hard, a faint squeal breaking from her. Her thighs clamp on either side of my face, and her pussy begins to spasm against my mouth.

I can't breathe. But if I pass out while she's coming on my face, I will count myself inexpressibly fortunate.

The tremulous rhythm of her orgasm continues, pulsating against my lips. I let her crush her sex against my jaw and nose so she can find the pressure she needs.

She clings to my horns, easing up on my face slightly. After a quick breath, I stroke into her with my tongue a few more times.

And then I realize what I've done.

I just tongue-fucked the Princess I cursed twenty-four years ago.

I permitted her to ride my face, though she was wounded in spirit, drunk on anger and wine.

She's sliding down my body, leaving a trail of her wetness on my skin.

"I shouldn't have let you do that," I say. "You're not in your right mind—"

"Hush." She presses her fingers over my mouth. "I need this, do you understand? I need to feel something that isn't the hurt and the lies. It's my choice. You gave me control, and now I'm using your body." A faint smile plays over her lips. Her blue eyes are softer now, brighter, and her cheeks are rosy from pleasure. The lamplight shines through her golden hair, turning it to woven sunshine.

She is so exquisite it hurts.

"You can use me anytime," I say hoarsely.

"Perfect," she says, "because I'm not done with you."

Hot, wet heat presses against the tip of my cock, and I jolt, a gasp of sheer sensitized need escaping my lips. She is backing right onto my cock—she's smiling at me, reaching down to push me inside—

"Oh shit," I pant. "Shit, shit, goddess… fuck…" I'm going inside her. My whole length is swallowed by her body, sucked into silky, slippery heat. I can't bear the stimulation—it's like the blazing light of the Triune Suns after the dark season, overwhelming and fucking divine.

Aura presses one palm to the center of my chest and begins to ride me. She keeps her eyes closed, as if looking at me might disturb her pleasure. A shadow of disappointment flutters through my heart, but I don't bother to analyze it—I'm too distracted by the heavy sway of her breasts.

Tentatively I reach for one of them, mesmerized—but at the brush of my fingers she knocks my hand away, pins it down with a sharp "No." Her delicate brows furrow, her eyes crinkle shut more tightly, and she bites her lip as she fucks herself on me harder, utterly merciless.

Heat and tension coil in my gut. I'm so close. "Shit, viper," I gasp, and she says, in a broken voice, "Fuck, Malec—"

Shock erupts through my body at that word, and I come—I come hard, pleasure stabbing through my body so violently my groan sounds more like a roar. The Princess slams her palm over my mouth. She keeps thrusting onto me, her sharp shrill breaths coming closer and closer together, until her second climax erupts, making her whimper and shake.

My cock jerks, compressed by the spasms of her inner walls, and another, milder thrill skates through my belly. I've spent myself so thoroughly inside her that I feel utterly drained. My muscles relax, and my racing heart slowly returns to a normal rhythm.

Aura lifts herself, and my cock slips out of her. She rolls over beside me, lying on her stomach, her face buried in my feathers.

Dazed, I lift one trembling hand and reach for her. My palm lands on one smooth cheek of her ass, and I don't move it. And she doesn't make me.

17

I don't regret it. It was glorious.

I want to do it again. I'll take longer next time, explore him more thoroughly. He's just as good as I thought he'd be.

Usually, after fucking someone, I take a tonic to prevent pregnancy. Fortunately there's no chance of my getting pregnant unless he's in heat—which, for Fae in this realm, happens once every five years or so.

Turning my head so my cheek is pressed to his huge feathers, I murmur, "You're not in heat, are you?"

"No."

"And how soon can you get hard again?"

He chuckles, a note of surprise in the sound. "I thought you might be wracked by guilt."

"For giving myself what I need, what I deserve? Of course not."

"I can get hard within minutes," he says, low. "But I revoke my consent. You may not use me again unless you unchain me first."

"What?" I sit bolt upright. My tone is half anger, half humor, because honestly, I'm in a fucking good mood, all things considered. I'm still rather drunk and I just had two very nice orgasms. "You said I could use you anytime. You liar. You dick-headed, shit-sucking, bull's asshole."

He smirks and cocks an eyebrow at me. "Harsh words, little viper."

I chew my lip, eyeing the cuff around his right wrist. Chaining him was a rebellious move on my part; I expected him to magic himself free the next instant. In the half-gloom of the chamber, I didn't even notice the cuff was bluesteel until I clamped it on him.

There's no permanent gain to be had by keeping him locked up here, unless I really do intend to kill him—which, let's face it—I can't.

Genla's voice in my head: *Selfish girl. You're being stupid and weak. Don't you know what others have sacrificed so you could live in comfort and safety?*

Her words, vented in anger so many times, hold a different meaning now. What would my true parents have said if they knew how she spoke to me in her rages?

Would they have cared?

I want to stop thinking about her, about all of them. And while I was playing with the Void King, I wasn't thinking about anything but his body. The way he made me feel.

I need more of him. "You said your room adjoins this one?"

The question is a candid admission that I want to fuck him again. He grins lazily, and I give one of his biggest feathers a vengeful yank.

"Ow!" He shoots me a glare of rebuke. "Yes, the door over there leads to my chamber. You should find the key to the shackles lying around somewhere."

I climb off the bed and scan my room until I locate the nightdress he said I might find. It's a thick, serviceable garment. I slip it over my head, in case I encounter someone on my mission to find the key.

I step into the adjoining room and close the door behind me. A massive canopy bed dominates the space, its thick black curtains patterned with gray swirls. The King's saddlebags are draped over a heavy wooden chair. All the furnishings in this place have a ponderous, practical look.

A few candles burn in a dish on the bedside table, and their light glimmers on a small key lying nearby.

As I snatch up the key, there's a knock at the door to the King's chamber. A moment later the door swings open, and Kyan fills the entrance. He's holding a broom.

I palm the key so he won't see it. "What are you doing in here?"

"The King told Ember and me to sweep all the rooms in the Chapel," he says gruffly. "Why are *you* in here? This is the King's room."

"And you thought you'd just come in? What if he was sleeping?"

"He said to sweep *all* the rooms," Kyan repeats, frowning. "Where is he?"

I purse my lips. "How should I know? He took me to my room and then left. I came in here looking for—an extra candle." I seize one and nod to him. "Good night. Happy sweeping. Oh, and don't bother sweeping my room. It's very clean. Very tidy. No need to touch it at all."

I back away, toward the door between the rooms, but Kyan says sharply, "Wait."

Heart racing, I pause.

"I wanted to apologize for threatening you." His words fall heavily, as if they weigh on his tongue as well as his heart.

"I should apologize to *you*." I bite my lip. "Your sister—I'm sorry."

The words are pitifully inadequate, but they're all I have to offer.

"You were doing the job you were given." His hands are white-knuckled around the broom handle, and his silver wings slump, trailing on the floor. "This war—everything has become so tangled I'm no longer sure what is right. Perhaps you feel the same way sometimes."

"You don't believe in what your King is doing?"

Kyan grimaces. "I never said that. I believe the King wants the best for everyone, and I trust his judgment, that the blood of the next Conduit is the necessary catalyst for the spell he wants to attempt. He would not claim such a thing without reason. He is a good man, though he doesn't always believe that."

"I don't think anyone is good," I mutter. "Everyone lies, cheats, murders, and betrays."

Hearing myself say it aloud—it hurts. My view of the world has darkened so much in just two days. When I stood beside Dawn at the Lifegiving I was so hopeful and excited because in three months' time, she and I wouldn't have to worry about the curse anymore.

The girl I was at the festival is gone now. Someone far more bitter, angry, and reckless has taken her place.

Kyan is watching me soberly. "I understand grief, as do others here. You may be an enemy by your birthright, but not by choice. So if you ever need to speak with someone… if that would bring you ease…" He clears his throat. "I would listen. So would Andras."

Drinking and fucking has formed a fragile shell over my emotions, but that barrier cracks at his words, and my pain spills out.

"Why?" I say hoarsely, incredulously. "Why would you show me kindness? I've killed your people, your sister. You want revenge on me, remember?"

"I want revenge on those who are truly responsible for this war. But if giving up my vengeance could secure lasting peace, that is what Forresh would want me to do." He steps back out

159

into the hall, pulling the King's chamber door half-closed. "You should sleep, Your Highness."

I can't find the words to say, so I slip back into my room and close the door. After setting the candle on the dresser, I walk to the bed and unlock Malec's bluesteel cuff, barely glancing at him. He gets up, stretches his wings, and preens a few of the ruffled feathers with his claws.

When I sit limply down on the bed, he says softly, "Are you all right?"

I lie down without answering and pull the covers over my whole body and my head.

A moment later, the mattress dips under Malec's weight, and his claws peel back the sheets. He scrapes my tangled hair away from my face.

"What happened?" he murmurs. "What terrible thing transformed my dominant mistress into a creature who hides under covers?"

I close my eyes tightly, but two hot tears slip out anyway. "Forgiveness."

"Ah. I thought I heard voices through the door. Who was in my chamber?"

"Kyan. Sweeping. I killed his sister, and he offered to listen if I need to talk. How could he say that? How could he— goddess, I can't bear any of this." I flop onto my stomach, burying my face in the pillow.

The King continues stroking my hair—well, combing it with his claws, really.

He's vain, insecure, impulsive, self-loathing, heretical, and careless with his powers. I should not find comfort in his presence. I should not know all those things about him, after so short an acquaintance—nor should I understand that he's also compassionate, determined, well-mannered, loyal to his knights, and considerate of his people.

I hate him for being here, for being a person I cannot truly despise. I hate him for touching me like he cares.

I flip over and knock his hand aside. He frowns as I scoot away from him on the bed, wrapping my arms around my knees.

"How long do I have?" I bite out.

He raises an eyebrow.

"How long until you take my blood and send me to sleep?"

A long sigh escapes him. "We'll ride hard to Ru Gallamet. There are a few preparations to be made, and then I will perform the spell. So... a day or two."

A day or two until I fall asleep for a century. When I wake, my real parents will probably be dead, and one or more of the Three Faeries may be as well. Dawn will be a hundred and twenty-five. That is, *if* the Edge hasn't consumed everything by then. There's a chance I may never wake at all.

"Where will I sleep for the century?" I ask. "Will you send my body home?" But even as I say it, I'm not sure where home is. My years have been spent traveling between castles or visiting my mothers' house in Arboret, near the winter palace. Somehow the thought of lying asleep in any of those places for a hundred years feels too exposed, too vulnerable. I don't want to trust my body to the mercy of the people who tricked me, lied to Dawn about her identity, and subjected me to soul-damaging magic.

"Never mind." I cut the King off as he's about to speak. "Don't send me back to them."

"One of your parents may wish to take your place."

"If they do, they can come *here* and kiss me," I retort. "I won't be at their mercy for a century."

"Then you'll be at mine." His dark eyes pry at my thoughts. "Is that what you want?"

I hesitate. "You won't fuck me while I'm asleep?"

He looks startled. "Of course not! If you resign your body to my care, I will see to it that you are protected and treated with the greatest respect until you awaken. A day I will look forward to with great anticipation."

But there's a shadow on his face, a hollowness to his tone.

I want to ask him more questions: about the day of my christening, about his interactions with my parents and his apparent feud with the Three Faeries, about the spell he plans to perform and how much it will hurt. But I feel vaguely nauseated, and I keep looking down at my fingers, noting the absence of my rings. I keep catching sight of the gold tendrils of my hair, startling inside, having to remind myself I'm not under a glamour, that the silken gold is my real hair. I keep thinking about the emptiness where my wings used to be. Those tiny unpleasant shocks happen over and over, minute by minute, and it's exhausting.

"You should rest." Malec rises, his hair spilling over his shoulder in a river of black. He's still naked, the carved planes of his pale body exposed to my view. He casts a regretful look at the carcass of a shredded feather pillow, and at the ripped fabric where his horns dug into the mattress. "I shall have to reimburse the Chapel for the damage. At least a couple of the pillows are still intact. You should be comfortable enough."

Doesn't matter. I won't be able to sleep.

Will you stay? Will you help me forget? But I can't bring myself to ask. The confidence that buoyed me earlier is slipping away.

Malec picks up his clothes, pauses beside the dresser, and peers into a small mirror. He frowns, taking a lock of his hair from the right side and switching it to the left before nodding in satisfaction. "Good night then, Princess."

I make a sound that's supposed to be a mocking scoff, but damn me if it doesn't quiver in the middle, far too much like a sob.

Out of the corner of my eye I see him hesitate, a tall white statue framed by black wings. I refuse to look at him. I will not show any more weakness tonight.

After a few moments he melts out of my line of vision, and the door to his room closes.

18

Screams rip through the night.

I startle out of sleep and leap from the bed. My wings whip out, feathers ruffled to twice their size—the damn things are a telltale indicator of my mood. No time to smooth them down—I charge through the door into Aura's room. She's thrashing among her sheets, fighting the fabric and screaming.

The other door of her room opens, and Ember peers in from the hallway. He snaps his fingers, igniting the lamp on the table, his eyes flashing reflective red in his dark face. Behind him I glimpse Vandel's freckled features and tousled red hair.

"My Lord?" Ember asks.

"I'll take care of it."

He nods and retreats, pushing Vandel back into the hallway.

"What the fuck is going on?" Vandel protests.

"The prisoner had a nightmare. Go back to sleep." Ember closes the door, muffling Vandel's protest that he isn't a child to be sent back to bed, Ember isn't the squad leader and therefore can't order him around, and so on.

I ignore them and approach the bed. By the dim lamplight I watch Aura's face—eyes pinched shut, a tortured, pleading expression furrowing her brow. Her head tosses on the pillow, and she cries out again.

"Princess," I say, before I remember she isn't used to being called that. "Aura."

She whimpers, but she doesn't wake.

"Little viper," I murmur, bending over her, laying my palm on her forehead.

Her eyes snap open. She lunges, catching my forearm with both hands and sinking her jaws into my wrist. Her small teeth punch through the skin.

"Damn it!" I shake her off, and she scrambles to the head of the bed, crouching there, wild-eyed.

I should have known she'd react like this. She was trained as a fighter her whole life, taught to expect attacks at any moment and return them with violence.

She was designed to be her own bodyguard. Concealed beneath a different racial identity, inhabited by the magic of three other beings, fragmented by their power. I will never understand the twisted logic that led her parents to risk her mental and emotional health for her physical safety. Perhaps they thought, being the future Conduit, she could handle it. Perhaps her mental state would have been worse if she hadn't been the God-Touched heir.

Or perhaps her parents didn't truly understand the risk to her psyche. Maybe the greater fault lies with the Three Faeries, for sinking their claws so deeply into a child's body and mind, for not considering that perhaps visceral glamours are forbidden for good reason. The three of them are so secure in themselves, so full of hubris.

I have my own blind spots, my own kind of pride. They damaged Aura, but I hurt her too. And worse still, I intend to stick to my plan and use the Princess for my great magical work.

I deserve all the pain she wants to inflict on me.

"Easy, little viper." I reach toward her again, my torn wrist dripping blood on the sheets.

"Don't touch me!" Her voice shrills with panic and revulsion.

"You were dreaming," I persist gently. "I'm not going to hurt you."

"I dreamed you ripped my wings off," she chokes out. "And then you—you fucked the holes where they used to be."

Horror sends a chill over my skin. "I would never do that to you."

She scoops up a pillow and pulls it to her chest, still eyeing me warily. "But we did fuck. That was real."

"Yes. You came on my face, and then again on my dick. You had all the control, Princess. You made the choices."

She nods, her expression softening. "Yes. I remember—it was good. I forgot everything for a little while. But my wings are gone for good. That much is true. I'll never fly again."

My heart swells, expanding, yearning. I struggle to keep my distance, to refrain from reaching for her. All I want is to pull her close, fold my arms and wings around her, and keep her safe. I want to soothe her sore heart with kisses. I want her to feel protected and loved and strong and whole.

The emotion welling up in my chest is the most powerful thing I have felt in years—maybe ever.

Aura hugs the pillow tighter, her eyes widening. "Why are you looking at me like that?"

"Like—" I clear my throat and attempt to neutralize my expression. "Like what?"

"Like you—" She hesitates, biting her bottom lip. "Like you want to hug me."

"Maybe I do."

"You're my worst enemy."

I make a wry face. "What's a little hug between enemies?"

She stares, and then her mouth twitches, her eyes brightening. It's an almost-smile.

"And who says you can never fly again?" I smile at her. "I'll take you flying right now, if you like."

"You're not serious."

"Serious as the Void."

"It's the middle of the night. It's probably cold, and you've only got those." She nods to the pair of black undershorts I'm wearing.

I square my shoulders and arch my wings. "Nothing that can't be fixed. What do you say, Princess? A midnight flight? I promise not to drop you."

She eyes me suspiciously. "What's your game? Your goal? Why are you offering this?"

"Call it repentance."

Aura shakes her head. "Repentance would be leaving me alone until my twenty-fifth birthday passes and your curse expires."

"I can't do that. So perhaps this isn't repentance, but reparation in some form. If you'll come fly with me, Aura, I will tell you why I can't simply let you go. You only know the vague shape of my plan—I will explain precisely what I intend to do. I will answer every question you have."

After a long, appraising look at me, she lays the pillow aside. "I need to use the washroom first."

I nod. "I'll find something warmer for both of us to wear."

19

AURA

I stand on the steps of the Chapel, warmly clad in the leggings and tunic Malec found for me. It's strange, not having clothes designed for my wings, not needing to work them through the slits in the back. My spine twinges occasionally, a phantom flexion of the nerves and muscles I once used to move the wings.

They were never mine. They were grafted onto me, fused and animated by magic.

The night wind rushes over my body, snatching at my hair, running invisible fingers through the blond strands. I relish the brisk cold, turning my face up to the sky.

The flow of the Void is thicker tonight, veiling the Triune suns until they resemble pale, distant moons. But with the concealment of the suns, other stars appear brighter, especially along the horizon, where the mounded forest meets the bluish-black of the sky.

Malec looms beside me, clad in black leather, with a high collar that flares up from his shoulders. The faint light of the night-veiled suns and the distant stars illuminates his elegant features. His is a crisp, pale beauty—cheekbones so sharp they could slice his skin, a jaw like a pane of cut glass.

In my nightmares of him, he was never this lovely. Sometimes he had veins of black cracking his skin, leaking shadows. He would drag Dawn into a cave or a tunnel while I screamed, or he would snatch me and fly away with me, into the dreadful Void. But in the worst nightmares he'd walk with me, a terrible, ominous presence. And I couldn't run, and he never said a word.

Maybe I'm still dreaming. Even now, his presence thrums in the air, a vibration so strong it's nearly tangible, a pulse synchronized to my pounding heart.

He turns to me in a rush of glossy feathers, catches me up in his arms, and leaps into the sky.

Wind whips the breath from my lungs as we streak up, up, into the dark, faster and higher than I've ever flown. The Chapel, its outbuildings, the courtyard—everything drops away, shrinking smaller and smaller. The forest of towering trees looks like tiny bushes.

We're shooting straight out of the realm. Right into the Void itself. Not possible, but that's what it feels like.

And then Malec drops me.

I scream—a keening panic ripped from my lungs—and then he dips under me and I drop into his arms, and we're off again, wheeling through the sky. He plunges terrifyingly fast, arrow-straight toward the ground—then pulls up with a mighty wingbeat and a pulse of green magic. Another whirl and a drop, and I scream again, while my belly thrills—but this time there's a laugh mixed into the scream, and when he twirls in midair and feigns dropping me, I shriek with terrified glee.

This is fun. It's like the dancing, the drinking, and the sex—it pushes all my fear and anger into the back of my mind. When I'm up here, flying with him, I don't have to think about anything serious—only about the shearing ecstasy of the wind and the thrilling anticipation of the next drop.

Malec is using magic as we fly, to enable faster speeds and smoother turns. He rolls onto his back in the air, with me lying on him, chest to chest, while his wings curve upward, feathers rippling on either side of me. We're falling, but it's a controlled flight, and it feels so wonderful I laugh again.

His eyes widen with pleasure at the sound, and a chuckle rumbles through his chest.

This time, I'm not walking with him in a nightmare. I'm flying with him in a dream, and there's music in my head, and a new, pleasant emotion quivering in my wounded heart—a sweet softness, a tender urgency.

He's still on his back, slowly falling with me draped on his chest. His lips are pale and full and smooth.

Don't think about anything. Nothing at all... do what feels good... give in to what you want right now... after all, in a few days you're going to sleep for a century... you deserve to have a little fun...

My hair tumbles against his cheek as I lean in and touch my mouth to those smooth lips.

A sound of impassioned relief rushes from him, and he pulls us both upright in the air, his wings beating heavily, keeping us aloft. His strong arms are banded around me, one warm hand cupping my rear, pinning my hips against his.

His mouth is heated breath, slick tongue, and a savory, addictive, midnight bitterness. My entire being soars at the contact, and I whimper with delighted surprise. I had no idea kissing him would be this good, or I would have done it sooner. He's like wine and sex and music, threaded through the rush of the night wind, and I'm carried away with him. I never want to separate my lips from his.

This man could be a very delicious and dangerous habit.

I hitch my legs around his waist and tighten my thighs, urging myself closer to his body. I need the pressure of him, the blessed friction of his hardness rubbing against my core. My arms wind around his neck. He keeps us in the air, high above the Chapel, while I take what I need—and what I need is his hot skin, his warm mouth, and the strength of his arms, holding me carefully, respectfully, except for that one naughty hand cupping my ass cheek.

I devour him open-mouthed, my tongue warring with his, my breath hot and frantic. He responds with a thick thrash of his tongue, a savage tug of his teeth on my lower lip. I bite him back, hard enough to draw blood and make him gasp.

"Fuck." His voice is a ragged breath.

"This is demented," I whisper. "It's perverse how much I want you." I squeeze him tighter with my thighs and arms, because I hunger for him and I'm still furious about it, about everything. With the terror of the nightmare gone, there's a reckless violence in me, a monster that wants to bruise and bloody him while I fuck him.

"I want to hurt you so badly," I hiss, grazing his cheekbone with my teeth, then ducking my head to the blood-warm skin of his throat.

"Fuck," he rasps again. He's trembling, but his hold on me is secure, and his wings beat steadily.

"I want to own you, to crush you." I scrape my teeth along his neck up to the corner of his jaw, then bite his earlobe until his breath hitches with pain. "You ruined my life, you beautiful fucking bastard."

"Destroy me then," he says hoarsely. "Be my goddess of doom, of vengeance. Kill me, and set yourself free. They've tried to end me, you know. So many have tried, from my own kingdom and yours. I know what it is to be hunted. Every one who came against me failed. But I would let you suck me dry, little viper—I'd drink poison from your mouth, lick venom from your tongue."

His words inflame my mind, fire racing along my spine, heat circling low in my belly. I want to rip open his pants and impale myself on him.

But a shape soars out of the night—black-winged, with beady dark eyes. A raven, clearly one of his, circling insistently over our heads.

"A message from the border," he says. "I need to take this."

We swoop lower, and he lands on a ledge that encircles the Chapel dome. It's a long, curved ledge, wide enough for me to sit with my legs fully stretched out. I wait, letting the breeze cool my face and my desire, while Malec allows the raven to perch on his fingers. He strokes its glossy breast with the knuckle of his forefinger, looking deep into its eyes.

Suddenly I realize that his hands are no longer gloved to the wrist in black. Perhaps, after a while, the color of the Void magic he uses ebbs away. I like his hands either way, moon-white or ebony.

Shit, I shouldn't be liking his hands at all.

The raven's head tilts aside, its bright eyes boring into Malec's.

"Our people are killing each other along the border," Malec says tightly. "And a few Caennith search parties have made it through the Daenallan defenses. They're hunting for you."

"To rescue me," I say wryly.

Malec casts me a look of hesitant pity.

"What?" I ask.

"This raven risked her life to get close to one of the search parties. She overheard that they have orders to kill you if they can't recover you."

A chill skates through my bones. "You're lying. Or the raven misheard something—it's a *raven,* after all."

"I wish I was lying. And I can tell when the ravens are uncertain about their messages." He runs a fingertip over the bird's small head, his touch incredibly gentle, full of fondness. "This one heard the instructions very clearly."

A hard, cold, sickening ball of dread tightens in my gut. "That doesn't make any sense. After going to such lengths to protect me, for so many years—why would they—"

But even as I protest, I know he's right. I can imagine what the Three Faeries and my parents are saying right now, how they would excuse such an order. *Better for her to die than be part of foul, heretical magic. Better for her to fly to Eonnula's light than be bound to a Spindle, bled dry by a monster.*

If I die, my father and mother will continue to be the Conduits until their death. They'll have time to produce another child if they want to.

I am disposable. Damaged. The cursed one. I've been a problem since my birth.

Malec was right. This game the Royals have been playing, the ruse they devised—it was never for my benefit. It was always about their rivalry with him.

"I'm sorry." There's an ache in his words, like he's apologizing for more than the message.

He lifts an elegant, pale hand, and the raven flutters away into the night.

20

The Princess and I sit on the ledge of the Chapel roof, watching the raven shrink into the distance and vanish. I'm not sure what to say. How do I comfort someone whose parents just ordered their capture or death?

"What is it?" Aura says suddenly.

I frown, confused.

She points up into the sky, at the veils of darkness shrouding the Triune Suns. "The Void. What is it? Despite the name, it isn't nothing. It moves in regular patterns. You pull things out of it with your magic—monsters like the Endlings. What is it, and how does it work?"

Only someone familiar with the dogma of the Caennith could understand how much it costs her to speak those words. To the followers of the Caennith religion, too much curiosity about the Void is considered foolish at best and traitorous at worst—just as fear of the Void is considered a sign of weak faith in Eonnula.

In the early days of my reign, I spent enough time learning the ways and religion of her people, thinking such knowledge might be the key to lasting peace. I was a fool. The attempt at understanding was one-sided. The Caennith Royals and their people expected me to learn their culture, but they made no attempt to understand mine.

Maybe Aura's curiosity is the first step toward something new. It's a pity she'll be sleeping for a century, unable to serve as an ambassador from my kingdom to hers. That's my fault, and the least I can do by way of reparation is to answer her questions.

"You're right," I tell her. "It isn't exactly nothing. More like a kind of energy we do not understand, the opposite of heat and light. The Void is all around Midunnel, pressing inward, as you know—but parts of it are more condensed, moving through its expanse. Think of those centralized currents as a monstrous serpent out in the dark, *made* of the dark, forever slithering and coiling in the emptiness that is also part of itself. When its coils loop around the suns, they are blocked out, while other stars shine brighter."

"So when you perform magic with the Void, you…" Her voice trails off, as if she isn't sure what specific questions to ask.

"I perform rituals in my tower at Ru Gallamet, to collect condensed tendrils of the Void. I have a wheel and a spindle of my own design, which siphons the dark energy and allows me to shape it into a form I can absorb and use."

"You perform rituals? Like blood rituals?"

"Yes." I sigh, rubbing my jaw. "The Void has no real consciousness that I've been able to discern. But when it encounters life, it attempts to consume that life, replacing life with Itself. Blood is the essence of life. So yes, blood is a necessary component of the process. Typically I use Fae blood, since I need quite a lot of it."

"That's why my parents didn't want you to have me. You were going to drain my blood."

"No!" I try to communicate my sincerity through my eyes, my voice. "No, I wouldn't have harmed you, not permanently. I planned to have a healer on hand, to replace whatever I had to take from you."

175

She scoots away, glaring, engulfed in the big woolen cape I found for her. Fierce and strong as she is, she looks so precious in that enormous cape that I want to scoop her up in my arms again.

"Listen, please," I beg. "Let me explain."

She pinches her lips together, but she nods.

"I've experimented with the Void ever since I was very young," I continue. "To my thinking, the only thing strong enough to hold back the Void is… well, Itself. My plan is to arrange a permanent flow of the Void around Midunnel, like a belt that passes around our realm multiple times. To use the snake analogy again—this would be a part of the serpent's coils that would constantly flow around the borders of our realm, like a moving wall. So if the rest of the Void tried to press inward, it would no longer recognize this realm as a foreign body or a threat, but as part of itself."

"And how is that different from what we already have?" She points to the night sky.

"That thick coil of the Void, the one that blocks the suns regularly, is very far away. I'm proposing to create a defensive belt that is much closer." Snatching a chip of pale stone, I begin to draw a diagram on the dark roof slates of the Chapel. "Here is Midunnel, a flat two-dimensional realm, but in three-dimensional space. There is already a protective dome above us, set in place by Eonnula. Not a dome of glass, but of layered air. The dome isn't compressing downward, thankfully—the pressure of the Void is concentrated along the edges of the realm."

Aura watches closely as I sketch the positions of the suns. I explain what I've charted of their movements, how they form the summer and winter seasons we know. Then I draw a wavy line and several circles to represent the path the Void follows at night.

"Always the same path," I say earnestly. "Yet the thickness of the Void varies in places, meaning some nights are darker than others. So it is capable of rhythmic, perpetual motion, yet accommodates for variance. I've forced pieces of the Void to take form and to do my will. You rode on one of them—the Endling on which I brought you out of Caennith."

She nods.

"So with magic, the Void can be solidified, formed, and bent to someone's will."

Her forehead puckers. "Eonnula's will is the only one that matters."

I close my eyes briefly, stifling my impatience. "Yes, I believe in Eonnula. It's difficult not to when the evidence of Her work is so clear. But I don't believe She is watching us anymore—at least, not constantly. I don't believe She plans to interfere or send a savior. She saved us once. This time we must prove that we're worthy. We must save ourselves."

Aura winces, brushing back a strand of blond hair. "That's a problematic concept for me."

"I understand. But bear with me a little longer. As I studied the Void, I began to realize that what strengthens the air-dome above us is the direct impact of the Triune Suns. Their light focuses on the dome's peak, then spreads outward, weakening as it reaches the edges where the Void presses most firmly. So the key to stabilizing the flow of the Void isn't simply learning to weave the darkness into a permanent barrier—I must harness the light as well. And who is best at channeling the light and power of Eonnula? Why, the Conduit of Caennith. Imagine it—if I could spin dark energy into a perpetual coil, a protective wall around Midunnel! Imagine a barrier the Void cannot breach, reinforced and stabilized by the power of Eonnula Herself!"

Aura's gaze lifts to mine, shining with renewed interest.

"I tried your father's blood," I tell her. "Your mother's Conduit power is the result of their marriage, but his is directly inherited. It seemed to be working, at first. But it failed, and I began to suspect I needed fresher blood—perhaps the blood of a Conduit who had not yet ascended, who had never received and transmitted magical power before. At the very least, I thought it would be worth a try. And then, if that didn't work, I thought I could try the Conduit's blood again after their ascension."

"How much blood?"

"Not enough to kill you. Although your body must be bound to the Spindle during the ritual, as bait for the darkness."

"Shit, Malec." She turns away, cupping her fingers over her mouth.

"I know it sounds horrible," I say gently. "But I've worked with the Void for decades. I can do it without risking your life, I swear."

"And you approached my parents with this request. On the very day of my christening, when I was still a tiny infant."

Memory darkens my mind and my tone. "You don't know the whole story."

"Tell me, then. Right now."

21

AURA

"My father faded in his five-hundred-and-sixth year, leaving me the crown," says Malec. "From the beginning of my reign, I was determined to be a different kind of leader."

I tuck my cape closer around me, sensing the start of a longer tale than I anticipated. "Was your mother still alive?"

"My mother lived on for another thirteen years before she faded. They had me later in life."

"How old are you?"

"Sixty-eight. Now hush, little viper, and listen to the story. I'll never be done if you keep asking questions."

"Very well." I wave my hand airily for him to proceed.

"I spent the first years of my reign wooing your parents and the Three Faeries. First, I ceased the hostilities along the border, ordering my people not to attack even if provoked, only to defend. Then I began sending small gifts into Caennith as gestures of goodwill. My overtures led to some cautious trade and sharing of resources, and finally to a tenuous peace. After a time, I invited delegates from Caennith to cross the border into Daenalla. I treated them like royalty, until at last the Three Faeries themselves deigned to set foot in my lands for a short visit. After that, your parents visited as well, and so did other nobles of Caennith. They would not admit they enjoyed my hospitality, and they made every effort to proselytize my people. They spoke against our beliefs, and though we showed them grace and tolerance, they gave us none in return.

"My people chafed under the perpetual disdain of the Caennith, but I told them it was the price of peace. Meanwhile I continued my research, cautiously gleaning what I could from the Three Faeries. I thought they might have some knowledge that could help me stabilize the Edge and hold back the Void for good. Some of our discussions helped to clarify certain things in my mind—like why the blood heir to the Caennith throne has the power to transform their spouse into a Conduit as well, and why the previous generation loses their Conduit ability once a new Conduit is established."

Intrigued, I swerve my gaze from the silvered landscape to his face. Malec half-smiles and says, "That explanation can wait, little viper. Suffice it to say, in those days, the connection between the kingdoms was beneficial for everyone, though heavily inclined in Caennith's favor.

"As time passed, I began to include your parents and the Three Faeries among my regular guests for special occasions at Court. In fact, since they were uncomfortable coming to Ru Gallamet because of its proximity to the Edge, I arranged for our most glorious and important celebrations to be held at Kartiya, a beautiful city, centrally located and closer to the border. Still, neither I nor any of my people had been invited to any celebrations or gatherings in Caennith. It was as if the Caennith regarded us like a muddy lake—too far beneath them to do any more than dip their toes in and then retreat.

"After giving, and giving, and receiving so little in return, I became frustrated. Perhaps I should have been content with peace, but I wanted respect as well, for myself and my people.

"Tensions began to increase again, slowly. I sent ravens into Caennith and discovered that the Royals and the Three Faeries were taking credit for the resources I was sending to needy villages. The Caennith Priesthood still called the Daenalla 'heretics' and 'lost ones' in their speeches to the people.

"My pride wouldn't stand for it. I began to try to correct some of the misinformation, sending ravens with missives to scatter over the towns where I'd given resources, letting them know who was truly responsible. I recruited a few dozen Caennith citizens to subtly spread the truth about the Daenallan religion and practices.

"But the Three Faeries caught on to my efforts much more quickly than I expected. They excommunicated my allies and shot down many of my ravens. From then on, my relationship with your parents was soured. I used up the last of their goodwill requesting a vial of the King's blood to use in my Spinning. It was grudgingly given, and I paid them handsomely for it. When the blood did not work, I asked the King if we could try again. I pleaded with him to come to Ru Gallamet and be physically present for the ritual. I wanted to explore every possibility.

"Your father told me he would consider it. Over and over he told me that, and I kept asking, because the Edge kept crawling ever inward. I'm not sure what you've been taught in your geography lessons, Princess, but both kingdoms have been losing ground steadily over the past few decades. The Caennith Priesthood claims to use the light to push back the Edge, but my ravens report that the decline has been nearly equal in both kingdoms—perhaps a little faster in Caennith. Yet no matter how many times I explained my magical theories in letters to your parents, they refused to offer any more help beyond that single costly vial of blood.

"When my ravens brought me word of your impending birth, I felt hopeful again, for the first time in years. Perhaps, with an heir in place, your father might be willing to come to the Spindle and try the ritual with me. Or perhaps, if I approached him at such a joyous time, in the right manner, he would be willing to entertain my new theory—that a fresh supply of God-Touched blood, not yet activated as the Conduit, could be the key to fueling my great work. The Void surely could not resist amassing at such a tempting intersection of life and light, and I would have everything I needed to ensure this realm's survival. So I waited for the right moment to make my request.

"Shortly after your birth, I began to hear of several noble Daenallan families receiving invitations to the christening of the Caennith Crown Princess. A truly courteous Royal would have invited me first, but nevertheless, I refused to take offense. I expected my invitation to arrive any day.

"As more nobles of Daenalla received their invitations, I began to realize what made my heart burn with humiliation and disbelief—that I was being purposely excluded from the event. I, whom the Caennith Priesthood still called 'the Maleficent One, Spinner of Darkness, Wicked Conjurer,' and such foul names, despite my beneficence. I who had supported Caennith for years without demanding anything but peace along the border and a modicum of respect. The Royals were shaming me publicly before my people and theirs.

"I could not allow it to stand. So I wrote a letter to your father. It was mostly about my concerns regarding the Edge, and my theories for stabilizing it. I hinted at my need for your blood, in the most delicate and reassuring terms I could concoct. At the end I mentioned the latest bouts of misinformation and slander my ravens had perceived occurring throughout Caennith. I told him that if I was granted an invitation to the christening, it would no doubt solidify our alliance and reassure the Caennith citizens that I was not some kind of Void-worshiping monster.

"In his reply, your father called me delusional and said that his daughter's christening should be a day of glee. He did not want the 'dark presence of a fear-mongering sorcerer to spoil his most joyful day.'

"Angry and desperate, I appealed to the Three Faeries, describing my magical research in detail, pleading with them to see the reason behind what I must ask, begging them to uphold the shaky alliance between our kingdoms. They sent a message overflowing with insipid flattery, but I could read the truth between the lines. They did not intend to help me, or to defend me before their King.

"That same day, I received word that the Three Faeries had held a gathering of all the elders among the Caennith Fae, and told them that I was causing the Edge to contract faster—that my 'dark magic' was hastening the doom of Midunnel. Utter lies.

"The following week, I appeared at your christening, uninvited, robed in black, wreathed in shadows, and filled with freshly-spun Void magic. The crowd shrank from me, leaving me a clear path to the dais where your father and mother sat enthroned, while the Three Faeries watched over your cradle.

"Perhaps I overdid the dramatics. I felt helpless to dispel their perception of me, and so I became the villain they wanted—green light, black shadows, a voice like doom. I demanded that your parents yield you to me. I promised them it would be temporary, that you would not be permanently harmed, and that I would prove my good intentions to all of them by stabilizing the Edge forever.

"I did not threaten. But perhaps my presence and my aspect were threat enough. Your father refused once again, vehemently, and your mother declared that my attendance without an invitation was an act of 'warlike aggression.'

"You have to understand, little viper—I was worn out from the strain of pacifying these people, giving them my time, attention, and resources for years. I played the role of both fool and villain that day. I pinned the Three Faeries to the wall with shadows, threw the guards across the room, and bent over your cradle to curse a tiny golden-haired infant who stared up at me with innocent blue eyes. There were so many things I could have

184

done differently—choices I could have made—but it is of no use to dwell on them. What I've done is irreversible."

Malec falls silent, his story complete. He stares at the darkened landscape below us, while I gaze at his white profile and the four black horns twining up from his hair, their ridges gleaming in the starlight.

"And you still believe my blood is the key to this ritual?" I say quietly.

"More fervently than I believed it then. I've had more time for experimentation and learning, and I'm more certain than ever that you are the key. Any young Conduit's blood would have worked for this, but we're running out of time, so you are the last hope. By my estimation, the Void will enfold this realm completely within another few decades. It's been all I can do to keep it clear of Ru Gallamet this long, and I can't hold it back much longer. I cannot be absent from my home for more than a week or so, or my palace, my tower, and my Spindle will be lost to the Void."

I draw in a deep breath of the bracing night air. Despite his terrifying prophecy for the fate of our realm, my anxiety has eased a bit. No one has ever taken the time to explain the origin of the curse clearly before—at least not without lurid language designed to provoke fear. Malec's calm, matter-of-fact explanation may have been one-sided, but it felt honest. He did not shy away from condemning his own actions.

I don't forgive him, but I believe he told me the truth. And I understand him better now.

Unfortunately, that doesn't make my fate any easier to bear.

"You would sacrifice me to the dark," I murmur. "You'd pierce my finger, spill my blood, and send me into oblivion. You'd steal my remaining years, on the slim chance that your ritual might save everyone else. What if my blood doesn't work?"

"Then I will try it again once your birthday passes."

"You'd bind my sleeping corpse to the Spindle and shed my blood a second time?"

He makes a wry face. "I would try it, yes."

I scoff, shaking my head and looking away from him.

"Perhaps one of your parents will take your place in the cursed sleep."

He means to reassure me, but he only stirs up the sharp-nailed fear scrabbling over the sore flesh of my heart. "You heard the raven's message. What if my parents don't want to save me?"

"Then they're fools. If one of your parents won't save you by their free will, I'll drag them into Daenalla and force their lips to meet yours."

"But if they're being forced, it won't work. It has to be a sacrifice by the person who loves me best—you said so yourself. Maybe one of the Three Faeries would do it—Elsamel or Sayrin. Or Dawn." I turn back to him, hope brightening my heart. "Dawn loves me, and I love her. We are sisters, she and I. Maybe she would—but no—goddess, what am I thinking? I can't ask her to give up a hundred years."

"*I* will ask her," Malec says firmly. "Saving the realm requires sacrifice. If it works, she'll wake up a century from now and live another century or two. It's better than dying in a few decades when our world collapses on itself. Besides, a secondary curse, passed from one person to another, is usually easier to break. I have a few books about dispelling curses—perhaps I can find a way to shorten the sleep of anyone who might take your place."

He doesn't sound entirely sure of it, but he speaks intensely, with fierce determination in his voice and visage. He wants so badly to make it better, this thing he has done.

"If only you hadn't cast the curse that day," I say quietly. "If only you had waited, and then met with me when I was older, and explained everything—"

"You think you would have agreed to go with me?" He arches an eyebrow. "You, raised by the Royals, knowing your birthright, and poisoned against me from the start? Face it, Aura—the only reason you believe me now is because I revealed the lie you've been living. And because we're—we've been thrown together like this, you and I—and I'm—there's an attraction—" He clears his throat, pushes his long black hair behind one pointed ear.

"I'm not that shallow," I say sharply. "I don't believe you just because you're pretty and you have a beautiful cock."

Then I clap my hand over my mouth.

A slow smile widens on his face. His dark lashes droop over eyes that glitter with delighted wickedness. "You think I have a beautiful cock?"

"No," I gasp, heat roaring into my face. "Cocks aren't beautiful, they're just—some of them are shaped better than others. Some are cleaner, less lumpy or smelly. Because, you know, some of them have too many veins like bulging snakes, or they're strangely purple, and they—oh Void take me." The last words are a humiliated wheeze.

He's grinning openly now, and it makes him twice as gorgeous, godsdamn him.

"Stop," I order. "Stop it, or I swear I'll slap that grin off your fucking face."

"I think we've established that you hurting me isn't much of a threat. I rather enjoy it." He bites his lip suggestively.

"Fuck you," I breathe.

"Oh, no, little viper," he murmurs, the tips of his claws trailing through my hair. "This time, I'll be the one fucking *you*."

The words are more than a challenge—they're a promise, directed to the pulsing ache between my legs, the hollow in my soul, the bleeding cracks of my heart that beg to be salved.

"I thought you liked the woman taking control," I whisper.

"I do. Trust me, I want to be on my face before you, kissing your feet, sucking each tender toe—and I want to be bound, with my back bared to your whip. I want to be lying prone at your mercy, straining for a release you refuse to give. But I like other things too. Like punishing naughty princesses who dance naked for my men and chain me to bedposts without my permission." He caresses my chin with his long fingers.

I knock his hand away. My heart is beating too fiercely, too hot—every breath incinerates on the way to my lungs. Punishment... *naughty Princess*... I remember him smacking my rear when I lay across his steed, and the memory makes my pussy quiver.

Malec rises on the ledge, a column of black leather and shimmering dark wings. He quirks his wrist, flexes his fingers, and his tall staff with the green stone appears, materializing in his grasp.

He slants his gaze down at me, as if he's checking to see if I'm impressed. Vain bastard.

I *am* impressed. But I harden my expression and shrug, pulling my knees up and propping my arms across them.

"Before I take you inside," he says in a velvety tone that vibrates right down to my clit, "I'm going to reinforce the boundary around this place. Can't be too careful, now that we know there are hunting parties after us."

"You're going to use Void magic?"

"I have access to a little, but not much. Only when I return to the Spindle can I collect more of that power. No, this magic is all mine, partly inherited, but with a few personal twists." He points to the farthest outbuildings. "See the crooked leafless tree, just beyond the corner of that slanted shed? The boundary I set is about twenty paces beyond it. Keep your eye on that spot."

I sigh, as if I can't be bothered, but I fix my gaze where he told me to.

He stretches out both his staff and his empty hand. The orb at the head of the staff begins to glow brighter, while dots of sparkling magic fly from it and from his other palm. Like green fireflies they dance through the air, traveling outward in a great ring before settling down to the grass and sinking into the earth.

Darkness. Silence.

"Was that *it*?" I mutter. "I expected more."

He holds up his hand, a mute directive for patience.

Slivers of green light jab out of the soil where the sparks vanished. They fork and branch and crisscross each other, higher and higher, until they form a tall hedge of vicious-looking vines all around the Chapel grounds. Each vine bears dozens of thorns so long, thick, and sharp I can see them even from this distance, by the verdant glow of the magic.

The green light disappears, soaking into the vines, finalizing and solidifying them. The entire valley is now encircled by a bristling wall of thorns.

"The magic extends above us as well." Malec sweeps his hand toward the arch of the sky. "If any Caennith Fae try to fly over it, thorns will shoot from the hedge and bring them down. I'll dispel it when we leave."

I shouldn't feel safer, now that he has cut me off from my people. He could be lying about them having orders to kill me. The "message" from the raven might be a trick, meant to keep me from escaping.

What if I could somehow break through his barrier and get away? What if I could run to my people and be safe, out of his reach once again?

Would I do that?

But what if he's right? What if my blood is the key for this ritual of his, this scheme that could protect our entire realm? The thought of being used for his dark magic makes me shiver with revulsion—but maybe that's only because I've been trained to view the Daenalla as twisted and heretical. My mind has been dipped into a bath of fear and hate so many times that it's saturated with those emotions, and the result is a physical recoil at the idea of Void magic.

I keep coming back to one fact—that the Royals and my mothers lied to me since I was old enough to know my own name. They fractured me, fused wings to me, falsified my magical abilities.

But Malec walked me through an agony of revelation to find the searing truth on the other side. Whatever else he is, I owe him for that.

I'm deep in thought, frowning heavily at the barrier of thorns, when Malec steps nearer to me, his huge wings flared. "Your thoughts look painful, little viper. Would you like to forget them for a while?"

When I don't answer, he takes a handful of my hair and pulls my head back so I'm forced to look up at him.

I twist my hips, shoot one leg out, and kick his ankle so hard his foot slips off the ledge and he tumbles into mid-air, his fingers sliding out of my hair. He catches himself on a wing-beat and rushes in again. His muscled arm clamps around my waist and he carries me right off my perch.

We plummet through the air so fast a half-scream dies in my throat. But with a quick flex of his wings, we slow our fall just in time to touch down lightly on the grass by the Chapel.

The Void King holds me against his chest, his profile brushing mine, his voice dark and heated. I have no idea what he's saying to me—I'm distracted by the nearness of his lips, by their crisply perfect shape, by the way they're hovering over my mouth without really touching. I'm delirious, inhaling the warm, delicious puffs of his breath.

His words register vaguely, a distant serenade to the urgency spurring my heartbeat. "I asked if you want to forget."

Breathless, I manage to nod.

"Thank the goddess," he groans, and he picks me up, throwing me over his shoulder with an easy Fae strength I envy.

The King heads for a side door of the Chapel and bursts through. He stalks down a corridor, flings open another pair of doors, and flicks his fingers to illuminate the candles in the room. As they blaze up, I inwardly seethe over the fact that I can't produce a spark for fire anymore.

Malec totes me to the front of the small prayer chamber, where there's a stone altar scattered with herbs and offerings—a shrine to Eonnula. With a low grunt of impatience he sweeps the little dishes of salt and the bundles of herbs aside into an irreverent jumble, and he throws me over the altar, with my toes touching the cold floor, my belly pressed to the stone, and my rear jutting out.

He shoves my cape and my tunic up around my waist. His claws scrape the flesh of my hips as he finds the waistband of my leggings and pulls them over my ass, down my thighs.

Cool air flows over my bare bottom, teasing the heated, slick groove of my sex.

Slowly, with a single claw, Malec begins drawing circles and spirals on one cheek of my ass. My skin tingles unbearably, and I squirm.

He smacks my rump. "Be still, Princess." His nails skate over my other ass cheek, tantalizing my sensitive skin.

I'm dripping on the altar. I'm sure I must be; my insides are a river of want. "Just fuck me already," I snap, and he spanks my ass again. A jolt of pleasure spikes through my clit at the forceful contact. I vent a tiny moan and press my mound against the stone edge of the altar.

"No." Another spank. "Be still."

I bite back a retort, feigning submission. I have to endure this so I can get his cock inside me. My memory of fucking him earlier is slightly blurry, but I recall a rich, satisfying fullness, like he was made to fit *me* precisely.

"Don't dance for my men again." His voice glides through the quiet of the altar room. He slaps one cheek of my ass, and my breath hitches. "And don't try to conquer me with bluesteel. I won't be so foolish next time."

"You're foolish far too often, aren't you?" I say wryly. "But you're never foolish in the same way twice. Maybe by the end of your long life, you'll be wise. If Midunnel lasts that long. Or if you can bear to stay alive until then."

The minute I say it, I realize how wrong the words are. How terrible it is for me to twist that particular knife in his soul, to mock the despair that has him wavering on the edge of self-destruction.

His palm slams into my ass, but it doesn't leave—his fingers grasp my flesh with all the strength of pain, or fury.

"I have never claimed to be the most intelligent of rulers," he says, low. "I often tell myself what an idiot I am. My mother always told me not to speak to my own heart in that demeaning way, but sometimes I deserve it." His claws swirl over my ass cheek again, and I close my eyes against the delicate tingling sensation. "I've told myself many times that Midunnel might have been better off without me, that it needs someone wiser and more gifted than me. I wreck things more often than I repair them. I've achieved none of the goals I set for my reign, and perhaps I never will. Saving the realm would justify my existence, but if that fails…" His voice fades into silence.

"Forget what I said," I beg him. "Forget it all, and do things to me… please."

But I've stolen his dominance, dampened his lascivious mood. I can sense the change in him, like false notes souring a melody. He's stroking my rear absently now, as if his mind is elsewhere.

Fuck his insecurity—I need him back. I want him driving into me, fierce and regal, with that compelling light in his eyes and his wings outspread.

I wriggle on the altar, and when he doesn't react I climb fully onto it and turn around, sitting with my bare ass on the altar's edge. My bottom smarts a little from the spanking, but he was more playful than cruel, so the sting isn't bad.

I kick off my leggings and scoot back on the altar, my legs arched and thighs spread. "Fine. If you won't do things to me, I'll distract myself." I trace one finger along the slick seam of my pussy, then dip two fingers in, parting the lips so he can see deeper into me.

It's working. His distant gaze refocuses, a lustful interest lighting his eyes.

My cheeks flame with the awareness of what I'm doing—where I'm doing it—and *who* I'm regaling with this little show. The Void King, of all people, is watching me touch myself.

But I've already ridden his face to climax. This is no worse—or better—or—ahh, forget the guilt, forget the confusion, the inhibitions. Fuck it all.

I hum softly, moving my fingertip to circle my clit. "Goddess, that feels good."

The Void King sinks to his knees by the altar, his dark eyes locked on my pussy. His beautiful wings arch more dramatically than ever, feathers practically trembling with his eagerness.

"Let me," he whispers. "May I?"

I lift my bare foot and trace my toe down his straight nose, nudging at his parted lips. He releases a blissful exhale as I push my toes against his cheek. "Kiss my foot," I order.

He takes my ankle in his hands and kisses each toe tenderly, just as he fantasized aloud to me. One Caennith guard I was with liked licking my feet; I hated the way he slobbered over them. But when Malec sucks my tiniest toe between his lips and bathes it delicately with the tip of his tongue, my body erupts in a glorious thrill.

He releases my foot, lifts pleading eyes to mine, and says softly, "Shall I make you come, my lady?"

"You may taste me." I struggle to keep my voice from quivering. "And then, I command you to fuck me like you promised."

Confidence flashes into his eyes again, and he grips my waist and pulls me to the edge of the altar. His face presses between my thighs, and as his tongue lashes over my clit, I vent a shrill gasp and grip two of his horns.

I'm sitting on Eonnula's altar, candlelight glowing on my bare legs, while the Void King kneels before me and bathes my sex with his tongue. He's magnificent like this, worshiping me with his proud wings outspread like a cloud of gleaming darkness. His black hair brushes silken against my inner thigh while he laps and suckles every tender bit of my flesh.

I love the curved shape of his horns, the flat ridges along their surface. The two front horns are just the right size for my hands.

"Look at me," I breathe.

He lifts his dark lashes, his eyes meeting mine as his beautiful lips nibble my clit.

"Shit," I gasp, shuddering. "Oh shit—I'm going to come—keep looking at me—fuck, fuck…" My thighs contract, squeezing around his head while my stomach tenses. Pleasure cascades through me, violent ripples of ecstasy making my legs shake.

He keeps licking me, savoring me until my thighs and stomach relax and I fall back boneless against the altar. I am a limp, willing sacrifice, soaked for him, too delirious from pleasure to say a word when he unfastens his pants and reveals the sleek length I enjoyed so much earlier in the evening.

Malec pauses, his jaw tense, lips tight. He's waiting for a protest, for a sign from me.

I make him wait for a moment, noting the gleam of liquid at his swollen tip. He's aching to be inside me. He needs me as fiercely as I need him.

I won't think about how strange and perverse this is, that I'm fucking my kingdom's worst enemy. Three days ago I would have boasted about how I'd kill him if I ever got the chance. And now—I nod to him, and he holds my legs up and slides every bit of that glorious length into my body.

I cry out softly, relief and surrender.

If my mothers knew I was letting the Maleficent One take me on Eonnula's altar...

"Harder," I grit out. "Fuck me as hard as you can."

Uncertainty crosses his features. "I'm Fae, and you're human—"

"I can take it." The words burst from me in a vicious sob. "Please. Please fuck me hard."

With a growl he plants both hands on the stone surface of the altar, on either side of my shoulders. His hips slam against my body, the first strike of a brutal onslaught. He drives into me so hard my back grates against the stone, and he has to curl one arm around my head to hold me in place while his body thunders into mine with the force of a battering ram. It hurts—his fingers clamped around my skull, claws digging in, the bruising slam of his hip bones against the backs of my thighs, the thick stretch of his cock plunging in and out with inhuman force and supernatural speed. I welcome the invasion and the pain—I revel in it, because I can feel the clenching build of pleasure deep in my gut, a raw, savage need climbing and climbing—I can tell that when it comes it's going to be the most intense climax I've ever felt.

I sink my fingernails into his shoulders, lacerating his skin. "Harder," I choke, and he snarls in response, huffing with the effort of obeying my demand. His arm tightens around my head, and he slows his pace for a moment to take my mouth.

His kiss is harsh and hot, a tempest over my tongue. I ravage him with my lips and teeth, and when I bite his lower lip he gives a whimpering moan of pained delight.

"Stop kissing me and fuck me," I whisper, and with a final violent kiss, he complies.

My eyes roll back as I'm pounded, shaken, hammered apart—as the sheer violence of his body batters the orgasm out of me. I come like a gate splintering, like a city falling, walls exploding and bricks crumbling into dust. I come so hard I can't even scream, or see. I can only convulse, rigid with bone-searing bliss, a faint cracked sound in my throat.

How he kept himself from coming for so long, I don't know, but when he feels me spasming around him, he lets go with a groan of agonized relief. His cock flexes in my channel, and I quiver at the sensation.

I reach up, gathering a handful of his hair in one hand and grasping one of his horns with the other. Pulling his face down to mine, I drag my teeth over his lips, twist and tug his hair, nip at his questing tongue. He moans a wordless plea into my mouth, so I finally kiss him softly, gratefully, while his wings curve inward, encircling us both, as if to shield this moment from the eyes of Eonnula herself.

While he was fucking me so mercilessly, I forgot everything. I'm sweetly sore now, but reality is oozing back into my mind.

The Fae who cursed me is kissing me like I'm the one thing he has always craved.

"Stop," I whisper into his mouth. "You have to stop. *We* have to stop."

Malec's eyes register what I'm saying. His body tenses over mine, and his lips leave my mouth.

Slowly he pulls back, resignation falling over his crisp features. He eases himself out of me, hands me my leggings, and refastens his pants while I arrange my clothing. When I stand up, I feel his cum leaking out of my pussy, dampening the crotch of my leggings. I have the strangest urge to scoop it up and push it back inside myself.

"We have a few hours until dawn," Malec says thickly. "We should both get some sleep."

22

My fist slams into Vandel's cheek, and his head whips to the side.

I'm restraining myself. He should be grateful for that.

Since dawn, I've already dealt out plenty of bruises to Ember and Kyan in the name of "training." They all know what I'm really doing—condemning them for stealing Aura's clothes in the bath-house, punishing them for ogling and touching her when she was dancing bare-breasted for them all. I gave Andras a few bruises too—minor ones compared to the others.

I've saved Reehan for last. He seems most interested in Aura, and I plan to clarify for him how I feel about that.

Vandel staggers forward, fists up, blood trailing from the corner of his mouth, his red hair wildly tousled. I grab his wrist, dart behind him, and deliver a sound smack to the back of his head. As he falls to his knees, I release his wrist before it cracks. He's human, and I don't want to damage him too badly. I need all my men in good fighting condition for the ride to Ru Gallamet.

"Go," I bark. Vandel hunches his shoulders in defeat and walks over to stand with the others.

"Reehan, you're next." I crack my knuckles and flare my wings as the blond Edge-Knight approaches.

His serpent's tongue flickers out while he paces slowly, eyeing me. "What's this little 'training' session really about, my Lord?"

Ah, so he's voicing what the others silently realized and accepted. He thinks himself courageous for confronting me.

As the youngest and least experienced, he also tends to be less respectful than the others. His lesson may need to be more— strenuous.

He's part Fae. He can take it.

"What do you think it's about, Reehan?" I ask.

"I think you favor the Caennith princess." His purple eyes hold my gaze.

"I demand you respect her. Which you have failed to do on numerous occasions." I tense as if I'm about to attack, and he dances backward nervously. Grinning, I expand my wings to their full width, and when his gaze flicks to them, I land a punch to his kidney.

Reehan grunts and retreats with a baleful glare. "There were some interesting noises in the Chapel last night."

"The captive had a nightmare."

"Some of us heard—other noises."

"Did you indeed?" I reply coolly.

"Yes. And some of us are concerned."

I face him, feet planted apart, fists at my sides. "Why don't you say it outright? Speak your concerns."

Reehan glances over at the other knights. Whatever he sees in their faces must embolden him, because he says, "All of us have sacrificed for your goals, Lord King. Some more than others. We would hate to see those sacrifices cheapened or wasted because you wanted to wet your dick in a Caennith hole."

Out of the corner of my eye I see Ember put a hand to his brow, shaking his head. Ember knows how much I value the thoughts and guidance of those who follow me. But I do require a certain level of respect. After all, I am their king.

What infuriates me more than Reehan's coarse words is the truth behind them. Aura fell asleep as soon as I saw her safely back to bed, but I prowled my room for the remaining hours until dawn, wracked by guilt and dread.

I am recklessly, helplessly attracted to her mind, body, and spirit. I've known her for two days, and already I crave infinite time with her. She is the blend of sweetness and violence I've always wanted in a woman. Her pain calls to mine, her prickly reluctance tempts me, and when she yields—goddess, the passion that surges out of her—it's exhilarating. The thought of losing her to the cursed sleep in just a few days—I can hardly bear it.

But Reehan is right. After everything I've asked of my people over the past decades, I can't let a personal attraction get in the way of what I must do.

"Nothing has changed." I fold my wings against my back and circle Reehan, while he adjusts his footing and raises his guard. "Today and tomorrow we will ride hard for Ru Gallamet, and when we reach it, I will bind the girl to my Spindle and bleed her. I will work the spell I've been crafting for years, and our realm will be saved. You have my word—I will not fail in this." I let my gaze roam over the others.

Reehan takes advantage of my apparent distraction, as I knew he would. When he leaps in, I block his incoming blow easily and smash a heavy punch to his jaw.

"But with that said," I continue coolly, grabbing him by the nape of the neck. "No one touches the Princess in the meantime. She is mine."

With a surge of muscle I throw Reehan to the ground, forcefully enough that he wheezes and stays put for several seconds. When I stalk away, Kyan approaches and helps the blond knight to his feet.

"Training is over." I pick up my leather cuirass and put it on, using magic to fasten the openings at the back, which seal around my wing joints. "Get something to eat, finish any chores you've neglected, and pack your bags. We leave within the hour."

23

AURA

I don't know who I am.

The thought circles in my mind over and over as I ride with the Void King and his Edge-Knights. Malec has chosen to fly overhead since we left Hellevan Chapel, so I've been riding alone. I'm not bound in any way, but the Edge-Knights keep my horse in the center of the group. There's no chance of breaking free, even if I wanted to.

I don't know what I want. I don't know who I am.

My life has consisted of training, guarding, and keeping watch—spattered with moments of violence. I didn't regret those kills, because I wasn't killing for myself—I did it for Dawn.

Except it wasn't for her, in the end. It was all for me.

My life, deemed more precious than the lives of others.

My parents' pride, valued above the welfare of an entire realm.

I have no magic anymore. No wings, no Fae heritage, no five-hundred-year life span. But I do have strength and skills. At least the Three Faeries taught me not to depend on magic for protection.

Maybe I should be glad for my years of excellent education at Dawn's side, for the countless memories of books read together, of swims in palace pools, of pranks played on servants and evenings spent giggling over my latest amorous conquest.

But it's all soured now, and I think that's the worst part—not the anger or the betrayal, or the peril of my true identity—but the fact that every good memory is now colored differently. None of it has the same meaning.

My head lying in Elsamel's lap when I was sick, her fingers brushing through my hair. Genla's look of grim approval when I staggered away from a fight, bruised but victorious. Sayrin's patient instruction in the use of my magic. Every remembrance is tinged with pain and lies.

Each encounter I had with the King and Queen is soiled, too. Every dinner at which I stood guard—I, the rightful Princess, just steps away from my parents' fake daughter. The time when the King came to watch me train. The time the Queen joined Dawn and me for our sessions with the seamstress. They so rarely spent time with Dawn—with me. I don't understand their reasons for any of it.

I don't know who I am.

When we pause for the noon meal, I sit listlessly on a rock, watching a stream gurgle over dark pebbles. Some of the Chapel attendants packed us food—flat bread folded in half, stuffed with meat and cheese and sauce, kept chilled within an enchanted basket. My wrap hangs between my limp fingers. It probably tastes good, but I can't bring myself to try it.

The horses are drinking and eating, and so are the men. They give me space, whether out of courtesy or by some directive of Malec's, I'm not sure. But I'm grateful to be left alone for a little while. I *think* I'm grateful, anyway. Being alone with my thoughts feels necessary right now, but also dangerous.

I don't notice Malec standing in the shadow of the trees until a raven soars across the stream and alights on his shoulder. He murmurs affectionately to the bird before letting it fly away.

Then he walks over, folds his arms, and props his hip against a higher part of the rock I'm sitting on.

He's in layered black-leather armor today, and his wings are folded up tight, pinned to his back. The sunlight catches on his horns as he tilts his head. "You're not eating."

I look down at the wrap in my hand. "I suppose not."

"You should eat something. Keep your strength up."

"Most captors would prefer weak prisoners."

"You're much more than a prisoner."

"Is that so?" I look up at him, too listless for anything but a faint spark of anger. "Who am I then? Because I don't know anymore."

"You are who you've always been. Certain externals and futures have changed, but you remain yourself."

"I don't think so. I feel different, inside. I'm solid, you know—not fractured anymore." I crook my fingers over my heart, digging my nails into the fabric of my tunic. "But it still hurts so badly that I want to—cut it out."

He answers in a voice of shadow and silk, of sorrow and certainty. "I know the feeling."

My throat tightens, and the inside of my nose stings with oncoming tears.

"In such moments," he says gently, "it might help to think of the little things that are still the same. They can often be the most important."

"What do you mean?"

"Well, let's start with your favorite food."

"This is silly—"

"Humor me."

I know the answer I've always given when asked such a question. "The spicy chowder Genla makes during the darkest days of winter. She says 'a fire on the tongue can light a fire in the cheerless heart.'" My stomach twists. "I won't ever eat that chowder again, will I? And if I did, I couldn't enjoy it."

204

Malec winces. "Let's try something else—your favorite color."

"The exact shade of blue that my hair used to be."

"Oh. Fuck." His frown deepens. "This isn't working like I thought it would."

His chagrin almost makes me smile. "It's all right."

"Someone asked me these questions, shortly after my mother's death. I felt like less of a whole person without my parents, but I went through the process of reclaiming each bit of myself, and it helped. Every type of grief and pain is different, but I thought perhaps—" He runs a hand over his face. "I apologize if I made it worse."

"It's all right." I reach up and touch his arm lightly, realizing with faint surprise that I don't feel the slightest impulse to hurt him right now. "It was kind of you to try."

He *is* kind. Despite what he has done, the mistakes he has made, the fate he still intends for me... he is a compassionate man. I find myself hungering for kindness, starving for it. "Will you ride with me?"

His lips part, surprise crossing his features. "I've been flying so I can keep watch."

"Don't your wings tire? Perhaps Ember or Kyan could take the watch a while."

"My wings rarely tire."

"Of course." I stiffen and drop my hand from his arm. "Forget I asked."

He leans down, warmth flowing from his eyes into mine. "I will ride with you, little viper, if you will do one thing for me."

"And what is that?"

"Eat your lunch."

Malec rides behind me for the rest of the afternoon. His broad chest at my back, his breath in my hair, and the firm press of his thighs keeps me warmly aroused for hours—not unbearably so, but pleasantly. We talk of religion, his and mine—their differences and similarities. With everything else I believed thrown into question, I might as well question that too.

To my surprise, our philosophies align more closely than I thought—with the exception that his theology allows for fear, doubt, uncertainty, and sorrow—embraces them fully, without shaming those who feel such emotions. Compared to mine, his faith is at once gentler and more terrifyingly open to possibilities.

The first skeins of the Void began to writhe across the suns, dimming their light to a deep orange. There's debate among Malec and his men—whether we should find shelter for the night or ride through it. Ravens have come and gone multiple times today, passing information into Malec's mind, but there have been none for a few hours, and that fact seems to concern him.

"We will pause for a meal, for us and the horses," he announces at last. "And then we will keep riding."

We've been traveling across broad plains thatched with grain fields and pastures, dotted with the occasional cottage and barn. In this part of the countryside there's nothing to break the monotony of the fields—tall golden-brown grass as far as the eye can see—except in the distance, where a few pointed smudges hint at the mountains where Ru Gallamet lies. There's a blackness behind those smudges—a deeper dark that I've seen only once in my life, when the King took Dawn and me to see the Edge.

"A future ruler should view the Void at least once," he told us. "It's important to know your enemy's face, to sit at his table and show him you have no fear. But do not let it trouble your minds. Remember that Eonnula's savior will come to defeat all such darkness."

I spoke to him directly then—not something I did often. "How will we know the savior?"

And he looked at me—my King, my father—and said, "The Priesthood will know. You need not trouble yourself with such things. Only trust, and rejoice, and worship."

Sayrin, who had accompanied us on the journey to the Edge, nodded and murmured her agreement.

Trust, and rejoice, and worship.

Have faith, and do not fear.

Easy enough for Royals and their retinue, living in the central parts of Midunnel. Not so easy, perhaps, for those living within sight of the Edge every day. Looking at it now, even as a gloomy suggestion in the far distance, I can't help wondering how the villagers abiding in its shadow manage to stay sane.

The Void King takes flight, leaping off the back of our horse and wheeling over the land high above our group. He seems unsettled, unsatisfied. When he finally descends again, he hovers and points down, to part of the field on the left of the dirt track we've been following. By the time we have plowed through the grass to the spot he indicated, he magically flattened a wide circle of grass, making space for us to camp. The grass surrounding the circle is slightly taller than me. I don't like not being able to see over it.

While we gather in the circle, Malec strides off into the grass, swearing as his wings drag against the stalks. He keeps his staff upraised, and the orb at its tip glows with a hectic light.

"He's trying to call ravens." Vandel takes the bridle of my horse, holding it steady while I dismount. He's got a black eye

207

he didn't have yesterday. "These fields are usually full of crows and blackbirds. Nothing to be seen now, and it worries him."

"That does seem strange." My instincts flare at once, suspicion tightening my nerves. "You think the Caennith are close?"

"If he thought they were too close, we wouldn't be stopping to rest." Vandel eyes me cautiously, as if he thinks I might leap at him with my teeth bared.

"The horses do seem to need a breather." I pat the heaving flank of my mount and glance around at the others—lowered heads, shining coats, froth on the lips of a couple horses. "We've been riding hard all day."

Reehan saunters up to me and flicks a lock of my hair. "Some of us were ridden hard last night, weren't we, Princess?"

"Careful," says Vandel warningly.

"Oh, she's been tamed. Haven't you, love?" Reehan grins at me, his purple tongue flickering out. "Not so vicious now. Like every princess, she just needed to be shown that her place is beneath a King."

Fitzell was wrong about this one. He isn't just young and stupid—there's real malice in him, and a lack of respect for anyone but himself.

Malec's body and voice soothed me this afternoon, but my anger never left. It roars up again at Reehan's words, a virulent river inside me, a molten flow that demands an outlet.

I shape my mouth into a sly smile and edge closer to Reehan, laying my fingers against his chest. "Maybe you'd like a ride, too."

"Reehan, don't." Vandel glances over his shoulder, but the Void King is nowhere in sight.

Reehan licks his lips and lowers his voice. "I'd be game for a roll in the grass."

"We'll have to be quick, while the others are feeding and watering the horses," I whisper. "Come with me."

"She's going to try to escape," Vandel says.

I laugh lightly. "On foot? Where would I go?" I grab Reehan's hand and pull him into the grass with me.

There is an upcoming scene of attempted rape (unsuccessful)—skip to the next break if you'd rather not read it.

I don't take him far from the circle. Just far enough that his grunts of pain won't be immediately audible. I need something to thrash, and he's practically begging for a beating.

"I knew you were a little slut," he says hoarsely, eagerly, gathering my tunic in both hands. I let him pull it off, revealing the chemise beneath. The fabric is ribbed, with cups designed for my breasts—not exactly a corset, but a pleasantly supportive undergarment I was grateful to receive this morning. And it shows off my breasts to full advantage, which Reehan seems to appreciate.

"Show me your tits," he rasps, unbuttoning his pants. "Goddess, I can't wait to fuck that royal pussy."

When he pulls his cock out, I strike, slamming my boot against his crotch.

A shrill whine of pain escapes him, and he clamps both hands over his bruised genitals. "Bitch," he wheezes. "Stupid Caennith whore… run if you want. You can't escape us."

"I don't plan on escaping." I whirl, slamming a roundhouse kick into the side of his face.

It's a good kick, and it nearly knocks him over—but not quite. Because even though I'm far stronger than most women my age, I no longer have the benefit of my charmed rings and their simulation of Fae strength.

And Reehan is Fae.

He rights himself and glares at me with murder in his eyes.

I charge him again, landing a punch to his jaw—but he catches my arm, his fingers compressing tendons and bones with brute force. Pain flares through my forearm and I realize with sharp alarm that my rings must have also helped me heal faster than humans. No chance of that this time.

I slam my foot into Reehan's stomach—almost, but he twists, so the impact I intended isn't as great.

My heart is pounding frantically now. I'm neither as fast nor as strong as I used to be, and I have no magic. This was a bad plan—I shouldn't have tried to use this randy Fae as a punching dummy.

Reehan knocks aside my next blow and catches me by the throat. He bears me down to the ground while the stalks of grass bend and crunch beneath me.

"You thought you could make a fool of me, Princess? You've been teasing and tempting me from the beginning. Don't deny it. You can't play the slut with a male and then turn him down, see? I'm going to show you what happens when little whores don't follow through on their promises."

This wouldn't be the first time a man has tried to turn my "no" into a "yes." I've always been able to extricate myself, by persuasion or by force. This time won't be different. It won't.

Reehan's body weighs heavy against mine, surging with a Fae strength I can't match. So I decide to try the truth.

"I wasn't planning to seduce you," I tell him. "I brought you out here because I'm angry, and I needed someone to fight."

"You like to fight?" he hisses, gripping my face in his hand, squeezing my jaw. "You like to be forced? Is that how the King took you?"

I can barely speak through the pressure of his fingers. "Stop, Reehan. Your king won't like this."

"He's weak. He can barely bring himself to punish anyone beyond a few chores and halfhearted blows." Reehan scoffs. "He'll think up some pathetic task for me as penance. Worry less about my punishment and more about yourself, love." His other hand creeps over my breast, squeezing.

"I told you, I just wanted to spar a little—let me up, and we'll talk about it."

"Why are you denying your desire?" he whispers. "You liked it when I touched you last night. You danced for me—you *wanted* me, before he took you away."

Reason isn't working. I reach toward his face, my thumbs aimed for his eyes, but he reacts with terrifying speed and a burst of glittering light. The next second my wrists are wrapped tightly with grass stalks, shackled as surely as if he'd locked me into metal cuffs.

I open my mouth to scream, but he stuffs his fingers in, shoving them down my throat until I nearly choke. I can feel the brutal strength of his grip against the fragile bone of my jaw; he could so easily press down and break it.

Reehan inhales through his nose, long and deep. "I'm not full-blooded Fae, but I've got a little magic, including one of the old tricks from the home realm. I can smell arousal. I can taste it on the air. And you, Princess, are saying 'yes' to me by your scent."

I'm not aroused because of him. Any lingering arousal is from riding in Malec's arms.

"I'll have to be quick." Reehan's free hand fumbles with the waistband of my leggings, and I buck my hips, kicking at him. Another burst of magic, and he has my ankles tethered with grass stalks as well.

The agony of helplessness floods my body. Braced over me, Reehan strokes his shaft a few times while I writhe under him.

Hot tears leak from the corners of my eyes, searing my temples, soaking into my hair. When will Eonnula decide I've suffered enough?

I'm going to have to endure this. A few minutes, and it will be over. Just a few minutes of pain—I can do this—I can take it—

Reehan tugs my leggings down on one side, over my hip, keeping the fingers of his other hand jammed into my mouth. He leers at me and leans in. His forked tongue skates out, smearing wetly along my cheek.

I squeeze my eyes shut.

Then—a squelching *crunch.*

More wetness, dribbling onto my face. Reehan's fingers relax in my mouth, and his heavy hand slides away.

When I open my eyes, I scream.

There's a giant black thorn sticking out of Reehan's forehead, like the spike of some deformed unicorn.

Even for a Fae, there's no healing from a wound like that.

Thorny vines lash around his body, yanking him backward, off me. Reehan's magic evanesces from the grass stalks, and they release my wrists and ankles.

Malec stands amid the tall grass, his horned head savagely outlined against the orange sky. His hand is lifted, almost like a casual greeting, except the clawed fingers are hooked, rigid. His magic holds Reehan aloft, while more thorns coil around the blond Fae's body. Blood drips between the vines, sprinkling the ground.

"My apologies if you wanted to fuck him," says Malec coolly, "but it appeared as though he was forcing you."

"He was." I climb to my feet. My legs are shaking from the horror of what nearly happened and from the violence of Reehan's death.

The Void King releases Reehan's body, which crashes to the ground. A thornless vine forms in Malec's hand, a leash by which he can drag the carcass.

"Walk with me," Malec says. "We'll return to camp."

He lifts his staff, and the tall grass *folds*. A huge swath of it simply lies down flat, creating a broad avenue straight back to the camp.

I manage to stay upright and mostly steady until we reach the circle of men and horses. The other Edge-Knights freeze as we approach—me, disheveled and stricken, accompanied by Malec's dominant winged figure, with the thorn-wrapped corpse of Reehan dragging along the ground behind us.

Ember is the first to speak. "You killed him."

From the stark disbelief in Ember's tone, Malec doesn't do this often. Which is somewhat reassuring.

"I kill rapists and molesters," Malec says icily. "He was warned, as you all were, to respect the Princess. No one may touch her. She is mine."

A terrifying, radiant thrill runs through my body at those words.

Defender, captor, murderer. My lover and my enemy. My comfort and my doom.

How can he be all those things at once?

24

I have not felt such fury since the day I cursed the Princess.

How could I have let this happen? How could I have missed seeing the evil in Reehan? I have been too distracted, too focused on the larger plan, not careful enough about the details.

I failed again. And this time my failure could have been catastrophic for Aura. Her mental and emotional state is already fragile, and for *this* to happen—

The fact that Reehan didn't get inside her doesn't diminish the trauma of the assault. She has every right to hate me for permitting this to occur while she's under my care.

I'd have killed Reehan even if he'd targeted some poor farm girl; but this was a vicious attack on someone I'm beginning to cherish deeply. The connection between Aura and me makes his betrayal so much worse.

My anger swells my chest until I feel as if I'm bursting at the seams. I kick Reehan's thorn-covered body to the edge of the camp and round on my men.

"You let them go off together," I snarl.

"She led him away, Sire." Vandel is bone-white under his freckles. "She hinted that they were going to—to—"

"And you let them go." I stalk nearer to him, my claws lengthening, the remains of my Void magic stirring under my skin. I'm tempted to plunge all five talons into Vandel's flesh and yank out his heart through his broken ribs.

Suddenly Aura is there, between us, her blue eyes wretched and pleading. "It's not his fault, Malec."

Andras sucks in a quick breath when she addresses me like that—so familiar, no honorifics.

"I just wanted to spar with someone," Aura says. "To beat someone up—I wanted to give pain, and maybe get a few bruises in return. I didn't expect him to—I forgot that I'm not as strong as I…" Her voice trails off, her face downcast.

"Vandel was stupid to let you two go off together. He should be punished."

"He didn't think I could escape. And he didn't suspect Reehan would go that far—did you?" Aura glances back at the red-haired knight, who shakes his head fervently.

"I made a foolish decision," Aura continues. "I led Reehan on, and I—"

"Stop," I bark. "There is no excuse for what he did. If you place one crumb of blame on yourself, I swear I'll—"

"What?" She looks up at me, a sweet, sad smile flitting across her mouth. "What will you do to me?"

I'm aching, burning, guilty, furious—a tempest I cannot quell. A passion I cannot allow myself to express, not here, not now.

"Nothing," I rasp. "I'll do nothing."

Her back is to the others, so they don't see her lips move. Two words.

Good boy.

That little phrase, and the tiny smile that accompanies it, lets me know she is all right. Or she will be. Relief trickles into the blended swirl of grief, anxiety, and anger in my soul. It gives me just enough strength to settle my usual calm expression into place.

I let my mask slip for a moment, and not in my usual way—casual jokes by the fireside, friendly sparring, merry songs. I allowed my men to see my cold fury, the darkness I keep locked away.

I was shaken. Out of control.

I killed Reehan without even thinking about it. Without asking questions, or considering laws and the fair order of justice. Excusable, since I witnessed the crime myself—but what if I had misread the situation? What if I'd murdered him, and then discovered their activities were consensual?

The impulsive nature of my actions disturbs me. I thought I had learned to consider more carefully before reacting. Despite Reehan's lack of respect, for me and for the Princess, he was right about one thing. Aura has affected me more deeply than I realized—shaken me to my core. When it comes to her, my self-control is questionable at best.

I must be more careful.

"We will ride on, and send someone back for Reehan's body later," I hear myself saying. "Take an hour of rest, and then we move. I don't like this place. There are no birds."

No birds, in a field of grass, with plentiful seeds on stalks. It isn't right. Yet I can't feel anything amiss—can't sense any magical influence. Nor did I see anything suspicious when I flew over the area and chose this spot. Of course there are cloaking spells and charms for the concealment of magic, but those take time to activate, and there's no sign of any Caennith arriving here before us. We should be safe enough for a short rest, as long as we set a watch.

My knights continue with preparations for the meal and the care of the horses, but they do so in heavy silence. Do they believe me, that Reehan was going to rape Aura, or do they think

I killed him out of jealousy? Either way I am still King, still their leader. But I'd like to know they believe me, and trust me.

How can I expect them to trust me when I don't trust myself?

And why, why am I thinking so much about *me*, when Aura is the one who suffered indignity and fear in the field?

She's standing beside the horse she rode, absently stroking its neck and shoulder. I should approach her and offer comfort—but I don't know what to say. Apologize for my knight's actions? Tell her I never imagined he would attempt such violence? He was a merry companion, a trickster, a teller of tales. Irreverent, gleeful, sometimes vulgar and offensive, but like a fool, I overlooked those instances.

"Sire."

I inhale sharply, tearing my gaze from Aura. "What is it, Kyan?"

His silver feathers glitter darkly in the fading light. "May I bring you some food? Some drink?"

There's understanding and concern in his eyes. No condemnation.

"I had to do it," I say under my breath.

He nods grimly. "I overheard him speaking to Vandel last night, after you carried the Princess away. I did not think he would act on his words, so I said nothing. I should have told you."

"I should have seen it in him. I used to be better at reading people." I sweep a hand over my face. "Fuck, Kyan. This is such a mess."

"I know, Sire." He lifts one hand tentatively, then places it on my shoulder, a brotherly grip. "I will bring you some wine, and something to—"

His body jerks, eyes blown wide, a faint grunt of surprise breaking from his lips.

A feathered shaft, gleaming with magic, protrudes from beneath his armpit.

His hand drops from my shoulder.

He's falling, crashing into the glitter of his wings. Blue lightning forks out from the arrow, caging his chest in virulent chains of flame.

With a roar, I grip the arrow and yank it out. Kyan's body arches, his face a rictus of pain. Calling on my magic, I spin to face the direction from which the arrow came. I can see nothing, so with a burst of power I flatten an immense swath of grass.

Two figures tumble and roll for fresh cover as I blow apart their hiding place. I send thorns racing along the ground after them, but my thorns are turned aside and crumbled to ash by some opposing force.

My knights leap to their feet, weapons ready, the meal forgotten. More arrows arch through the dusky sky, over the towering grass, curving down into our hollow. They don't behave like normal arrows—they swerve, seeking targets.

"Seeker arrows!" Vandel calls out.

These missiles are a Caennith specialty—arrows that are charmed when they're crafted, then animated by a specific spell. They don't just fly from a bow; they pursue their target. Glamours do not fool them.

Shit. The Caennith *were* lying in wait for us—they guessed where we were going, got ahead of us somehow, and set a trap. They shot down all the crows that could have warned me of their presence in the field.

Whips of green light lash from my staff, turning aside most of the incoming projectiles. A few arrows manage to skewer the legs of two horses, who whinny their terror, staggering and rearing as the magic eats into their flesh. Aura darts away from the thrashing animals, barely escaping their hooves.

The Caennith aim to pin us down, incapacitate us, and take the Princess. The seeker magic guiding the arrows takes time to produce, and it requires a stationary anchor, which means the Fae performing the spell can't follow us if we leave this place. We have to keep moving and get clear of this trap, or we'll have no chance. Judging from the quantity of arrows, we're far outnumbered.

The thoughts skim through my mind in an instant, and I'm already shouting "Mount and ride," when the next volley of arrows rains down on the hollow. An arrow skewers one of my wings. Instant agony shears through my bones and nerves as the magical toxin chases along my wing, heading for my torso, intent on reaching my heart. I crash to one knee, momentarily stunned, but I manage to slam the butt of my staff against the ground and call on my powers, transforming some of the grass into thorns, urging them to grow high, high above, forming a protective circular wall around our camp, with a single path of escape.

A gleam of golden hair, a strong tug, and the pain in my wing recedes. Aura tosses the arrow aside. "On your feet, Your Majesty." Her blue eyes blaze in her flushed face.

Andras is dragging Kyan onto his own horse. Ember's fire magic incinerated several of the incoming arrows from the last volley, but he ignited some of the dry grass as well. If we don't move quickly, we'll be roasted, along with our enemies, in the burning field.

Despite what Reehan did, my heart suffers a pang as we leave his body behind and ride out of the hollow on our four undamaged horses. Andras holds Kyan steady on his mount, while Vandel and Ember ride their respective steeds, and I ride behind Aura. Ember and I dare not take to the sky, not with seeker arrows in play. Besides, I can't leave Aura to ride alone, unprotected. In close quarters she might be a match for these warriors, but not at this distance, not weaponless. Not without magic.

She could have run into the grass while I was injured, and escaped from me—rejoined her people. But she pulled the arrow from my wing, and she mounted the horse readily. She doesn't fight me as I ride behind her, pinning her close to my chest with one arm.

Is she really a prisoner if she's choosing to come along with us—with me?

Flames lick through the fields at an alarming rate. Mine is not the type of magic that can douse them. If I had more Void magic, maybe. But I must save the bit I possess, and I must take care not to run out of energy before the Caennith do. So I use my natural abilities sparingly, sending bolts of green light to dispel or redirect incoming arrows. Some of them are trickier than I expect; they dodge my countermeasures, whizzing between us as we ride and then darting in to strike the horses.

Our enemies are trying to bring us down. Trying to keep us from getting clear of the spell's range.

"Faster!" I bellow to Kyan and Andras. Kyan seems to be recovering—he's fortunate that I pulled the arrow out immediately. When the invasive magic of a Caennith seeker arrow reaches the heart, healing becomes impossible. It's a death sentence for Fae or humans. Fortunately for us, such spells are difficult to cast, short-lived, and require a rooted point of origin. They also drain the caster's energy swiftly.

I suspect more than one caster is hidden in the grass, because even as we streak across the fields, arrows continue to chase us, diving and swerving, trying to break through our scattered defenses. My men are wearing armor, but the arrows seek out the vulnerable joints and grooves, any tiny crevice where they can touch skin and begin spreading their magical toxin.

"Eyes open," I cry to my men. "Watch the sky, but keep an eye on the field as well."

Scythes of green light whirl from my staff and slice through the grass ahead, clearing our path; but I can't expend too much magic on that. Since worship yesterday evening, I've used greater amounts of magic than I usually do, and I can't afford to run dry at such a time.

Aura has her slim, strong fingers buried in the horse's mane, and she's leaning slightly forward, as if mentally urging him to run faster.

"Not so eager to return to your people, Princess?" I ask. "Maybe they won't kill you. It seems the seeker arrows aren't spelled to hunt you, but rather to eliminate the horses, and me, and the Edge-Knights."

"If I wanted to go with the Caennith, would you let me?" Her voice is taut and sharp.

"No. Too much at stake."

"As I thought."

The arrows are thinning now, fewer in number. We must be clearing the caster's field of influence, or perhaps the fire took out some of the archers.

I risk a glance behind. Someone among the Caennith must have a water gift or an air gift, because the flames devouring the grass have died, leaving stretches of charred black stalks.

None of the Caennith have emerged from hiding to confront us directly. Is it because they fear me, or simply that they wish to accomplish their goal with as little risk to themselves as possible?

Our horses are running up a slope now as we move into the hilly country between us and Ru Gallamet. There used to be fine orchards here, and fields of berries, but most of the people have moved inland at my urging, so the trees and bushes lie untended. Soon the Edge will devour them all.

"I think we have cleared the ambush, Sire," Ember calls to me.

I'm about to respond when a tall, robed figure rises atop the peak of a craggy hill ahead of us, silhouetted against the gloomy sky. On either side of the figure rise more shapes—archers, eight of them.

The robed figure lifts their hands, and a whirlpool of rainbow magic forms in the air above them. The magic forks outward, sparks catching on the tip of each arrow as the archers let them fly.

These arrows are seekers, too. They do not fly in a prescribed arc—they dip and rise, shearing through the air, streaming light—and they're not branching off to target the horses and knights. They are all converging, focused on a single point.

Aura.

I vanish my staff and yank her off the saddle into the air, just as the first few arrows reach us. One of them slices the side of my horse's neck, releasing a spurt of lifeblood—another carves a deep groove in the saddle. The other arrows turn and shoot up toward the Princess as I carry her higher, buoyed by frantic beats of my wings.

When the arrows were spread out, targeting anything they could reach, fighting them off was easier. But now they're all aiming for her. So many of them, streaking toward us.

I clutch Aura to my chest and bolt sideways, barely avoiding two more arrows, which immediately turn to follow me. My wings flay the wind as I streak across the sky, faster than I've ever flown in my life. The rolls, spins, and dives that I usually do to show off are far more vital now, and I add bursts of magic to enhance my speed and agility.

My men are roaring below us, bellowing their rage and fear. Ember manages to target a couple of the arrows and incinerate them, but he nearly singes my wing with a fireball, and after that he stops trying to help for fear of making it worse. I'm barely tracking my men—I'm moving too fast for that—but I think they're heading for the hill, aiming to take down the final caster and the archers.

The earlier volleys targeted everyone but the Princess. And now that the ambush has failed, this group of Caennith is tasked with eliminating her.

She's clinging to me quietly, gripping my body with her arms and legs so I can have one hand free for magic. I send pulses of green light at the arrows, destroying several, but more are coming, and they're too quick, too agile—

Thump.

A pinching pain at the top of my spine, right at the junction of my neck and my shoulders. I swerved to avoid one arrow, and another lodged in my back.

The initial pinch explodes into savage agony. I convulse with the force of it, barely able to hold onto Aura.

I can't stay aloft like this. I'll drop her. She'll be smashed on the hillside.

Shuddering with pain, I let myself fall, holding her close as we plummet to earth. I flare my wings at the last moment, but the landing is clumsy—Aura falls backward from my arms and crashes onto her back in the short, weedy grass.

My magic is stalled by the influx of the toxin. I struggle to access it, but all I can do is groan and shudder. A glance over my shoulder reveals more arrows tracing tails of rainbow fire across the sky, headed for us. My knights haven't taken down our attackers yet. They need more time. I have to protect Aura a little longer.

My jaw locks in place, fused by the invasive magic. I can't speak, but I manage to lean forward stiffly on my knees, and plant my fists on either side of Aura's head. I curl my wings around her. It's the best shield I can manage—my wings and my body, forming a protective dome over her body.

For the fate of the realm, I must protect her.

It's a game I can't win. If she dies, I lose the blood I need for the ritual. And if I die in her place, there will be no one to work the great spell to save our realm.

But this is no longer about the fate of the realm—not entirely. If only one of us can survive, I want it to be her. Not for any logical reason—simply because her existence is paramount. It is all that matters.

25

AURA

I lie beneath Malec, staring in horror at the rigid paralysis of his features, at the toxic branches of light crawling over his shoulders from the arrow in his spine.

He's braced over me, his wings and body forming a domed barrier. Every time another arrow hits him, he shudders, and his eyes brighten with pain.

An arrow pierces his wing—I can see the tip of it. It's struggling to get all the way through the flesh and feathers, wriggling in an effort to break free and reach me. Then it halts, and more virulent light stabs outward from its tip, spreading over Malec's wing.

I've never seen these arrows at work, but I've heard of them. In the hands of certain Fae, they are the rarest and deadliest weapons my people own. I never thought they would be used against me.

Another thump of an arrow's impact. Another jerk of Malec's body.

He doesn't have a sword that I can see, only a dagger, and he vanished his staff. There's no weapon I can use to help him.

I could wriggle out of the shelter of the feathered dome—but I'd be shot through the heart by a seeker arrow the moment I emerged. How would that help him, or anyone?

Still, I can't lie here and watch him die. Why is he doing this? He's the only one who can perform the spell to save Midunnel—

Shit, have I actually started to believe in him? To trust that he can save us?

"This is stupid, Malec," I gasp. "You'll die. Give me to them."

But it's too late. Too late to parlay, to bargain, to make a deal. Too late for both of us.

"Use your magic," I plead, but his beautiful face is stony, his eyes beacons of anguish. I don't think he can move anymore, except to shudder as arrow after arrow plunges between the seams of his armor.

All I can do is lie helpless, in the shadow of his wings, while he takes the death that was meant for me.

I begin to sob, each heaving breath jolting my body. He's dying. He's *dying*, and I can't stop it. I can't pull the arrows out of him from this position, but if they stay in his body much longer, he can't possibly heal from this. He's going to die right here, right now, and I have to watch it, and I *can't*. I can't bear it.

The shrieking panic in my soul shocks me, rips apart the last shreds of what I knew about myself. My sobs surge and expand in my chest until I have to scream, wordless and agonized.

Mine, mine, he's mine, I need him, I want him...

"Eonnula, help me," I choke out. "You have to save him. You *have* to. I'll do—anything—" I hitch a ragged breath, more sobs clogging my throat— "I'll offer you anything, everything—he can't die—no, no—no, please no, please."

The toxic lightning flickers along the swaying locks of Malec's dark hair and creeps with crooked fingers up his throat. His fixed eyes are slowly emptying of life.

I will never recover from this. Never. I will walk straight to the Edge and fling myself into the Void—

"Are you listening?" I tell him, angry, wretched. "If you die here, I will walk right to the Edge and jump in. Don't you fucking dare let yourself die."

The crawling light-poison has nearly succeeded in encasing all of him. I can only see its outer spread, the acidic burn of the light on his armor and skin—but I don't know if it has reached his heart yet.

"Push it away," I whisper through tear-slicked lips. "You still have the Void in you. Use that. Protect your heart, and push back the light with the darkness. Don't stop fighting. Don't you ever fucking stop fighting, not *ever*. From now on, you are not allowed to give up on yourself. It's not even an option, you hear me? You're mine. You're mine, and I want you here, you maleficent bastard—"

Something's happening outside, beyond the dome of his wings and body. Malec jerks, but this time it's not an impact— it's as if something is being pulled out of him. Yes, someone is yanking out the arrows, one by one, thank Eonnula.

"They're coming," I murmur, more tears bathing my cheeks. "Hold on. They're coming."

Minutes later, Ember and Kyan finish pulling out the arrows and roll Malec onto his back. With the arrows gone, he's no longer suffering the toxic paralysis, but he's strangely gray, and his eyes are distant, unfocused.

"He's fading," mutters Ember. "It's a miracle he isn't already dead."

"He had some Void magic left," I manage. "Maybe it helped him survive."

Ember nods. "It won't last long, and none of us have the skill to heal this kind of damage. We must ride for Ru Gallamet with all speed. We killed the Caennith on the hill, but more may be coming from the field soon. We're going to ride on, using our enemies' horses. Andras saw them in a hollow and went to fetch them. Those mounts have had a chance to rest, standing around while their masters waited to attack us. With those fresh horses, we'll cover ground faster. Are you with us, Princess?" His red eyes pierce mine.

I nod. "I'm with you. With *him*."

"Good."

The remaining four knights are all wounded—minor injuries, thankfully. Kyan appears to be healing, though slower than usual for a Fae, thanks to the toxic arrow. Even though it was only embedded in him for a few seconds, it weakened him dramatically. Malec had multiple arrows in him for several minutes. He should be dead. He *will* be dead, unless we hurry to a healer.

When Andras arrives, leading the horses, I notice that he has open cuts which don't appear to be healing at all, despite the faint blue of his skin marking him as not entirely human. Apparently he doesn't have Fae healing abilities, and he doesn't seem to be Fae-strong, either. He's probably the result of generations of Fae and human intermarriage.

The Caennith Priesthood would shake their heads at a man like him. "What a pity," they would say, pointing him out as an illustration of their personal dogma, that the races should never breed. They would have missed his kindness, loyalty, and diligence, noting only the absence of the traits they wanted to see.

I brush aside thoughts of the Caennith as the Edge-Knights lift Malec and his immense wings onto a horse. I want Malec with me, but I don't protest when Vandel is appointed to ride with him and keep him in the saddle. The mare they're riding is huge, with shining muscled shoulders and massive haunches, capable of both strength and speed. I'm given a slim, swift horse, and although the knights discuss tying my hands to the saddle, they decide against it.

The knights work swiftly, transferring saddlebags to the fresh horses. Haste is vital, because there may be more Caennith in the fields behind us, preparing for another attack, this time under cover of darkness.

In mere moments, we are mounted and galloping over the shadowed hills, under the pallid nighttime glimmer of the three veiled suns.

We ride all night. Never have I suffered such long hours of strained anxiety and strenuous physical exertion. We stop once, briefly, to piss and cram food into our mouths. My heart drags me toward Malec, but I manage to resist the urge to fly to his side. Instead I use the precious minutes to relieve myself, eat, and drink. But I cast furtive glances at him as we mount up again.

From what I can discern in the dark, he's still gray—the color the Fae take on when they are fading, dying.

I remember Kyan's sister—her olive skin losing its warmth, changing in tone. Blood dribbling from the corner of her mouth. My sword in her gut.

When the flesh turns smoky and translucent, the faerie is past hope.

We ride on, and I stay abreast of Vandel and the Void King, dreading the signs of that final change.

Malec's wings trail on either side of the horse, nearly brushing the ground. His head hangs forward, his face hidden by his long black hair. I can't see the color of his skin, and I'm too proud to ask Vandel how he's doing. I can't help Malec anyway—knowing his condition won't change my utter impotence in this situation.

So I pray to him, quietly, in my mind. *Stay alive, stay alive. Fight.*

I intersperse those mental commands with prayers to Eonnula—if she's listening, if she even cares. Maybe the Surges and the gifting of her power during worship is something she set in motion long ago, before going far away, wherever gods wander. Maybe she's not intimately or directly involved in our realm anymore. As Malec said—she saved us, and we must now save ourselves.

It's a frightening thought, one that turns my universe huge and empty. But it's empowering, too. Because maybe that means anyone can choose to be a savior.

Malec chose to protect me, knowing that he might die, and that if he died, all his plans would be for nothing and our realm would perish.

Saving me wasn't just about him defending the ingredient he needs for a ritual. It was something more. Something sweeter.

In those long, dark hours of travel, and throughout the morning of the next day, I take the pieces of everything I once knew, everything I have been, and I begin to reassemble them. I pick out the truths, lay them side by side, and build upon them. I explore my feelings about the faeries who raised me, about my true parents, about Dawn herself. I inspect my view of the Caennith Priesthood and dismember their teachings about the Daenalla. I assess and dismantle my prejudices, my false assumptions, and my fears.

Last of all, I confront my feelings for *him*.

Enemy. Captor. Caster of my curse.

Truth-teller. King. Companion.

He is all those things, and he is the man who let me use him as a pleasure toy. He's the faerie who fucked me on the goddess's altar. He's the soul so wracked with insecurity about his own worth, so burdened with heavy responsibility, that he would consider ending his own life.

Maybe that's why he gave himself to protect me. Not out of some imagined affection for me, but out of the desire to be done with it all. The thought sours the tender hope in my heart.

I don't do tenderness or softness with men. I fight them, and I fuck them. I don't befriend them and crave their love. That

231

would be pathetic and foolish. Especially since my life will end in just a few days, if Malec lives.

Why did my existence have to be so complicated? It's a puzzle I can't reassemble perfectly—the pieces are broken and warped, cut into the wrong shapes.

I cast another look at the King. It's morning now, so I should be able to discern the hue of his skin—but he's still slumped over so far I can't see his face, and his hand is hidden by his wing.

And truth be told, I'm somewhat distracted by my current surroundings.

We're riding through mountains now, picking our way along narrow, winding paths. The Void is a line of absence slicing through the landscape, as if the mountains are loaves of bread shorn in half by a knife of darkness. Beyond the rocky crests is empty space flecked with stars, a great Nothing that extends forever downward, and outward, and upward. Overhead, the blackness fades into the layers of bright, sun-soaked air that arch over our realm—the protective, invisible dome Malec mentioned.

As we navigate the mountain road, I stare into the Void, at the tiny stars in its vast depths. They shift constantly, winking out and reappearing. Malec was right. The Void isn't Nothing—it moves and changes. It exists as motion and chaos within its own emptiness, like a brain exists in a body.

My attention veers from the Edge as Ember leaps off his steed, spreading his leathery wings and soaring above our group. He calls down to me and points ahead, to a gap between two bluffs. That gap should empty straight into the Void, but instead there's a tunnel through the Edge, like a hallway with black walls extending up to an infinite height.

"The passage to Ru Gallamet," Ember calls.

My stomach soars with horrified expectation—because Ru Gallamet is actually *in* the Void. It's located on a peninsula of ground stretching out into the Nothing. Or perhaps it's more like a cave within the mountainous Void, a solitary refuge accessible by a long tunnel.

We don't need to fear my people pursuing us here. The Caennith would never venture into such a place… would they? No wonder some of my people believe Malec worships the Void, that he's mad and untrustworthy and wicked. Who but a madman would maintain residence in such a dangerous location?

Yet he has managed to keep this spit of land from being swallowed up, even in his absence. There is something solid about his theories, something reliable in the spellwork he crafts.

Chills roll over my skin as we ride between the walls of the Void, along the narrow bridge into the Nothing. My brain keeps switching its perspective, sometimes viewing the Void as a solid mass, sometimes as the most terrifying emptiness, as if I could topple off the edge of the road and fall forever. Perhaps both are true. The darkness seems to thicken the farther we go, surging and writhing like smoke, like tenebrous serpents.

At the end of the narrow road rises the mountain of the Void King, with the castle of Ru Gallamet jutting from its peak like a clawed hand bursting out of black rock. The tallest tower has a flat peak, atop which sits the great Spindle, pointed to the churning Void overhead. Beside it is a massive wheel of gleaming black metal. We're still some distance away, but they're both so huge I can see them clearly, as well as part of the mechanism to which they're attached.

It's a terrifying sight. No wonder my parents didn't want to give me up to the Void King—although judging by Malec's story, Ru Gallamet hadn't yet been encompassed by the Void at the time.

If Malec survives, that Spindle is where he plans to bind and bleed me. That's where I'll sink into the enchanted sleep and lose a century of my life.

The Edge-Knights urge their horses forward faster, racing toward Ru Gallamet, and suddenly I understand Malec's men a little better. It takes a reckless kind of bravery to ride into the Void itself—a loyalty that approaches insanity. It's easy to see how Reehan's particular brand of youthful arrogance and boldness might have been mistaken for the qualities necessary in an Edge-Knight.

"There's a healer at the castle?" I call to Vandel.

He turns to me, his skin paler than usual beneath his freckles. "There is."

"And he's still alive?"

In answer, Vandel cups the King's face and turns it toward me. Gray skin—frighteningly gray—but no translucence. Not yet.

I lean forward in my saddle, urging more speed from my horse.

Ru Gallamet must have been glorious once. It still is, in a gloomy, terrifying way, but the pressure of the Void all around it has taken a toll. Nothing grows on the bare ebony rock. No wind stirs the black-and-gold pennants that hang limply from the spires. No horns or heralds announce the return of its master.

The gates part with a groan that echoes against the rocks before soaking into the soundless dark. Vandel and the Void King enter first on the massive chestnut mare. Her coat shines like amber fire beneath the smoky drapery of his wings.

The horses are all exhausted. Mine barely makes it up the cobbled slope of the road into the courtyard, and I slip from the saddle the moment we halt.

Everything in me wants to run to Malec. He's my anchor in a world that has tumbled upside down.

But I hold myself back. Arms folded, I glare, and I wait, even though I want to scream, *Why isn't the healer out here? Why isn't your king already being mended? Hurry, hurry, you idiots, you imbeciles, can't you see that he's dying?*

I trap the screams of fury behind clenched teeth, and I wait.

The knights move around me, as if I'm a dark rock in a river of shadows. A few servants appear to greet them. They lead the horses to a stable, tend to the knights' wounds, and carry the King into the castle out of my sight.

And I, the Crown Princess of Caennith, the treasure they've been seeking for decades—I stand alone. I might as well be invisible.

The gates have closed behind us. No chance of escape. Not that I would try to leave, and perhaps they all know that, somehow. Or maybe my expression keeps them at bay. If I had Malec's magic, I would be producing thorns right now, creating walls around myself, so thick and impenetrable that no one could ever hurt me or help me again.

When I look up, all I can see is towers, the sharp tip of the Spindle, and the blackness of the Void, soaring above me. The Void to which I will soon be offered in sacrifice. It will come to feed on me, and when it does, Malec will spin it into magic, on a Spindle wet with my blood.

Whatever good he has done for me, he still intends to subject me to that horror.

My mind closes in on itself, my thoughts congealing into a kind of frozen dread. I feel somehow separate from my body—disconnected.

A servant approaches me—a round-shouldered woman with small antlers and a motherly face. She reminds me of Elsamel.

She speaks to me, but I can't reply. I can only stare at the towers and the Void.

When she reaches for my hand, my body reacts automatically, my teeth bared in a vicious snarl. I can't bear for her to touch me.

The woman's eyes widen, and she backs away.

A man tries next. His black beard is streaked with gray, like the King of Caennith, my true father. When he grabs my wrist, I respond with a quick backstep, twisting his arm around, pinning it to his spine while he gasps with pain. It's an automatic response, a move I've practiced countless times. A little more pressure, and the man's wrist will snap—or I could pop his shoulder out of the socket.

"Princess." Andras's voice.

My consciousness links him with kindness. A little of my tension eases, and I feel my mind reconnecting with my body again.

"Yes?" My voice sounds distant, hollow.

"Come with me. You need food and rest." He doesn't try to touch me. He simply walks past me, calm and confident, as if he expects me to follow.

After a moment, I do.

Andras leads me into the castle. "They're preparing a room for you now. I'll take you to the parlor where you can eat and—"

"Where is he?"

Andras glances back at me. His shoulder and arm are wrapped in bandages, probably a temporary measure until the healer finishes with the Void King and can tend to him.

"His Majesty is in his chambers, at the foot of the central tower."

"I need to see him."

"He's being healed—"

"Andras." I stop walking in the middle of the stone hallway. The tapestries look as faded and frayed as my mind feels. I have not slept enough lately. I don't think I can sleep, or eat, or be at peace until— "I need to see him."

Andras turns, his blue skin faintly lavender in the orange light of the torch on the wall. "He's weak right now, Highness. Vulnerable. Can I trust you to be with him?"

"He was weak and vulnerable the day I met him, when his magic ran out. I had a knife to his throat. I could have ended him then. You and Fitzell both saw us in that clearing, so you know

I'm telling the truth. And truth be told, I am less inclined to kill him now, after everything."

We exchange a long look, and then Andras ruffles up his brown hair with his fingers and says, "Shit. All right," and continues down the hall. We take a left turn, then follow another corridor to a pair of heavy doors which stand open.

The Void King lies naked on the bed, his horned head nested in pillows, his wings spread out beneath him. His eyes are sealed shut, and his skin still bears that awful shade of gray—the mark of a Fae injured beyond his own powers of healing.

A tall Fae with milky eyes, feathery antennae, and pale moth wings bends over him, murmuring a spell and waving smoky incense through the air. The Fae casts me and Andras a rebuking look, but they don't cease the healing chant or make any further objection to our presence.

Andras points me to a comfortable chair, and I sit down. I'm suddenly, heavily aware of my own exhaustion. I'm not sure how I stayed on my feet as long as I did. Despite my sturdy leggings, the insides of my thighs are chafed from the long ride, and every joint in my body is sore. I'm still earth-stained from when Reehan pinned me under his body, and from when the King shielded me. I smell like horse, and sweat, and the bitter afterburn of magic.

I am broken, and the last time I felt whole was with Malec. In his arms I was safe, and that makes no sense, yet it's irresistibly true.

When Andras leaves to fetch food and drink, I slide out of the chair and crawl toward the bed, unable to resist the pull any longer. I need to be near Malec, touching him.

The tall healer raises their eyebrows, still chanting, as I kneel by the bed and push one of my dirt-stained hands across the covers toward Malec's limply curled fingers.

I slide my fingertips across his palm, then grip his hand in mine.

A tremor runs through his body, and he sighs. The healer looks at me, surprised, and nods encouragement as they keep chanting.

Just holding his hand centers me, settles me. It's a foolish response, weak, pathetic—I'm an idiot, an imbecile—

No.

No, I'm not weak for caring about someone, nor pathetic for wanting support. I'm not a fool for taking what I need, and giving back in return.

I won't say those things to myself again. I will allow myself the freedom of needing more than this man's lust, of craving more than his body.

I want *him*. All of him.

"Fuck you," I whisper. Lifting his hand to my mouth, I place soft kisses on each of his knuckles.

The Void King's chest rises with a deeper breath, and he moans.

"Keep doing that," says the healer hastily, before picking up the chant again. "He's responding to you."

I kiss Malec's knuckles once more. I press my lips to the back of his hand, then the inside of his wrist. The gray drains from his face, his natural pallor returning.

The healer ceases the chant and tips a bottle against Malec's lips. When he swallows, the moth Fae sighs with relief. "He will recover within the hour."

"Thank the goddess," I breathe.

The healer looks at me quizzically. "You are the Princess of Caennith, are you not?"

"So it would seem."

"Yet you—and he—" They raise an eyebrow, jerking their head toward the King.

Panic stirs inside me—the terror of my weakness being perceived. I have to stifle the urge to react with caustic words, or with violence. "Yes. He and I."

238

"Well now." The Fae's antennae twitch. "Who would have thought?"

"Certainly not me," I mutter.

"It's fortunate Andras brought you in here. His Majesty was blocking me somehow, holding Void magic in place within his body. He was protecting himself. Your touch eased him and allowed my healing power to pass through."

Tears pool in my eyes. "Are you sure?"

"I felt it happening."

"Shit," I whisper, holding Malec's hand to my cheek.

Andras re-enters the room, carrying a tray with a plate and a goblet. "It's not much, Your Highness, but—" He hesitates, noting my position on the floor by the bed, eyeing the King's hand clasped in mine.

He and the healer exchange a glance, and then Andras gives me a sympathetic look. "I suspected something like this. It's beautiful, and godsdamn tragic." He sets the tray on the bedside table. "Will the King be all right?"

The healer reassures him, but I barely listen. My mind is growing slow and sleepy.

Andras takes up a post in the open door of the chamber, and from there he berates me until I grudgingly nibble at the food. After the first few bites, my hunger roars to the surface, and I devour everything, emptying the goblet as well. Reluctant though I am to leave Malec's side, I yield to Andras's insistence that I bathe in the adjoining room. The water is delightful, but though I want to linger, my need to be near Malec is stronger. Fear gnaws at me, fear that his condition will revert and he'll fade if I'm not there. So I rush back to the bed, skin still damp and hair bundled into a sopping golden braid. I wear a simple dress someone brought or conjured for me—creamy white, with a lace-up front and a skirt wide enough for kicking and fighting.

Again I kneel by the bed and clasp Malec's hand in mine. He's still the right color, though he hasn't yet regained consciousness.

My own consciousness is barely intact. My eyelids droop, weighed by the ponderous bulk of everything I've had to bear these past few days. I'm not sure when my head drops onto the mattress and my body slumps beside the bed. But I'm vaguely aware of low voices—Ember and Vandel, I think—and of hands grasping me cautiously. I'm too sodden with sleep to react, and when the hands place me on something soft, I sink into dreams again.

26

I'm awakened by a light peck on my cheek. Not human lips, but a bird's beak. A raven.

Opening my eyes, I recognize one of my most faithful birds, Roanna, a female with more intelligence, courage, and cunning than the rest. I've permanently enhanced her with greater speed than the others—a difficult spell to perform, one that requires Void magic. Even with that extra speed, she must have strained herself to reach me this quickly if she came here from the battlefront.

Two of her tail feathers have a purple tint—a subtle mark of mine, to identify her to my people.

"She was insistent," says a voice at the door of my chamber. "So we let her in."

I lift my head from the pillows and glimpse Kyan standing there, arms crossed. His olive skin is a shade paler than normal, and his heavy brows are lowered in a somber expression, but he looks well. Healed. Thank the goddess.

"You did well to admit her," I say.

"Andras let the other one in." Kyan nods to the bed. Confused, I look down, suddenly conscious of a warm pressure on my right side.

Aura is nestled against my ribs and hip, her hair loosely bound in a golden braid and her cheeks pink with sleep. Her lids are faintly lavender along the edges, and purple shadows paint the delicate skin beneath her eyes.

"The healer says her presence helped you recover, that you only responded to the curative spell when the Princess arrived and spoke to you." Kyan's voice carries a hint of reproach.

"Ask the question," I say stiffly. "Go on."

Kyan puckers his lips. "Reehan was wrong about many things, including the way he addressed you when he spoke of this. But I must know, my Lord—can you do what must be done? Can you perform the ritual, despite what is between you and the Princess?"

"What do you think is between us?" I shift my arm so I can stroke my raven's wing.

"You know best, Sire."

"I don't, though. I only know that I'm drawn to her, that I like her as much as I lust for her. That her absence would wound me and her death would destroy me."

Kyan clears his throat. "I believe that's called love, my King."

"It's terribly inconvenient."

"Love usually is." He flares his wings slightly. "On that subject, Sire—would it be a difficulty if two knights were to—join in a sort of relationship that—well—"

"You and Andras." I nod.

"It has been growing for a while," he says quietly.

"I have nothing against it, as long as the two of you maintain your loyalty to me and your fellow knights, protecting us with as much devotion as you protect each other."

"Of course." He clasps a fist against his heart and bows. "Always, Sire."

"Then you have my blessing, if you need it. Wait here a moment, and let me see what Roanna has to say. Then you may run and tell Andras the good news."

I turn to the raven, locking my eyes with her beady dark ones. Her visions unfurl in my mind, linked with snatches of overheard conversation, and one clear message from Fitzell.

Two of our border fortresses have fallen, and Caennith soldiers are streaming through a breach in the wall, riding hard for Ru Gallamet. They aim to stop me from using the Princess for the ritual.

Fools. Don't they understand I'm trying to save them?

The images bursting in my mind are painful. The Caennith Priesthood, mostly Fae, are surprisingly skilled at designing cruel weapons. One might think they'd be a peaceful bunch, dedicated as they are to the worship of the light and waiting for Eonnula's savior. Yet they work closely with the military forces of Caennith, designing spells that can batter bluesteel armor until it cracks. They have concussive bombs and poison-laced spears, not to mention the most awful of curses—blood-steamers, nerve-rippers, lung-shredders, heart-bursters. Our defenses are strong, but their hate is stronger. Their fanatical belief in Eonnula's sovereignty makes them incredibly dangerous.

Roanna shows me what she last saw as she flew over Daenalla during the hours I was asleep—a contingent of Caennith Fae speeding across the plains toward this castle. We don't have much time before they reach us.

They have slaughtered so many of my people. When they arrive, I will deal with them quickly and mercilessly.

"Reinforce the gates. Set defensive spells." I sit up, relieved that I can do so without pain. "And see if anyone is willing to help me at the Spindle. I need to replenish my magic and fight off this first wave of Caennith Fae before I do the ritual with the Princess. That spell cannot be interrupted."

"At once, Sire."

"Oh, and tell one of the servants to feed Roanna." I wave the raven gently away, and she flies to perch on Kyan's shoulder, eyeing his silver wings.

As they leave the room, Aura stirs and pushes herself up to a sitting position. She's wearing a white dress, and the laces at the front have loosened while she slept, allowing me a generous view of her breasts. My cock twitches and lifts slightly at the unexpected treat. That's when I realize I'm entirely naked. Healers sometimes prefer that, especially in cases of widespread injury—clothes can hamper their access to certain energy centers of the body. Unfortunately that means my reaction to the Princess's cleavage is all too obvious.

"What's happening?" She brushes blond wisps of hair back from her flushed cheeks.

"An attack within the hour." I reach for a blanket at the foot of the bed and drag it over myself. "I need to siphon Void magic so I can fight off the Caennith."

"You'll kill more of my people." Her tone is flat, resigned—yet with the fragility of grief in the sound.

"I don't want to. But I have no choice. I need to get rid of them so I can perform the ritual with you, uninterrupted. You can remain here while I regain my magic."

She tugs the laces of her dress tighter, closing off my view of her breasts. "Why would I stay here when I could watch the Spinner of the Void at work?"

On the way up the steps of the tower I devour a bowlful of potato-bacon dumplings. I offer one to Aura, and after finishing it she darts her hand around the edge of my wing to steal another.

"Greedy little viper."

"You saw nothing. Keep climbing."

Chuckling, I mount the last of the steps and open the door to the tower roof.

Aura doesn't gasp as we step out onto the black stone under the shadow of the great Wheel—but when I glance her way, I can tell she's impressed. Her eyes are wide, her jaw immobilized right in the middle of chewing a mouthful of bun.

"I built this decades ago, and I've been working on it ever since, perfecting this and that. Forged some of the pieces myself." I clamp a hand on the railing of the metal steps that wind upward, to the peak of the Spindle.

One of the castle servants, Iyyo, is already standing at the top of the skeletal stairway, ready to serve as the catalyst for this ritual. He has done it before; he knows it's safe. Any blood he loses will be swiftly restored by our resident healer, Szazen.

"You may stand here in the doorway and watch, Princess. Do not come too close, understand? This magic is dangerous. But you should be safe as long as it's not your blood being shed. Stay perfectly still, if you can."

She swallows her bite of dumpling. "Of course I can be still. I was a bodyguard, remember?"

"How could I forget?" I rub my throat where her teeth tore it, and I give her a wry grin.

She smiles back, and a thrill floods my chest.

I cannot indulge in these feelings. It's not fair to my people, who have supported me for so long. I wipe away my own smile, trying not to feel a pang as her face falls.

Turning my back on her, I start to climb the stairway to Iyyo.

And then I spin around, march down the steps, hook my hand around the back of her neck, and kiss her.

She makes a savage little frustrated sound into my mouth and presses her lips hard against mine, her fingers running deep

246

into my hair, nails grazing my scalp. I'm wearing lightweight black robes and nothing else—appropriate garb for the spell I plan to perform—and the thin material lets me feel far too much of her body against mine.

"It's unfair," I mutter against her cheek. "You and I—we have so little time."

"We are a tragedy," she agrees. "We don't make sense."

She tugs on my hair sharply, jerking my head back so she can press a hot kiss to my throat, right where she ripped into it once before. I gasp, shuddering against her as she lets her teeth graze my skin.

Pulling away is a monumental triumph, because all I want is to crush her against me and surge inside her again.

But I must prepare myself to fend off the Caennith attack.

Aura lets me go. But I feel her gaze, a sweet malevolence following me up to the peak of the Spindle, judging me and desiring me while I press Iyyo's fingertip to the spiked tip and bind his body in place with thin black chains. His feet rest on a metal strip bracketed halfway up the Spindle. His arm remains uplifted, his finger pressed to the Spindle's point, while blood begins to drip from that spot and trickle over the polished surface.

I carved the Spindle from emberwood hardened in white fire. It bears a glaze infused with my blood, sweat, and tears, linking it intrinsically to my body, soul, and mind. It's taller than three Fae, thicker than my body, sleek and round in the middle and tapered to a dangerous point.

When I descend from the Spindle, I glance at Aura. She looks horrified at the sight of Iyyo, bound to the device, blood trailing from his finger. I rather expected her reaction, but it pains me nonetheless.

I will do what I must, whatever she thinks of me. But I can't help saying, "Iyyo is willing to serve. He is under no obligation to offer himself."

"If he's doing this willingly, why are there chains?"

"The chains aren't to restrain him. They're to keep the Void from taking him."

Her mouth forms a startled "O."

I busy myself with the final preparations—the lighting of incense, the casting of the oils over the Wheel, the potion I always take before a Spinning, to prepare my body for channeling the Void Magic.

"All right there?" I call to Iyyo as I seat myself behind the Wheel.

"All right, my Lord!" he calls back.

"Does it hurt him?" Aura asks.

"No. They drink a potion before they serve me in this way. It softens any discomfort."

She looks somewhat mollified, then anxious as she notices the increased violence of the wind spiraling around the tower.

"Stay still!" I call to her. "The Void is coming."

I place my foot on the treadle and extend my fingers. Green light stabs from my claws, crackling over the Wheel, setting it in motion.

No matter how many times I do this, it always terrifies me. I sense the advance of the Dark, a sucking pull on my soul. I smell it, like the air before a storm—a crackle of bitterness, the aching sting of endless cold. Most of all, I feel its pressure on my skin— a slithering brush of shadow, a crawling lust for the vitality of my body and mind.

But I am the one in control. The Void is not exactly sentient, and though it shudders with raw power, it is a force of nature as well. This mechanism I have built is science and magic combined, a heretical device in the eyes of the Caennith, but marvelously effective here in Daenalla, where our religion does not interfere with the pursuit of scientific exploration.

I wish I could show Aura the technologies we've implemented in Daenalla's central cities—the plans I've drawn up for more devices and mechanisms, once the war is finally over and I can devote more resources to invention.

But there is no time to show her any of it. Once I drive the Caennith forces away from Ru Gallamet, she'll be taking Iyyo's place on the Spindle.

The Void is nearer now. I glance over my shoulder to assure myself that Aura is well out of the way, behind me and the Wheel. She's rooted to her spot in the doorway, her eyes fixed on the star-flecked emptiness beyond the tower, where a deeper darkness writhes and swells against the Nothing.

"You see it?" Despite my efforts, the strain of fear and awe tightens my voice.

"I see it." Her voice filters faintly through the wind. The Void dislikes the consistency of this place, the breathable pocket of air around Ru Gallamet. It strives to disturb it as much as possible. If I allowed it, the Void would swallow the air and suffocate us all. But the magic I've woven around this mountain holds, as long as I reinforce it from time to time.

The Void swirls nearer, flinging out coils of impenetrable shadow, nosing closer to the tip of the Spindle. I redouble the magic surging out of me into the Wheel, and it spins faster, green light traveling along the mechanism, up the Spindle, flowing harmlessly over Iyyo, snaking all the way to the sharp point, where my servant's finger is still pressed, still leaking blood.

I don't have much magic left to spend. I used the remainder of my Void magic to shield my heart from the Caennith arrows' poison—and the rest is pouring out onto the Wheel. But it doesn't matter. In moments I will possess more power than I can use.

My Spindle sucks in the first tendrils of the Void—siphons them from the emptiness, winds them around itself. Shadows spiral along the machine, rushing past Iyyo as the Wheel pulls the darkness in, whips it around and around, its gears groaning. I press the treadle firmly, while one of my outstretched hands guides the Wheel and the other accepts the inbound flow of magic.

The rush of power hits me like an orgasm. It's a terrifying pleasure, because the roaring flood is intense enough to tear me apart if I don't remain focused, in control. I press the treadle, spin the Wheel, and chant the words I devised when I first crafted this spell.

"Mastery of the arcane, confinement of the abyss. Let me be blind to the light, deaf to the world. Come to me, father of destruction. My bones shall house your infinity, and my mouth will bleed your shadows. I tether you, bind you, pour you into me. Your violence shall be mine to tame, and your monsters shall answer my call. Because I have need of you, Formless One, Endless Depravity. Glorious Abyss, inhabit me. Spill into my soul, split my veins, fracture my heart. Submit to me, reside in me, yield to me. I am the residence of the tempest, the cup of endless wine, the guardian of your greed."

The Void responds, a wave of dark energy crashing into my mind. My hands turn black from claw-tips to forearms—my sight vanishes in a blaze of green flame. I throw back my head, and I scream.

27

Clinging to the doorframe, I take in the spectacle before me. The servant boy, bound to the Spindle, his blood gleaming dark crimson. The shadows flowing along the Spindle, curling around the Wheel, blending with the flickering green fire and then racing in dark threads into the fingers of the Maleficent One. He is wreathed in shadow, his robes streaming darkness, his horns twined with smoke, his wings outspread.

Behind him, behind the great Wheel and the enormous Spindle, hunched and roiling in the endless black, there is a gargantuan shape—a fathomless entity feeding itself into the machine Malec has built.

In this moment, I understand why the Fae of Caennith fear him so much. And I understand why he is called the Void King.

I've seen him vulnerable. Uncertain, powerless, insecure, troubled. In the desirable, self-deprecating Fae male I've come to know, I had almost forgotten the sorcerer who overturned the royal carriage with shadows, the one who has single-handedly stopped the Void from overcoming this bastion of his.

I forgot to be afraid of him.

Malec's head snaps back, a violent scream roaring from his throat. His eyes are twin emerald flames, and my breath stops because what if the magic burns them out—what if he becomes blind, like the words of the spell I heard him chanting?

He doesn't sound like he's in pain, exactly. The arch of his body, the heave of his chest, the rigidity of his wings—he looks as if he's either being tortured or fucked. Maybe both.

A horrified thrill races through my body as Malec pulls himself upright again, as if he's reclaiming control over himself, over the shadows. He keeps spinning for several long minutes, while the Void writhes around Iyyo and the Spindle as if it wants to swallow them both.

And then the green light glimmering on the Wheel fades away. It slows gradually, and the remaining shadows along it flow into Malec's hands. The Void stirs, uncoils, and melts away into the dark, like a predator who has lost interest in its intended victim.

Malec rises from his stool, wavers for a moment, then steadies himself. He lifts his hand, and the chains around Iyyo loosen and fall away.

As the young servant staggers down the metal steps, someone brushes past me. The healer must have been quietly watching from behind me, waiting until they were needed. They give me a pleasant nod and a soft "Your Highness" as they move out onto the tower roof and hand Iyyo a vial. They loop his arm across their shoulders and help him back inside, while I shrink against the wall to let them pass.

When they've descended the stairs out of sight, I cautiously move out of the doorway onto the roof.

Malec is standing by the battlement, staring down at the road that leads through the Void, back to Daenalla. His horned head is bowed, and shadows still flow in smoky ribbons from his wings and robes.

"That spell," I murmur. "You devised that yourself?"

"Yes."

"It's terrifying."

"Of course it is. I invited the Void into my body. If I did not have a healthy fear and respect for It, I could never hope to control its power."

"And what can you do with this power, exactly? Tangible shadows that do your bidding, Endling monsters—what else?"

He glances at me, his eyes still luminous green. "You want to know all my heretical tricks?"

"I suppose I'm curious."

He looks more like the monster of my nightmares now—yet I don't fear him. Maybe it's the knowledge that he needs me, or the sacrifice he was willing to make to save me—or the way his lips curve slightly, the way his eyes dip to my mouth.

"Your people are coming," he says softly. "Look below, and you'll see. I must greet them unpleasantly, I'm afraid. I hope you don't have friends among them."

I follow the elegant wave of his pale hand. A contingent of Caennith soldiers are advancing along the narrow corridor through the Void, approaching Ru Gallamet. Most are on horseback, but some are aloft—winged Fae, circling above the heads of the riders.

"So many of them," I murmur. This isn't the full power of the Caennith army, but it's a significant advance force. I can't imagine him and his handful of knights holding off this attack. "Why don't you have more soldiers here at Ru Gallamet? It's a site of strategic importance, and so close to the border."

"I won't risk the lives of too many people here, where the Edge could advance beyond my control," he says. "Trust me, little viper—I can handle this. You may want to step back."

He leaps onto the edge of the parapet and whips out his immense wings. The rush of power exploding from him strikes me in the chest, and I stagger back with a gasp. He looks over his shoulder at me, his eyes green flame, his teeth bared in a menacing grin. And then his body begins to expand, to change. The inky color of his fingers spreads up his arms, flowing over his skin. His shoulders swell, ripping through the black robes, and rows of black scales solidify along his lengthening form, while his face darkens and extends into a long, slim snout. His hands become clawed feet, and his feathers shift into the leathery black wings of a dragon. As he springs into the sky, his tail whips out, lined with bristling spikes.

This is a full-body transformation, something not even the most gifted Fae in our realm can accomplish on their own without great effort—and Malec did it easily, with the power of the Void.

He rises above Ru Gallamet, a sinuous scaled form flanked by dragonesque wings. Shadows gather around him in great smoky clouds, and green lightning rips across the sky, flashing luridly on the approaching soldiers below.

When he dives, I rush to the parapet and lean over it, holding my breath.

Malec wheels over the incoming Caennith troops, sending out spears of green lightning and whips of shadow to sear and flay the winged faeries who attack him. Bright pulses of their magic burst through the dark, but though he screeches at the impact from a few of them, none seem to seriously injure him. One after another he blasts them from the sky. Some of them spin out into the Void and vanish, while others fall to earth like severed leaves in the storm of his rage.

Then the shadow-dragon swoops lower, opens its throat, and vomits rivers of green fire over the riders.

The fire blazes up, unquenchable, while the shrieks of the dying soldiers and their mounts echo into the Void.

I press my hand over my mouth, holding in a scream.

He's slaughtering them.

I want to condemn him for it, but how is it any different than what I've done, killing the kidnappers and assassins who came after Dawn? This is war. And if Malec did not kill the Caennith, they would slay everyone in Ru Gallamet, including me. He can't risk imprisoning them all, not with so many Fae in the group who could perform magic to escape. He needs to end them quickly so he can proceed with the ritual to save the realm.

My blood chills with the sudden realization that I have mere hours left until my hundred-year sleep. A sleep from which I may never wake, if the ritual fails.

Malec does another pass over the last few Caennith invaders, spraying more lurid fire before skimming back up to the top of the tower. He alights, his claws clasping the parapet, and his shape convulses briefly as the scales evanesce and the wings revert to their usual feathered state.

He's himself again, a tall, masculine figure—stone-white muscle, long legs, glossy black hair, and a pair of storm-dark wings. Naked, because his robes were shredded during the change. As he steps onto the roof he sways, and I step forward impulsively, catching his arm. His wingtip brushes along my back.

When he meets my eyes, I glance away. The memory of the screams and the burning soldiers is too fresh in my mind.

"I understand," he rasps, a trail of smoke issuing from his lips. "You can't face me after that. But I'd do it again—I'll be the monster over and over until this is done, until our realm is saved, do you understand?" The green light in his eyes has faded; there's only darkness in them now, and the glitter of tears. His voice is hoarse, fervent, violent. "I'll do whatever it takes. Sacrifice anything and everyone. Myself. You." He grips my shoulders, teeth bared.

I jerk away from him, my combative instincts kicking in. "Do it then. Chain me to the Spindle right now. Pray to the Abyss, and beg it to come feed on the future Conduit. I've been nothing but a pawn in everyone's game all along, and I have no moves left."

"You're not a pawn to me," he grits out. "You're the Queen, the King, the entire endgame. You're the answer to your own salvation, because if this works, you'll wake to a world you can enjoy for decades. A world in which your heirs can live safely, without fear of the Edge."

Fists clenched, I stare at him, struggling with clashing waves of hope and anger.

"You believe me now, don't you?" he murmurs.

I vent a frustrated hiss through my teeth, whirl away from him, and stalk toward the metal staircase leading up to the Spindle. "Let's get it over with."

"Don't you want a last meal first?" he says wryly.

On the third step I pause and turn back, raking my gaze along his toned body, up to his handsome face.

Awareness flares in his eyes, and he strides forward, sinking to one knee at the foot of the steps, his wings draped against the smooth black stone. He bows his head briefly, then lifts his face to mine. "I'll be your last meal, Princess. Yours for an hour, to use as you please."

I can taste my heart on my tongue, a pulsating weight.

The last time we did this, I was half-drunk with wine, grief, and rage. Desperate for relief.

This time, I am desperate for him.

One hour is not enough. And I want to weep for its ending, before it has even begun.

Malec turns an ornate hourglass upside down on the bureau. Then he comes to me and unlaces me gently, opening the front of the gown, revealing my breasts. Pushing the fabric off my shoulders. With my face turned aside and my eyes brimming, I let him slide the dress from my body.

He has locked the doors of his suite with bolts and with magic. We won't be disturbed. We can do anything we like in here, for a single hour. And then I will bleed, and I will sleep.

"Are you sure this is what you want?" Malec asks again, softly. He asked me once already on the way down the stairs from the tower, and I snapped, "Yes. I'm going to make you *hurt*." But my anger has ebbed and left me strengthless. I want that rage back. It's better than this yearning sorrow.

"Do things to me," I whisper. "Be cruel to me, so I'll want to fight you."

"I'll hurt you if you promise to hurt me back."

"Agreed."

He strokes his fingers along my neck, then collars my throat roughly with his hand. The familiar defensive instinct sparks inside me, a sharp counterpoint to my aching sadness—and I exhale with relief.

I breathe in his smoky scent, bitter blackthorn and leather, with a hint of fresh rain. "Take me hard. Like you did on the altar, but worse. I'll tell you if I want you to stop."

He's already naked, and he's been erect since he promised me an hour of his time. I reach down and touch the glistening bead of precum at his tip, painting his cock head with it.

"Fuck," he grits out, and his grip on my throat tightens. At the constriction of my breath, the malaise of peril floods my body, alchemizing my emotions into heightened sensation. I can feel the press of each parallel finger, the prod of his thumb against my neck. His precum is slick and viscous between my fingertips.

A buzzing warmth wakes between my legs, cloaking my melancholy in desire.

He pulls me in with his other hand. His palm rushes over my back, my waist, my rear, greedily sweeping along my skin. A predatory growl ripples from his throat and he whips out his wings, curving them forward to encircle my body. Shadows unspool from him, slithering up my bare legs, and they don't stop this time—they glide across my center, tantalizing my pussy lips until I can't help a sharp gasp. They're soft, wicked shadows, delicately nudging me open and probing between my folds, inserting themselves gently and writhing deep into my body, where they pulse with exquisite malevolence.

I'm paralyzed, prey to the new sensations. My mouth is parted, barely taking in enough air.

Malec is caressing my bottom, and each graze of his claws resonates through my belly like a summons to ultimate bliss.

His shadows are prying me wider, and some of them have passed between my ass cheeks to tease open my other hole. There's a cool slickness to their influence, as if they're applying some magical lubricant.

My eyes lock with Malec's, and he gives me a merciless grin.

He releases my throat, steps back. His shadows coil around my naked body, catching me up into the air, whirling me around, bending me over. They bind my arms, torso, and thighs so I can't straighten, or touch anything. The shadows are soft, yet with a tensile strength I can't resist. They hold both my holes wide open.

My pussy feels swollen, warm and damp, unbearably sensitive to the air, exquisitely alive and tingling, alert to the slightest touch. I'm practically dripping with lust. My heart shudders in my chest as I wait for Malec to take me.

A thick, hot length plunges into my center, and I release a faint scream.

Malec's hands and shadows haul me against him, bracing my hips as his cock pummels into me. He's a cyclone of tormented passion, and I'm consumed by his darkness. I relish the stab of his claws into my soft flesh, the low groans wrenched from him with each thrust. I want to end with *this* as my clearest memory—the swelling thickness of him pounding into my core.

"Fuck me like it's the end of the world," I beg, my body jerking with the force of his onslaught. "Fuck me to death."

"I'm going to fuck us both into oblivion, little viper," he promises. His flesh smacks against mine, and the lewd liquid sounds of fucking fill the room as his shadows hold me steady. "Shit, you feel better than Void magic. Far better than anything I've ever—fuck, I'm already coming—oh gods—"

He bucks hard against my ass, his hands clutching my hips as his cum jets inside me. At the same moment his shadows squirm across my clit and pussy, vibrating with the force of his orgasm, and the buzzing pulse of power sets me off. Bliss shatters through my lower belly, a release so violent I twist uncontrollably, my legs shaking, harsh screams of ecstasy searing my throat.

Malec stays inside me, heaving great gasps. A moment later he pulls out, though I can feel he's still hard—and he wipes the head of his cock on my ass cheek. The next moment his fingers find my pussy—he's scooping up the cum leaking from my slit, and he's poking it back inside me.

"I'm not done with you yet." His voice is unsteady.

His shadows pull my ass cheeks apart, tugging at the sphincter of my second hole. My feet are still planted on the floor, my body bent double and tied in place, my arms bound along my sides. Having my ass presented so boldly to the Void King is devilishly thrilling, especially when he runs the rigid length of his cock along the groove of my bottom. He pats my wet pussy with it—and then he shoves himself into my ass.

I bite back a scream. Even with the magical lubrication, his invasion burns. I can't think about anything else, nothing besides the horrible tightness of his shaft, stretching me to the point of bursting.

It's exactly what I wanted. Sensation to erase my anxiety.

Malec doesn't move for several seconds. His palm cups my ass cheek, a reassuring pressure, and inside my channel I feel the shadows leaking more of that cool, soothing substance until it saturates all my tissues and eases the burning tightness.

"I'm going to fuck your sweet little ass now, Princess," he says thickly. "I'm going to come inside you again, and fill up this hole, too. You'll go into your cursed sleep full of my cum. Is that what you want?"

"Yes," I whimper.

"Good, because I couldn't stop myself from coming again if I wanted to. Goddess, you're tight—I don't think I can move without—fu-u-uck—" He's shifting, dragging himself out a little before pushing back in. "Oh fuck, I'm coming in your ass, viper. Can you feel it?"

"Yes, I feel you coming," I breathe. His cum is hot, pulsing through me as he shoves in hard. My pussy is soaked and my clit aches to be touched.

Malec's breathing slows, though it's still uneven. He drags a claw down my spine, all the way to the spot where he's nestled inside me. He teases the puckered skin of my asshole, and a bolt of pleasure snakes through my clit.

"How does it feel, little viper?" he murmurs. "To be fucked and filled by your enemy? To know that you smell of sex, that you carry my scent on you, inside you? And yet I'm the one you fought against all those years, the one who haunted your nightmares. Don't you want to punish me for the curse, for troubling your dreams—for all of it?" He reaches beneath me, rubs a fingertip over my clit.

I jerk at the contact. "Yes, I need to punish you," I manage.

A hum of anticipation rolls through his body as he pulls out of my ass. When his shadows release me, I nearly fall over, but I manage to stumble to the bed and grab one of its posts for support.

Malec has stepped over to a bureau, and he's removing something from a drawer. He turns around, holding up a riding crop and a pair of manacles—not bluesteel this time. "I'm ready for my punishment," he says.

28

I lie prostrate on the floor of the bedroom, my cheek pressed to the rug, my wings tucked close to my sides, and my hands cuffed behind my back.

Aura is sitting directly in front of my face, her thighs spread. The juicy lips of her sex, the delicate creases of flesh between them, and the wet pink slit are all wide open to my view. Her fragrance saturates every inhale—sour sweetness, delicate richness, and a faint scent of *me*, of my cum pooled inside her.

She's fucking herself with the handle of the riding crop. Her head is thrown back, her beautiful throat exposed, lips parted, hair tumbling back from a brow damp with passionate sweat. She's exquisitely gorgeous.

This woman's fantasies align with mine so well. I could lose so much time playing with her. Beyond that, she is intelligent, quick-thinking, forceful—and yes, she's impulsive, like me. Despite years of being saturated with Caennith dogma, she was humble enough to listen to me. She opened her mind to me, as well as her body.

I want her. All of her, forever.

"A taste, Princess, I beg you," I murmur.

She makes a frustrated sound, pulls the riding crop out of herself, and strikes me across the rear with it. The sting on my buttocks makes my cock twitch. I've had several blows from her already, across my shoulders and ass. I crave more of the delicious pain.

"You distracted me," Aura pouts. "I was about to come." She smacks me again, then holds the handle of the riding crop to my lips. "You may taste that."

I put out my tongue and lick her arousal from the leather-wrapped handle. She smirks at my rumble of pleasure.

After a few seconds, she sets the riding crop aside and unclasps my cuffs.

"Turn over," she orders, and I obey gladly, rearranging my wings. When I'm finally settled on my back, my cock juts straight up, a pathetic testament to how much I crave her.

Aura picks up the riding crop again and drags its tip along the underside of my dick. I hitch a sharp breath, half-terrified, half-delighted.

"Do you deserve another orgasm, wicked man?" She nudges my balls with the riding crop.

"No, Princess."

She eyes me, her head tilted. Then she tosses the riding crop aside and settles herself astride my hips, with my cock pinned between her pussy and my stomach.

My head rocks back, a groan issuing from my throat as she begins to rub herself along my rigid length. While she's stroking her pussy along my cock, she reaches out and traces tiny circles around one of my nipples.

"Mercy," I croak. "Mercy, please."

She plants both hands on my chest and drags herself along my cock faster, her cheeks flushed and her eyes hooded with oncoming bliss. "Oh gods—oh gods—" She rocks forward, and her luscious body goes rigid for a moment, her pussy quivering against my shaft. She squirms—blissful friction against the sensitive skin just beneath my cock head—and I spurt, coming all over my own heaving chest as pleasure quakes through my body.

The bliss is scorching, transcendent—our bodies and voices entwined in a melody old as time.

Aura collapses on top of me, almost crying, her skin stippled in goosebumps from the thrill of her climax. I stroke her hair with a trembling hand.

And then I turn my head aside to look at the hourglass on the bureau—

Just as the last grains fall into the bottom half.

Our time is up.

I let loose a long string of curses in my head while I wrap both arms around Aura's body, clutching her to my chest.

I can't give her up. I've had sex many times, but never like this—never with someone like her. Never with this much passion, this agonizing tug in my soul.

Her golden head moves on my shoulder. She's looking at the hourglass too.

Impulsively I move one hand to cover her eyes. But she has already seen it. I can tell by the sigh she releases.

"How long will it be, from the moment I prick my finger until I fall asleep?" she whispers.

"It will happen swiftly. Within a few minutes." I stroke my knuckles over her shoulder, down her arm. "I need confirmation of something, Princess. Do you want me to keep your body here in Daenalla?"

"Yes." She pushes herself upright. Goddess, her breasts are beautiful. Swallowing hard, I lift my hand to stroke one of them, to compress the soft, warm flesh under my palm. She doesn't protest.

There is another question I must ask, though I hate to do it. "If this ritual doesn't work, do you consent to your blood being used again, after your birthday?"

Her lips tighten as she slides off my body, sitting beside me on the rug. After a moment, she relents. "Yes."

"I won't let you die. You'll be cared for with the utmost respect. I swear it on my own life."

Softness wakes in her blue eyes. She leans down, presses her mouth briefly to mine. "I believe you."

That gentle kiss breaks me. Panic roars through my body, wild and reckless—a frantic rejection of the idea of losing her.

Fuck everything and everyone else. Fuck the Edge, the Void, and the curse. Fuck the whole realm—let it be swallowed into oblivion. I'll suffer the End gladly, if only I can have a few years of joy with this precious woman.

29

AURA

Malec is gazing at me with worship and agony in his eyes.

"I can't do this," he bursts out. "I thought I could deny myself again and focus on the needs of Midunnel, but I can't. I can't yield you to the curse, Aura—not when I've just discovered who you are. We don't have to do the ritual now—we can wait awhile—a week, a month, two months. A few years."

His words send a warm, tingling thrill through my heart. They heal pieces of me that are still jagged and bleeding.

And they reveal the truth, with a sharp, sweet clarity.

He'd spare me, yes. We could spend more time together. But larger Caennith armies would come. Battles would be fought along the border and throughout the country, with people perishing on both sides.

Every day costs more precious lives from both our kingdoms.

But Malec looks so wretchedly hopeful, so intent on this new plan—I need to handle him carefully.

"We'll wait, then," I murmur, stroking the firm ridges of his muscled abdomen. "And now, I want you to do something for me."

"Anything."

"Turn over on your belly again."

Obediently he flips onto his stomach, readjusting his wings. I run my palm over the smooth curves of his ass before smacking it lightly. "Are you my beautiful whore?" I say softly.

"Yes, Princess," he breathes.

I slap his ass cheek again, and he moans with delight.

"And you'll do exactly as I say?"

"I promise."

I pick up my dress and pull it on, not bothering to lace it up.

"Close your eyes and count to a hundred," I tell him. "And then come find me. I won't be far away."

I take a moment to admire him—the swelling muscles of his back, the joints of his gorgeous wings, his big shoulders, his silky raven hair, and his four proud horns. And that perfect rear, and those long, toned legs.

I wish I could keep him forever. But I can't let him betray himself like this. I can't let people keep dying in this war, while he and I fuck each other in the tower chambers of Ru Gallamet.

This needs to end, and there's only one way to force his hand.

I slip from the room and climb the tower steps as silently and swiftly as I can, counting in my head. I hit sixty-five as I reach the tiny room at the top, where there's a small table, a chest, and a tall cabinet—probably containing ritual supplies.

I count seventy as I push open the door to the roof, eighty-five as I climb the metal stairway that twists halfway around the Spindle. Ninety as I step onto the grate, the ledge where Iyyo stood. Ninety-five as I reach up, my fingertip hovering over the sharp point of the Spindle.

"Aura!" Malec's cry rings out from the doorway of the tower. He's naked, his eyes wild and his expression frantic.

"You didn't count to a hundred," I sob out.

"I know you." His voice is strident with anguish. "I knew what you'd do. But it took me a few seconds too long to guess it. Aura, please wait—"

I press the flesh of my finger against the Spindle's tip until it punctures my skin. Pain surges from that tiny prick—and I recall what Malec said, how he usually gives his blood donors a potion so the process won't hurt.

"Fuck, Aura!" Despair cracks his tone. "There are preparations to be done—"

"Then you'd best do them quickly. And chain me in place, so the Void can't drag me away."

"Fuck!" It's nearly a sob, cracked from his chest. He disappears into the tower, returning a moment later with the small chest. He flings it open, pulling out the supplies he used earlier. I don't watch him prepare; I stand with my chest against the Spindle, my forehead touching its polished surface.

My finger hurts, my whole arm hurts—but something else is happening inside me, too—a droning sound, reverberating through my very bones, a dragging weight along my limbs. My eyelids droop, suddenly heavy.

A chain coils around me, then another, then more, lashing me tightly to the Spindle.

Malec's cool fingers brush my cheek. "Little viper. You struck before I was ready. I would have spared you, after all."

"And condemned so many others," I whisper. "Selfish."

"I *am* selfish." His lips tremble as he kisses the corner of my jaw, then my temple. "But you are not. You never have been. That is a truth about you that hasn't changed, no matter what others did to you—you beautiful soul."

The wind soars around us, a gale that catches my hair and his, blending them into black and gold, the colors of Daenalla. Beyond the curve of the Spindle, I can see the coiling serpent of the Void. It's coming to swallow me. But I'm sinking, sagging— I won't be conscious when it arrives.

"Bind me tighter," I gasp, struggling to keep my eyes open. "Don't let me fall. Don't let it eat me."

"I won't." A sob in his voice, while the chains tighten, pinning my body in place, binding my wrist and hand as well, so my finger won't slip from the Spindle. "I promise I'll do this, darling, and you'll wake to a safer world."

"You'd better save everyone," I murmur, my lashes drifting shut. "And you'd better be alive when I wake up, or I swear... I'll fucking... kill you..."

Malec's lips crush against my cheek, and then the gust of his wings joins the rushing wind. I force my eyes open a crack and turn my heavy head. He's alighting by the Wheel, his lips moving in a chant. He gathers handfuls of herbs and glittering black dust from his supply chest, flinging them over the spokes of the machine.

I can't watch anymore—my head is a stone, clunking against the Spindle. Through the fringe of my lashes I see the Void coming for me—the titanic Abyss, an entity beyond the strength of humans, Fae, or gods.

And my lover figured out how to tame it.

A faint smile twitches on my lips. "Come on then, you maleficent fiend," I whisper. "Come and taste me."

Then my eyes close, and I'm lost to the roaring wind.

30

I am a god.

Darkness blooms from me in infinite surges, crashing in wave after wave upon the world. My veins are starlight, my blood is darkness, and my eyes are twin suns, everlasting.

Such power has never flowed through any mortal being, human or Fae.

All I want is to exist in the rush of this endless ecstasy forever.

But something scratches at my mind. A duty. A purpose unfulfilled.

A promise.

I don't know who I am, or where I am. There is too much raw magic to permit that level of self-awareness. But I am vaguely conscious that something besides me exists. Something I must protect. Something small and golden.

It takes form—the gleaming image of a tiny golden viper, hissing at me, its mouth wide, showing curved fangs. Adorable, savage, powerful and poisonous—and yet helpless. Because even as it strikes, it goes limp, the light fading from its eyes.

No.

I want it to stay whole and living.

A whisper through the screaming wind. *You'd better save everyone. And you'd better be alive when I wake up, or I swear I'll fucking kill you...*

My awareness flares, bright as the sun, my mind lit up with purpose, fusing my consciousness to my body. I am myself again, and I have a reason for the magic surging through me.

Aura.

Her realm and mine.

I gather the Void, its violence thrumming through every sinew, every joint, every organ I possess. Tenacious, implacable, I match its will with mine. For all my moments of doubt, of self-hate, of despair, I am not weak. I have never been weak. If nothing else, my inner torment prepared me to withstand *this*, because I have plunged myself down into the bowels of darkness and I have clawed my way out again, every time.

The Void has always lived within me, and I with it. And that is why it can never win. Because no matter how it howls and rages, I am stronger.

My will pulls the Void over the Spindle, through Aura's blood, wraps it around the Wheel, sucks it into myself. My will forces the absorbed magic out of me again, this time with form, intent, and purpose. I am myself, but I am larger than myself, enshrouded in the starry emptiness, standing tall above Midunnel. I can see the great serpentine coil of the Void—the coil I am creating. It races along the Edge, along the borders of the realm. Around it goes, a solid wall crafted of darkness, a serpent chasing its tail in a neverending circle.

I keep pushing, pressing my will into it, using a variation of the spell I've used to keep Ru Gallamet from being swallowed up. This work is far bigger—alarming in its scope, but I refuse to let myself doubt, or dream of failure. I keep pushing and chanting, until a flutter in the magic makes me hesitate.

The Spindle is coated with Aura's blood.

Too much blood.

How much time has passed between the moment she pricked her finger and now? I have no way of knowing.

Shit...

I send one last pulse of my energy and will into the barrier that now borders Midunnel. It will have to do. I can't risk Aura's life, and that flutter in the current of magic—it means her vitality is fading.

I let the rest of the Void go, let the Wheel spin to a stop as I race forward, waving my hand to release Aura's chains. She falls backward, and with a wingbeat I spring up and catch her in my arms.

No need to bellow for the healer—Szazen is already there, waiting in the doorway of the tower. In fact, all my men seem to be crowded into the small space at the head of the stairs, and I glimpse a few of the servants behind them. My great working of the Void did not go unnoticed.

Szazen pries open Aura's lips and pours a tonic between them. "Take her to your room, Sire. I'll ensure that she's healed."

"She won't wake." My voice comes out as a throaty rasp—I must have been screaming during the ritual, though I don't remember it. "I cursed her. She won't wake—she won't come back. A hundred years..."

"I understand, my Lord," Szazen says gently. "Lay her in your chamber, and I'll see that she's resting safely. And then I should see to you."

I don't understand why they want to tend to me. I don't understand until I've laid Aura down, and they're caring for her, and I have a chance to look at myself in the full-length mirror near the bed.

My flesh has been carved open in dozens of places, and I'm missing great swaths of skin from my chest and limbs. My hair is gone, and my face—my face is a mask of glistening red tissue and white tendons. My nerves must have been seared away, because I don't feel any pain. My eyeballs bulge strangely from their stripped sockets.

"I'm not healing," I whisper. "The fuck?"

"You should lie down, Sire." Ember's deep voice, just behind me.

"My face." Nausea spikes in my stomach, and I gag. "Szazen—Szazen, you can fix me. You can—you have to. But it doesn't matter, of course—*she* matters. The realm matters—goddess, I look horrifying. Szazen, tell me Aura will be all right."

"I'm replacing her blood now," the healer says soothingly.

"Good, good… And tell me this isn't permanent." I risk another glance at the mirror.

Szazen casts a sidelong look at me. The worry on their face is answer enough.

My hands fall limply to my sides. "Well, fuck."

TWO MONTHS LATER

I sit before the mirror in my dressing room, staring at myself. Seeking any hint of change.

It's all the same. Striated red tissue. White tendons and pale bone.

I work my jaw, watching the muscle pull and flex. My horns emerge straight from my exposed skull, gray at the roots before they darken to black. I look like the monster Caennith has always believed me to be.

It's laughable that they have faith in me now. Once the Caennith rulers verified the stability of the Edge, the Priesthood began to call me "Eonnula's savior." I was lauded, celebrated. The fickle masses praised my name, and peace talks began.

I've let Fitzell handle the peace negotiations. The treaty was signed just yesterday, in a fortress near the broken border wall. Neither I nor the Royals attended, so our emissaries signed in our stead.

The bastard Royals barely spoke of their princess during negotiations. There were some vague demands for Aura's body to be sent home, but when I returned assurances that she was resting safely in my palace at Kartiya, they didn't press the matter. Nor have they responded to my pleas for someone to come and wake her. Perhaps they will, now that the treaty has finally been signed.

It should not take eight fucking weeks to secure a peace agreement.

Meanwhile, I've passed the time in my study, poring over every book I could find about the dissolution of curses. I can't break my original curse, but if it's passed on to someone else, it will be weaker. I've written out most of a dissolution ritual, including ingredients and an accompanying chant, but since my great work, my magic has been unpredictable. I need to wait until it stabilizes.

Still, having the dissolution spell on hand is one more incentive for someone who loves Aura to consider kissing her and taking her place. I'm not fool enough to think I could break the curse. I only knew the Princess for a few days, and the breaking of the spell requires the person who loves her best. There is no way that person could be the selfish, foolish King who ruined her life in the first place.

A knock from the next room draws my attention and I rise, wincing as my robes brush over the open wounds on my body, none of which have healed, despite the best efforts of every healer in my kingdom. As it turns out, my nerves were not gone, only temporarily shocked. Since my great work, I have suffered more agony than I ever thought I could endure sanely. Potions take the edge off, but I only take them before sleeping. I need my mind sharp during the day.

My wings remain undamaged, but flying is torture. I can't bear the flow of the wind over my exposed flesh.

If there's anything to be grateful for, it's that Midunnel is no longer shrinking. My spell worked. The two kingdoms are at peace, and Aura is alive, sleeping peacefully in the north tower of the palace, under constant rotating guard.

The knock occurs again. Stiffly I walk into my bedroom. "Who is it?"

"A visitor from Caennith, my Lord." Kyan's voice is muffled by the door.

"Have Fitzell deal with it. Or Andras. Or the Chief Steward, or Lord Wiggam. Anyone else, Kyan. I'm indisposed."

"At the risk of inciting your wrath, my Lord," Kyan says. "This visitor is one you'll want to see. We're coming in."

"A moment," I growl, snatching one of my masks from the bedside table. Another delightful trait of my new visage—it can't be concealed by any glamour. It's a permanent kiss from the Void, all over my body. Even my cock bears a long slit up the side. No pleasure to be found there, only anguish.

Even if a glamour worked on my mangled form, I could not assume one here. My palace in Kartiya, like the royal castles of Caennith, is spelled to prevent glamours from working within its walls. A visceral glamour would stay intact despite those precautionary spells—but I've been torn apart enough. I won't let someone fragment my soul just to make me beautiful again. I'm not desperate enough for that—yet.

Placing the mask against my raw facial muscles sets my teeth on edge. But the mask is lined with a soothing gel Szazen concocted, so once it's secure, it offers me a little relief.

"Come in," I snarl.

Kyan opens the door. "May I present Dawn, princess of Caennith." He nods to a yellow-haired girl, who steps forward into my room.

"Just Dawn now," she says quietly. "No title or surname."

I don't recognize her, though I know she was the girl who crawled away from the wrecked carriage on the day I captured the Princess. She and Aura were kept within coaches and castles, always protected by walls and spellwork that prevented me from ever seeing their faces clearly through my winged spies.

Dawn is pretty, and sad, and her bearing reminds me enough of Aura to hurt. She gives me a deep curtsy, bowing her head for a moment.

"I heard what happened to you, Your Majesty." Her blue eyes take in the gouges along my arms, the gaps where skin is missing from some of my fingers. "Thank you for what you did."

Her gratitude—simple and succinct—means more to me than all the odes, poems, and prayers I've received during the past weeks.

"There are things I regret deeply." My voice grates through my throat. Like the rest of me, it hasn't been the same since the day I secured the Edge.

"I'll get to the point, my Lord." Dawn's eyes meet mine—fearless, kind. No obsequious adulation, no maudlin pity. I can see why Aura liked her.

"Neither of us are happy with the way things have gone," she says, "but there may be one thing we can change. I overheard a rumor last week, that there's a way to break Aura's curse—that someone who loves her can take her place."

"The Royals were supposed to speak to you about that weeks ago." I almost frown before I remember the pain the

278

expression will cause me. "I didn't know how to contact you directly, so I sent the message through them."

"They failed to deliver it," she says crisply. "Perhaps because, since Aura's capture and my discovery of the truth, they have treated me like a servant. Worse—they've treated me like someone hired to play a role, and now that I've completed the part, I have no further place in their home. It doesn't seem to matter to them that I thought it was real. That I thought they loved me."

"I am sorry for that."

Her eyes glitter with tears, but she tips her chin up resolutely. "I didn't come here for your pity. I came here for Aura. She's a sister to me, and she was duped, like I was. She doesn't deserve any of this. I'm an orphan, trained as a Royal, with no throne in my future. I have no place, no purpose, no family, except her. She is the Crown Princess, the future Conduit—and she will make a far better ruler than either of her parents ever did. So it is my duty, as her sister and her subject, to make this sacrifice for her."

I stand frozen, galvanized with hope. "You understand you'll have to take her place? Sleep for a hundred years?"

Dawn pales a little, but she nods. "I understand."

"I'm working on a dissolution spell that will free you—within a week or two, I hope. But unless my magic stabilizes soon, I'll have to call on some other Fae to cast it. Rest assured, I will do everything in my power to ensure you are awakened as quickly as possible."

"That's kind of you." Dawn gives me a small smile. "I trust you will honor your word. But even if it's not possible to wake me before the century is over, please tell Aura that I did this willingly, because I love her."

A wave of exhilaration rushes over me at the thought of Aura being awakened *today*. I might see her within the hour.

And just as quickly, dread fills my soul, because there can be no future for us as long as I'm locked in this tortured form.

I've tried to use Void magic on my body, but it would not heal me, nor could I take any form besides the shadow-dragon. Perhaps, now that the treaty has been signed, I could ask the Three Faeries for help with my wounds. It would grate against my pride, but if it means being with Aura again—I'll do anything.

"My Lord?" Kyan speaks from the doorway. "Are you all right?"

Suddenly I realize I'm hunched over, clutching the bedpost for support. I unclench my fingers slowly, wincing as moist, exposed flesh peels away from the wood. "I'm as well as can be expected, Kyan."

"Shall we see Aura then? I'm ready." Dawn presses her lips together, her eyes bright with purpose.

"Would you like anything first?" I ask. "Food, drink—"

"No thank you," she says firmly. "Just my sister."

Oleander, shadeflower, and white jessamine cluster in delicate vases, unfurling their fragrance throughout the quiet room where Aura lies under silken sheets. Her body is in a kind of stasis—she needs no sustenance or physical care, but the years of her life will slowly tick away under the somnolent veil of the curse.

Her golden hair swirls on the pillow, a halo to her lovely face. I'm still not used to seeing her like this—placid, motionless, peaceful. She is a creature of fire and blades, fueled by anger, duty, and passion. I miss the light of her eyes, the strength of her body as she rode me, the nip of her teeth, the taste of her arousal. I miss the way she hurt me, and the way she understood me.

I'm still masked, but something in my demeanor must give Dawn a hint of my feelings. That, or Kyan mentioned something to Dawn before he brought her to me. She touches my knuckles where the skin still exists and murmurs, "You care about her."

"You can laugh," I croak. "I know it's idiotic. We only knew each other for a few days."

"But your lives were bound together for longer than that."

"Bound by my stupidity and pride."

"I would say you have overpaid for any mistakes."

She is gentle, this false princess, this girl who was duped more cruelly than Aura. She doesn't seem angry about it, only faintly bitter and deeply sad.

"You have to kiss her," I say. "And then the curse will pass to you."

She gives my knuckles a final pat and moves to Aura's side. Her traveling dress is a simple one, brown with a creamy lining, slit up the side to permit riding, with sturdy leather leggings beneath. A servant's garb, but rich enough to denote her royal connections. Her hair doesn't have the golden, glossy abundance of Aura's—it's thinner, paler, and neatly plaited. Dawn is a shadow of the Princess she was raised to be.

And yet, she has a heart of love and sacrifice, unlike the Three Faeries who raised Aura as their own, or the Royals who used their only daughter as a pawn in political games. This orphan girl, this child they claimed and then cast off—she is worth more than all of them.

"Gladly I take your place, sister." Dawn leans over and presses her lips to Aura's rosy ones.

I hold my breath.

Seconds tick by.

No movement. No response.

"Fuck." A shattered whisper from my tightening throat. Tears sting my eyes.

Dawn rises, smoothing her riding frock. She faces me, nods grimly. "It's you, then."

"What?" I rasp.

"I love her more than any of them, and my kiss didn't work. It's you. You love her best. Or did you know that already?"

"It can't be me. How could it, after so short an acquaintance—"

"Stop making that excuse." Dawn's eyes spark. "Sometimes, in a time of crisis, you come to know a person more intimately than you could from years of placid existence. You're the one who can wake her, Majesty. Whether you do it or not is up to you."

I'm about to reply when a searing pulse of energy strikes my body, an invisible concussive wave. It hits Dawn, too—I see her sway on her feet.

"What was that?" She stares, eyes wide.

Alarm convulses my heart, and I turn, racing down the steps of Aura's tower. I ask each servant and guard I pass if they felt the disturbance—every single one of them did, human or Fae.

Something has happened. Something widespread, something terrible.

I run to the parapet above the palace gates, raise my staff, and call my ravens. They come to me in a great flock, drawn from the forests, the fields, the palace aerie, the watchtowers.

"Go with all speed," I tell them. "Find out what has happened." And I send out a burst of Void magic to hasten them on their way. For once, my magic works as intended. Perhaps it is settling into place again.

Or perhaps—

Perhaps I already know what has happened. But I don't want to believe it. My soul rages against it.

I stand on the parapet, my robes tossed by the wind, my wings pinned to my back.

One by one, my knights arrive. Fitzell, newly returned from the border, is first to come to my side. Her brown, freckled face is tense with concern. Then I spot Kyan, wheeling high above the topmost tower of Kartiya, surveying the distance. Ember perches on the tower's peak, his bat-wings outlined against the sky.

Andras moves in on my left, with Vandel beyond him. A few more gather as well, silently waiting with me for news.

A few hours pass, and during that time, my wounds begin to close. Slowly they seal, and the skin regrows over raw muscle, leaving faint scars to mark the edges of each wound.

My face is tingling as well, alive with a strange crawling sensation. I remove my mask and turn to Fitzell, a question in my eyes.

"My Lord," she says quietly, confirming my unspoken question with a nod. Her smile says she is happy to see me healed, but her furrowed brow echoes my own fears about what that healing could mean.

At last my favorite raven, Roanna, glides down from the heights and lands on my right arm. Her tiny claws graze my new skin gently, almost a caress.

Ember and Kyan swoop down to us, eager for the news the raven brings.

This time, when Roanna locks eyes with me, there is reluctance in her glossy black gaze. She doesn't want to communicate this message. But she has no choice—our minds are already synchronizing.

I see it as she did—the explosion of the protective barrier around Midunnel. The barrier I created bursting into fragments, dissolving into nothing. I witness the resurgence of the Edge, encroaching even farther into this realm, swallowing border towns and farms, blotting out Ru Gallamet entirely.

Thank the goddess I brought the servants and Szazen to Kartiya with me, but my Spindle and Wheel are gone. They took years to construct, and they required materials so rare I'm not sure I can replace them.

It's over. And with my equipment gone, I will not be able to try Aura's blood again after her birthday passes.

Our realm will end in a few decades—sooner if the Edge moves faster this time, which seems to be the case.

I've made things worse, as I always do.

My great work, and it barely survived long enough for a peace treaty to be signed between Caennith and Daenalla. A treaty that will now be useless. I can picture it now—the way the Caennith will mourn their lost villages and roar for my blood.

And I should give it to them. I am a fucking monster.

I crash to my knees.

"What is it?" Fitzell's urgent voice echoes in my mind, dim and distant. "You must tell us, my Lord. What report did the raven bring?"

"Ask her."

Fitzell holds out her hand and Roanna hops onto it. Though I'm the only one who can summon and command ravens, the birds I've gifted with higher consciousness can link their minds with other humans and Fae. Fitzell and Roanna are well-acquainted, with a long history of such communication. As their eyes lock, Fitzell gasps.

I bow over, hunched against the pain in my heart, gripping my staff for support. I'm half-aware of Fitzell telling the other Edge-Knights what has happened.

"Have three dozen men ride to the new borders of the Edge," she says tightly. "We need to know where the lines fall, how much is gone, and how fast the Edge is moving. Any citizens who are too close to the Edge must move inland. Do these orders please you, my King?"

"Please me?" I haul myself to my feet. "No. They do not please me. None of this pleases me. But they are wise words, from a wise woman. Fitzell, you are now in command, as I am no longer fit to rule. I hereby abdicate my throne, and I offer all of you my deepest remorse for having failed you once again."

Before any of them can speak, I spread my wings and leap from the parapet, soaring up to the balcony of my suite. I alight there, push open the balcony doors, and stride across the sitting room, my heart pounding with dark purpose.

On the way to my study, an oval mirror on the wall catches my attention, and I pause.

I'm still bald, but I have my skin again, and I am beautiful—save for a long, thin scar that travels across my forehead, down my temples, and along my jaw, outlining my whole face. There are scars on my throat, too, and when I tear open my robes—more scars, thread-thin and white, marking the borders of every injury I suffered during my great work.

I am no longer the flawless Fae I once was. But I am healed. It's more than I deserve.

Seating myself at my desk, I begin to write.

A flapping rustle from the balcony catches my ear, but I don't look up. A moment later, silver feathers appear in my peripheral vision.

"Kyan," I say evenly. "Fitzell sent you to check on me?"

"To ensure that you do yourself no harm, Sire."

"I'm no longer your King. I abdicated that role just now, or didn't you hear me?"

"You will always be my King."

"I let your sister go on that mission, and she died." I glare at him. "You should hate me."

"I hated the one who killed her," he says calmly. "And that hatred changed once I began to know Aura better. We are all victims of a war that began generations ago. You are perhaps the greatest victim, because you torment yourself with this belief that you must save us all."

"I don't think that anymore. Goddess, Kyan, you've made me misspell two words. Stand there and be silent, while I do what must be done."

Sighing, he props his shoulder against the wall and leans there while I write, and write, and write. I finish the first document and pull another sheet of paper in front of me, adding lines to what is already there.

As I write the last few words, I let tendrils of living shadow seep from my body. They wind swiftly around Kyan, binding his legs, arms, and wings before he can react. He opens his mouth to protest, and I direct a skein of shadow across his lips, silencing him.

"I'm sorry for this." Rising, I clasp his shoulder. "But there is something I must do, and you'll try to stop me, because you're a good man. A loyal man. Take care of Andras—he's a good man too. I'm happy for both of you. When it's done, show these papers to my successor."

Kyan bucks, trying to break free, straining to yell muffled words through his shadow-gag. I turn my back on him and head for the door of my chambers.

Before opening it, I draw on my Void magic again. It's been swirling inside me for weeks, but I've had only haphazard access to it. Now it is fully mine once more, and I may as well use it up.

I allow more shadows to leak from my body, and from them I form a pair of Endlings, with the bodies of panthers and the heads of dragons. I send them into the hallway ahead of me, with mental orders to fight, but not kill. Shouts of alarm rise, and I smile as I recognize the voices of Vandel and Ember. As I suspected, Fitzell sent more than just Kyan to guard me. But my men are used to defending themselves against me with swords and fists; I've never attacked them with my Void magic. They underestimated my determination in this matter.

I will not be deterred from my purpose.

With the two knights occupied fighting the Endlings, I stride casually past them and continue up the hallway, using my shadows to gently move aside any guards or servants who attempt to intercept me. Some I leave bound in chains of darkness, which will dissipate once I do the thing I intend.

Up the steps I climb, to the tower bedroom where Aura sleeps.

And there, before the door, stand my final two obstacles: Andras and Dawn.

Dawn—I'd forgotten all about her. Shit.

"Don't try to stop me." I lift my hand, shadows writhing from my fingers like smoky serpents.

"We won't. We only want to talk." Dawn glances at Andras. "He told me what happened with the Edge. He guessed where you would go, and what you plan to do."

"It is madness, my Lord." Andras's blue skin is paler than usual. "We need you now, more than ever. You cannot send yourself into a hundred-year sleep."

"It may not be that long. I've left instructions for breaking the curse." I swivel my hand palm up, gathering my shadows amid my curled fingers. "But my successor must consent to my waking, and you will need the cooperation of the Three Faeries, the Regents of the Caennith Fae."

Dawn's eyes widen. "They would never agree to such a thing."

"Exactly. Only when both kingdoms are united in common purpose can the curse-breaking come to pass. The deaths that occurred today when the barrier failed—those are mine to own. This is my atonement to Eonnula for my arrogance. I do not deserve to be awakened."

"But who will lead us?" Andras's voice cracks. "Fitzell?"

"I've selected someone who deserves a chance to rule. The one person who may be able to unite both kingdoms at last. You must honor my choice in this matter."

"Of course, my Lord," Andras murmurs.

When I wave them aside, Dawn and Andras both step back, allowing me to pass by them and enter the tower room.

"Sire!" calls Andras, and I glance back.

"You've been a king worth serving." He bows to me, his lips trembling.

If I reply, I will break. So I close the door quietly between us, and I turn toward the bed where my Princess sleeps.

There is no question in my mind that Aura would consent to this kiss. She knew the path to breaking the curse. She wants to be awakened.

Will she be surprised, I wonder, that it was I who released her?

Maybe it's cruel to wake her, to make her face this shrinking world. But she would want a chance to step into her power, to rule as she was meant to. She would want all the time I can give her.

I am under no delusions about my future. I doubt I will ever wake again. The Three Faeries will not agree to restore me, not since the spectacular failure of my spell—and the realm will be swallowed before my enchanted sleep expires.

Still, I can do one good thing before the end.

I lean over Aura, enchanted by the shape of her face, lured by her soft red mouth.

"I am the monster who cursed you, little viper," I whisper. "And I am the supplicant who adores you. If my imperfect, wretched, diseased love can save you, take it. Take it all."

And I press my lips to hers.

31

I'm so comfortable. I don't want to move, ever.

A fragrance teases at my nostrils—blackthorn and leather, rain on fresh grass. A long sigh at my ear, like someone deeply weary who is finally sinking into rest.

I frown, searching the dark of my mind for memories, for understanding.

My eyes blink open.

I'm in a strange room with a peaked ceiling. A room at the top of a tower, maybe?

As I sit up, silken sheets slide from my body. I'm wearing an inky gown, like a river of midnight, with lace along the neck and sleeves.

On the bed lies a broad-shouldered figure, on his side, facing me, with his dark wings draping off the edge of the mattress. Four horns arch from his smooth skull. Scars outline the edges of his face, while more scars decorate his throat and the part of his pale chest that shows through the V of his torn black robes. His hands are marked too—white scars against Void-darkened skin.

Malec. Something terrible happened to him—

He's asleep, and I'm awake—and that means—

The door of the bedroom creaks open, and a familiar face peers in.

"Andras," I gasp. "What is happening? What does this mean? Did the King—did he kiss me? Is that why he's—oh goddess. Oh shit." Frantically I pat Malec's scarred face. "No, no, no—please—shit, you impossible idiot, why would you do this?"

"He took your place," Andras says quietly. "There is more to tell you, but only when you're ready."

"But—Dawn," I gasp. "He was going to ask Dawn to do it, and then he was going to awaken her…"

"I tried." The door opens wider. The second figure standing there is as familiar as sunshine, as dear to me as my own self.

"Dawn." Tears burst from my eyes, and sobs lurch from my throat as Dawn flings herself at me. I clutch her like she's my tether to life.

"I'm sorry," I sob, over and over. "I'm so sorry."

"No," she hisses fiercely. "You did nothing. It was them, the Royals and the Regents. They were cruel to both of us. I love you, you know that. I always will. And you're all right now, because he—" She glances at the handsome, sleeping face of the Void King.

I stare at his pale hand arched against the sheets—at those strong fingers that caressed me so skillfully, so worshipfully. The hand that spanked my ass, broke my glamour, cupped my chin, stroked my hair, held me securely as we flew through the night.

Pulling away from Dawn, I pick up that hand, now laced with fine scars.

"He loves me best of all," I whisper.

Dawn's smile breaks through the tears on her face. "Yes, he does. And it's strange… but it's wonderful, Aura."

I lift the King's hand, kissing each of his knuckles before laying it gently back down. Then I turn to Andras. "Tell me everything."

ONE MONTH LATER

Wingless and wordless, I stand before a silver mirror, staring at the dark purple gown that flows from my shoulders to the floor. The palace seamstress dithered between pink and blue before I selected this fabric—a deep, rich, royal hue, softened by a black gauze layer dotted with scintillating crystals. Sheer sleeves part at my shoulders and trail down to mingle with the skirts pooling on the polished floor.

My maid brushes out a few locks of my golden hair before arranging them over my shoulder and smoothing the rest of the curls that tumble down my back.

A quick rap of knuckles at the door of the dressing room, and Dawn enters. She's clad in the fashion of the Daenallan nobility, with peaked puffy shoulders on her dress and a cascade of ebony-and-gold beaded necklaces down her front. She seems far more comfortable in her role as a Royal Advisor than I am in my latest identity.

"They're here." Her eyes meet mine in the mirror. "They actually came."

"Of course they did." I adjust the rings on my fingers. "It's their daughter's twenty-fifth birthday."

She shakes her head. "Maybe you were certain they'd show up, but I wasn't. It has taken us weeks to convince them you're in control here, that they're safe."

"And those weeks gave us time for other important preparations. Hold our guests at the palace entrance, would you, Dawn?"

"Yes, Your Majesty."

"I told you not to call me that."

She smirks, but her smile drops quickly. "Are you all right, Aura? This noonday celebration—it's an immense number of people, most of whom hate each other. And you have to address them all. You've prepared notes, haven't you? Please tell me you have."

"Obviously I prepared notes." I've done no such thing, and by the way her lips tighten, she suspects as much. So I hurry into another topic. "Are *you* all right? With them being here?"

She hesitates, lips pursed. "I'm better than I thought I would be—thanks to you, and my new work here. I'm going to face them with all the regal grace of my upbringing. And when you overturn their expectations, I'm going to laugh." She breaks into a gleeful smile. "I can't wait."

"Neither can I."

"They'll wish they hadn't played us for fools." With a swift kiss on my cheek, she leaves the room.

I'm glad I can provide her with this small taste of revenge. The King and Queen of Caennith lied to Dawn in the most intimate way, every day of her life. Despite what she said, I can't imagine her facing them without any hint of anger or bitterness. Throughout the past month, our communications with them have occurred at a distance, usually in the form of written letters since they don't trust any magical missives coming out of Daenalla.

I've refused to meet with them in person until now, on this most joyful day, the twenty-fifth anniversary of my birth.

Before he kissed me and took my place, Malec appointed me as his heir. A bold, controversial move, and a brilliant one—because as the Crown Princess of Caennith, the future Conduit, *and* the Queen of the Daenalla, I am not easily ignored.

It's comical how much more attention people pay to you when you have not just a title but the authority and the army to back it up. I've always been the Caennith Crown Princess, but that identity meant nothing while it was a secret. During the few days I knew of my true parentage, I was a captive, powerless to decide my fate.

Malec's sacrifice gave me back my future and all the choices I never thought I could have.

Not that claiming this throne has been easy, of course. There was opposition among the Daenalla. But the King's last written words were a binding contract, magical as well as legal, cursing the crown and the throne unless both were given to me.

Fitzell's staunch support and the loyalty of the Edge-Knights helped to secure my new role. And even the most crotchety of the Daenallan nobles had to admit the wisdom in Malec's choice, because my appointment as Queen immediately softened the tension between the two kingdoms. The Caennith were furious when the barrier failed, and they would have gone to war again if Malec hadn't left me in charge.

I've been a restive Queen, chafing at all the paperwork and diplomacy, the meetings, the flattery, and the endless communications that have been necessary during these past four weeks. Since the day I woke, I've ached to see my plan through to its conclusion. To turn the tables on the ones who fooled me for so many years.

Today's gathering is part birthday celebration and part worship festival. I wanted the biggest possible crowd from both sides, so I sent invitations to every citizen of both kingdoms, from the humblest servant to the richest lord, from the toddling child to the wrinkled elder. I need them all.

"Enough fussing," I chide my maid gently. "You've done your work well. Go on and see the festival. Enjoy yourself."

She curtsies, thanks me, and hurries off. I've already sent the other servants away—not that I've allowed many to serve me these past weeks. I'm used to doing things on my own.

My skirts swish across the floor as I glide into Malec's study. No one protested when I took over his rooms in the Kartiyan palace, while he lay in the tower where I slept for two months. There was some fuss about whether or not I, as a Caennith Royal, should be allowed access to the former King's study and his personal documents, which might contain state secrets. But when the objection was brought up in a meeting, I said sharply, "What secrets? What do any of us need to know, beyond the fact that our realm is shrinking faster than ever and we're powerless to stop it? If the King had any clandestine knowledge that could help me deal with this, you should be on your knees scrabbling through his private documents to help me find it—not twiddling your lace cuffs and pontificating about 'state secrets.'"

I smile as I recall how effectively that shut their mouths.

From a drawer I take what I need and stow it in my pocket. I insisted on pockets for this dress—two of them, cleverly concealed amid the sparkling purple folds of the gown.

One last look in the mirror before I leave the suite. Goddess, Malec was vain. Mirrors hang everywhere in these chambers. I'm getting used to the sight of myself, golden-haired and wingless, but sometimes it still unsettles me for a moment—a jarring dissonance between who I thought I was for almost twenty-five years, and who I've been since that night in the Chapel.

I shove the doors of my suite, but I barely get them halfway back before Kyan and Ember pull them all the way open for me. They took it upon themselves to serve as my bodyguards today.

"Your Majesty." Ember's eyes flash crimson, an approving smile spreading on his dark face at the sight of me.

Kyan bows low as I step forward. He's looking especially well-groomed today, from his neatly brushed beard to his silver wings.

"Are we ready?" I link my arms with theirs, not caring that a Queen probably shouldn't be so companionable with her bodyguards.

"Andras told me to assure you that everything is prepared," Kyan replies.

"And Vandel told me to give you this." Ember pulls a small flask from his vest and passes it to me.

I take a long swallow, then wheeze a little at the afterburn of the liquor. "Oh yes, that's the stuff. All right then… let's go make the King proud."

By the laws of courtesy, I should have met my parents and the Three Faeries at the city gate, or in the festival square, or at the very least in the courtyard. But I made them wait for me, held at bay on the steps of the palace. Fitzell stands with them, and Dawn is there, too, speaking to them with a cool, easy grace I envy. I've played this moment in my head so many times, and yet I find myself woefully unprepared, unsteady, nearly unmade again, like I was on that horrible night in Hellevan Chapel.

My father, the King of Caennith, stands on the palace steps, feet set wide apart as though he's staking a claim on the place. His black beard is streaked with gray, a sign that he has entered his third century. The graceful Queen hovers at his side, her hooded eyes and primmed lips proclaiming her disdain for everything around her.

Beside them stand the Three Faeries. Elsamel, round and motherly, with gauzy blue wings and the large dark eyes of a doe. Genla, black-eyed and angular, with scarlet horns sweeping upward from her brow. Sayrin, tall and brown, her yellow butterfly wings folded against her back.

My three beautiful mothers. Sweet and sour, unpredictably indulgent at times and caustically bitter at others. Linked in a trinity of love no one can penetrate. I suppose part of me always sensed they didn't have much love left for anyone else. Still, I thought they loved me as best they could, in their own way, because I was their precious daughter, born of their union.

None of it was real.

But the bile churning in my stomach, the acid stinging the back of my throat, the nervous pain in my gut—that's real. I'm trembling all over. I've let go of Ember's arm, but I don't dare release Kyan's or I might fall.

He looks down at me, a shadow on his handsome face. He's thinking of his sister, and how the Royals before us bear part of the blame for her death. This is difficult for him too.

"For our King," he whispers.

"For our King," I reply under my breath, squeezing his arm.

Together we surge forward, while a herald nearby proclaims, "Her Royal Majesty, Queen Aura of Daenalla, Crown Princess of Caennith, the God-Touched Heir, the Conduit of Eonnula's Light."

The change in my true parents' faces is almost comical. All traces of haughty disdain or arrogant possessiveness vanish, and they assume expressions of passionate delight. They both rush forward with quivering lips and tearful eyes. Such excellent actors, both of them.

"Sweet Aura!" The Queen reaches me first, moving to cup my face in her hands the way I saw her do with Dawn a thousand times.

I recoil. Rude or not, I can't bear her caress.

Ember steps in quickly, his leathery wings flaring slightly to shield me. "The Queen does not like to be touched."

"Not like to be touched?" The Queen gives a little surprised scoff. "But I'm her *mother*. I've gone without touching her for so many years. For your safety, sweet child. All of it for your safety. You understand—of course you do, because how could we let that horrid beast have you?"

"I'm not a child," I say firmly, and I stop myself before I add, *And you are not my mother.* But I hold back those words, because my plan isn't yet ripe. I need to seem pleasant and amenable.

Forcing a charitable smile is the hardest thing I've ever had to do—harder than pressing my finger to the Spindle. I only manage it by picturing Malec looming behind my parents, giving me his most wicked grin over their heads.

"I'm sure you did what you thought best." I hold the smile in place while I nod to my parents, to the Three Faeries.

Elsamel smiles at me, then nudges Sayrin and points delightedly to the rings I'm wearing—the rings they gave me, every single one in its usual place. To her, it seems to signal that I bear no ill will about the deception under which they raised me.

"Yes, we did what was best. And you should be grateful," Genla says sternly. "Placing that visceral glamour took a toll on us. And maintaining all the little tricks and trappings over the years—that was fucking exhausting. All that effort, and it would have gone flawlessly if you hadn't let Dawn leave the summer palace. And then you fucking took her place? How many times did we warn you never to do that? If you had only followed our orders—"

"But all's well that ends well, isn't it?" Elsamel strokes Genla's arm appeasingly. "And Aura managed to take down the wicked King in the end, didn't she? Took his throne, his lands—everything!"

"I only wish it had happened sooner." Sayrin's eyes narrow, curiosity etching lines between her brows. "How did you manage it, child? How did you get him to turn over the kingdom to us?"

"He didn't turn it over to *us*," I say smoothly. "He yielded its care to me, while he took a much-needed rest. You may remember that only the one who loved me best could take my place—"

"Or so he claimed." Genla scoffs. "I've never heard of such a condition for curse-breaking. Are you trying to imply that the Maleficent One was a secret romantic?"

"I'll wager there wasn't much romance involved, eh, little one?" The King winks at me and lets out a coarse, boisterous laugh. "You seduced him well, you did. Turned his head right round! What a little temptress."

The Queen's lip arches. "You would know a temptress, wouldn't you, husband? Forgive me if I cannot laugh at the thought of my daughter playing the whore to that detestable worshiper of darkness. I can barely stomach the idea of her ruling over this... rabble." She casts a dismissive look at a group of servants clustered nearby, their faces bright with the joy of the festival.

Rage heats my face, but luckily I catch Dawn's eye, and her slight shake of the head helps me maintain my composure. "Enough talk of the past! We can discuss such things later. First, please accompany me to the dais that has been set up for us in the city square. From there, we'll have the best view of all the festivities, including the worship session to be conducted at noon. And there is a banquet prepared for us, as well."

"I could use a drink and a plateful." My father nods, hands gripping his broad belt. "But after worship, I expect to discuss the matter of this kingdom's future. Surely you realize that someone of your age and inexperience cannot rule Daenalla. You'll need a Caennith regent, and Caennith advisors to help you manage these wild Daenallan folk."

"The King speaks true," pipes up a man in my parents' retinue. I recognize his goat horns and flowing hair—he's the very Priest Dawn and I saw at the Lifegiving Festival. He steps forward, a fanatical intensity in his eyes. "We must teach Daenalla the true way, the path of the coming savior."

"The coming savior?" I meet his gaze. "While the Edge races ever inward, you would rejoice and pray to the goddess, and do nothing?"

Too far. That's too far—I may have shown my hand.

But Dawn comes to my rescue. "Her Highness is merely illustrating the kind of opposition you may expect when you attempt to convince the Daenallan people. They will ask you this question and others."

"I have Eonnula's light to overcome their doubts," says the Priest, beaming at her. "It is all I need."

"How sublime for you," I reply, with only a fraction of the acid I want to inject into my tone. "Come, let us celebrate the gifts of the goddess." I lift my hand, and servants come forward with awnings to hold over the heads of the royal procession. Guards fringe our group as we pass through the crowds, walking for nearly a block before arriving in the main square. An avenue has been cleared for us, with more Daenallan guards to hold back the people while we climb the steps to the dais and settle into our thrones.

Pretending to sip the wine that's handed to me, I watch my people step into their assigned positions—Kyan, Ember, Fitzell, and Dawn. Andras and Vandel have another task, one that will keep them out of sight for a while.

The lavish celebration I have arranged floods out beyond the main square of the city, continuing for street after street and spilling into the fields beyond the walls of Kartiya. All the food, drink, and entertainment is free, courtesy of the much-diminished treasury of Daenalla. I needed it to be a celebration no one could resist, not even those who rightly deemed it an inappropriate waste.

Because it *is* inappropriate. It's idiotic to be singing, dancing, eating, and drinking while the walls of the universe close in on us. It's painful to smile and chatter with the Three Faeries and the Royals, when I know how many lives our kingdoms have lost in recent months.

It should have been harder to convince the Caennith Royals, Fae, and Priesthood to abandon all their caution, worries, and weapons and come to Kartiya. But once they ascertained that I was firmly in control, they were all too ready to rejoice over the end of the war. The people of my kingdom have one great weakness—they will always say "yes" to a celebration. The prospect of food, wine, music, and sex is too tempting for them to ignore.

And there is one more thing they can't resist—the thing I promised to every living creature of this realm—a Surge of magic and ecstasy the like of which none of them have ever experienced.

The first Surge by a new Conduit is legendary in its intensity. And every Fae and human in this vast crowd, whether they be Daenallan or Caennith, is eager for the chance to experience the rush of Eonnula's power. Andras told me the Daenalla are especially curious about it, since they've been deprived of the Conduit's influence for generations due to the ongoing war.

This will be the first time in millennia that the Daenalla and the Caennith have gathered for a Surge. The larger the gathering, the greater the rush of magic will be. And this time, since I'm no longer blocked by the visceral glamour, I'll get to feel it.

But first, there is a sequence of events to follow, in precise order. For hours I've pored over the plan with my Edge-Knights, Fitzell, Dawn, and a few trusted Fae, including Szazen the healer. I've accounted for every eventuality, from my parents' over-cautious guards (who will be plied with drinks by attractive Daenallan servants) to the possibility of an assassination attempt by some desperate soul. I will consume nothing that might contain poison, and there are spells in place to intercept any arrows, daggers, or magic that might be thrown my way. Edge-Knights move through the crowd, eyes open for anything amiss, freeing me to focus on the plan.

I wait until the wary looks on the faces of the Three Faeries have faded into complacency, until my father is deep in his cups and my mother is licking honeydust off her fingers after delicately consuming four pastries. I wait until several troupes of dancers, jugglers, and merrymakers have delighted us with their antics, until the crowd is thoroughly relaxed and liquored.

I wait until Regents and Royals believe we're a happy family of Caennith conspirators, poised to control this entire dying realm.

I wait until they believe they have nothing to fear.

Just before noon, when the Triune Suns are at their brightest, I rise and step to the front of the dais.

The crowd quiets, eager for my speech. I've spoken to groups of Daenalla a few times since I became their queen, but it's the first time the Caennith have seen their true princess in person. And I've never addressed a crowd this immense—like a swarm of ants over a pile of sugar.

Dawn was right. I should have prepared notes.

I press my hand over the pocket of my gown. The lines on the paper I've concealed are the only notes that matter today.

"Thank you all for coming," I begin, and the Fae herald near me amplifies my voice with his magic, carrying it across the square, through the streets of the city and beyond. "This is a historic occasion—the joining of two kingdoms. Despite the events of a month ago, it's good to know we can still rejoice and worship together."

A murmur of approval runs through the crowd, though half of them still look more concerned than carefree.

I'm sounding too much like a Royal. Too much like the fucking Priesthood, and the Daenalla don't like it. Neither do some of the Caennith.

It's time for some hard truths.

"The End is coming." My words ring out like a death knell, silencing everyone. "The Void King tried to save all of you—he tore his own body apart to do it. All his life, everything he has done has been for *you*. Not just for Daenalla, but for the entire realm. Some of you were loyal to him, and you loved him. But too many of you were ignorant of his sacrifice, which is bad enough—or ungrateful, which is worse."

Shock, guilt, wonder, and fear etch the faces staring up at me. I may not have magic, or wings, but I feel more powerful than I ever did as a Fae bodyguard. Malec gave me this power—his love, his crown, his years, his people. The whole realm. Gratitude wells up in my heart, stinging my eyes with hot tears, but I take a deep breath and force myself to keep speaking, in the strongest, smoothest tone I can manage.

"You know the Maleficent One broke my sleeping curse—we've spread that news to the far reaches of this realm. The condition of breaking that spell was his love for me—*me*, the heir to his greatest enemies, the woman he cursed at birth. The Void King loved me like he loved all of you—with everything he had, even when he was maligned and misunderstood. If this is our last great celebration, he should be with us."

Six Daenallan Edge-Knights, armored and helmeted, approach the dais. I recognize Andras and Vandel by their height and posture. The six knights carry a silver bier, on which lies a bulky figure draped in silky black cloth.

I glance back at my father, whose mouth is forming words—I think he's saying, "What is the meaning of this?" His voice is probably meant to be blustery and commanding, but no sound emerges. No one can hear his protests.

A slow, wicked smile curves my mouth as I realize that it has actually worked. The first step in my plan is a success.

The Three Faeries would have noticed any dramatic, aggressive spells, but they overlooked the mild muting spell on the wine they drank, which took effect gradually, as intended. They didn't notice the comfort spell Szazen laid on their chairs, which drains them of the will to take any action. Bound by seemingly harmless magic, the Regents remain in the same state as the two Royals—voiceless and docile, unable to speak spells or rise from their seats.

The Three Faeries won't remain placid for long, though. I have mere moments in which to activate the rings they saw on my fingers. My mothers must have thought the rings were inert; a reasonable assumption, since they haven't been around to recharge them for me.

But these rings don't represent reconciliation, or any nostalgia about my childhood.

The High Priestess of Hellevan Chapel brought the rings to Kartiya for me, and at my request, she tweaked their original purpose. They were always designed to hold the magic of the Three Faeries and allow me to channel it in specific ways as if it were my own. And now, the rings will act as siphons, sucking every bit of magic from all Three Faeries, channeling it into my body in a raw, malleable form, so I can use it for any purpose I desire.

The sole purpose of my heart at this moment is to have my Maleficent King standing at my side.

The High Priestess is in the crowd near the dais—I can see her there, half-concealed by an elaborate festival headdress. She gives me a nod, her lips moving beneath the edge of her half-mask.

I never noticed a tangible change in the rings when my mothers recharged the magic. They must have done so with great care during our "worship sessions," so I wouldn't realize what was happening.

But when the High Priestess activates the rings, the sudden influx of power is more than the charmed jewelry can absorb quietly. Every ring vibrates on my fingers, warming my skin, sending pulses of energy into my body. I focus on my palms, following the process the Three Faeries taught me—drawing their power from my hands, along my arms, into my chest, through my heart—then transferring it to my mind, where my thoughts can shape it.

I've never held so much magic at once. It rushes along my veins like icy water, like liquid fire, like sizzling sugar. The power of the three Fae Regents of Caennith is mine to command.

From my pocket I extract the spell Malec left behind when he took my place—the spell to dissolve the curse. He said it would require the power of the Three Faeries. And he knew they would never willingly agree to awaken him.

But perhaps he also knew I wouldn't let that stop me.

I look over my shoulder at the Royals and the Regents, all staring at me mutely, unable to speak, and so comfortable they can't quite bring themselves to move, or to panic.

Their eyes tell me they did not expect this. They expected me to be grateful, to rejoice over seeing them again. They expected me to be ready to hand over the reins of my new kingdom to *them*. As if they haven't lied to me all my life.

They expected to reclaim a pawn. But they found a queen.

My gaze swerves to Dawn. When my eyes meet hers she laughs aloud, pure exultant triumph.

Invigorated by that joyous sound, I turn back to the bier, which the guards have lifted onto the dais. The Edge-Knights stand with their backs to the platform, ready to defend their sleeping King against any threat.

The crowd is half-fearful, half-excited—they stir and murmur as I scatter herbs and ashes over the silken drapery. Next, a sprinkle from a vial Ember hands me—some of my blood, and a little from each person who loves him best—Fitzell, Szazen, his knights, a few favored servants and nobles whom I permitted to know my plan.

Then I lift my hands and begin the chant Malec wrote. I change the words a little—the High Priestess told me it would be more effective if I spoke from the heart.

"To the curse transferred, to the slumber imposed, I call. To the magic infused and the somnolent mind, I call. To the soul adored and the spirit beloved, I call."

I hesitate, tension building in my throat, tears gathering in my eyes. But the power thrilling along my limbs is a promise and a caution—a reassurance that I have the magic to do this, and a warning that if I waver, the tether will fail, the power will slip back into the Three Faeries.

If I falter, I will lose my only chance to save him.

The crowd remains utterly silent as I continue.

"Release your bonds, for they are satisfied. Relinquish your darkness, for the light is here. Yield your sacrifice, for it is no longer needed. What was woven in hate is unlaced by love. The caster has recanted, and the cursed one has been freed. Your conditions are fulfilled. Let the sleeper arise. I call to you, Malec, maleficent ruler, I summon you. King of the Void, I adjure you to wake."

The magic of the Three Faeries rushes out of me in a torrent, a wave of compulsive power crashing against Malec's sleeping body. The aftershocks ripple through the crowd, eliciting gasps. People rise on their toes, crane their necks—some winged Fae even take to the air, eager for a glimpse of what's happening.

Behind me, Genla manages a faint hiss, a protest at the theft of her magic.

The Regents have been drained entirely now. I have nothing to fear from them until after the Surge. Maybe not even then.

I kneel beside the bier, lay back the gauzy covering, and trace my fingertips along Malec's pale, scarred face. His hair has grown back in somewhat—short, glossy curls, like raven feathers.

The curse should be inert now—unable to pass back to me when I kiss him.

This has to work. It *will* work, because I'm the one who loves him best.

I lean over him and touch my lips to his.

His soft mouth yields under mine. I press deeper for a moment, then ease away from him.

I count in my head as the seconds pass—twelve of them. And then...

Malec's black lashes part, and he stares up at me.

It fucking worked.

A gasping laugh cracks from my lips. I grip his hand, holding it against my heart.

He blinks, lifts a hand to his brow.

At the sign of movement, the crowd breaks into a frantic roar of gladness, and Malec startles. "By the Void, what is going on?"

"Your awakening is a rather public affair," I murmur, leaning in. "I'm sorry for it, but it had to be this way. And we're not done yet. We have to save the realm. Do you trust me?"

He blinks again. Then a smile widens on his scarred face, transforming it into the most beautiful thing I've ever seen. Confidence shines in his dark eyes. "I trust you."

"And you love me?"

"And I love you."

"I love you, too," I whisper fiercely, clutching his fingers so hard he winces. "Sorry." I let go, and he chuckles.

"Little viper." His voice rolls beneath the ongoing joy of the crowd. "What's next?"

"You greet your people."

Anxiety tightens his features. "After my failure, Aura, I can't—"

"Today isn't about that. They don't need your apologies right now—they need you, on your feet, by my side."

"I probably look awful." He touches his hair self-consciously.

"Nonsense. I had the servants comb your hair, preen your wings, oil your horns, and line your eyes with kohl."

He grins, delighted. "My heroine."

"I knew you'd want to look good for your wedding."

"My—my what?"

With a laugh I rise, helping him up. The servants dressed him in shimmering black robes for the occasion, complete with a collar of glossy feathers. He flares his wings, eyeing the feathers before giving a satisfied nod. Then he lifts both hands to the crowd, and they roar thrice as loud as before.

"My what?" he says out of the side of his mouth to me.

"I'm the Queen, you're the King—it's a matter of course." I nod to the Hellevan High Priestess, and she mounts the steps of the dais.

Malec catches my hands, pulls me to face him. "You'd bind yourself to me before the goddess? Me, the Spinner of Darkness, and you, the heir of Caennith? It's unheard of."

"Exactly." Now that he's awake, I can barely contain my excitement. "It's so simple, Malec. It's always been this simple—so plain we refused to see it. I don't have time to explain, just—marry me. Please."

"You don't have to beg, little viper." His eyes darken with desire, and he tugs me closer, my body pressed to his. "You and me, fighting and fucking for the rest of our lives? It's all I've wanted since I met you."

The herald had ceased broadcasting our voices, giving us privacy; but for some reason he reactivates the spell during Malec's "fighting and fucking" speech. The entire city breaks into frenzied cheers, so loud I can barely hear the High Priestess as she takes her place, facing the crowd, with Malec and me before her.

I glance over at the Three Faeries. Tears glaze Elsamel's cheeks; I'm not sure if they're tears of joy or heartbreak. Sayrin stares, tight-lipped and stony-eyed. A vein bulges in Genla's forehead, a complement to her ferocious frown. My father's face is purple and swollen with rage.

But my mother—my real mother—has a sly smile on her lips, a glint of approval in her narrowed eyes. When she meets my gaze, she gives me a single nod.

She may have ruined all chances of my loving her the way I should. But perhaps she and I won't be enemies. Not forever.

I exchange a look with the Caennith Priest, too, letting all my defiance shine through my eyes. I'm violating the Caennith law, the rule that says Fae and humans may not marry or procreate. The Priest looks utterly horrified and disgusted, which makes me grin more widely as I prepare to repeat the vows.

"Before the goddess I bind you," says the High Priestess. "Here in Daenalla we do not use the same vows for all couples, because every pairing is unique. I will lay hands on you both, and you will be free to speak what is in your hearts." She reaches up and places one palm on Malec's head, right in front of his horns. The other hand she lays on the top of my head. "When you feel so compelled, speak, and swear to each other."

A brittle silence falls over the dais, over the square, over the city.

And then Malec speaks, his velvety voice sending chills over my skin. His eyes are soft and serious.

"My soul was cloaked in shadow," he says quietly. "Every dalliance with the Void soaked it in a heavier darkness, weighed me down with dread. Eventually, it would have killed me. But you, with your beautiful savagery of spirit—you sliced right through the heavy shroud over my soul. You kicked down the doors of my heart and stabbed me with the splinters, and I bled, and the blood reminded me that I was alive, that I was more than the dark hope to which I clung. You kissed me, and you woke me from death's embrace. You gave me hope, rapture, agony, laughter. I want to stay awake, for you. Alive, for you."

I'm shaking with the raw intensity of his confession, the naked truth of his heart exposed before all his people. No more masks or shadows. No more pretense.

"I was always wrong inside," I begin, tremulously at first, but my voice strengthens with the urgency to communicate what I feel for him. "I was different. Crooked. *They* made me crooked, put their fingers into my mind and body, saying it was to protect me, claiming they knew best. And they lied to me—but you— my curse, my captor—you told me the truth. You unmade me and put me back together as I should have been. And you didn't mind that I was angry, wounded, unhealed. You didn't mind my scars—the ones I will always carry."

Malec releases a shuddering breath, and I know he's thinking of his own scarred face and body. My eyes blur with tears, and I clutch his hands tightly in both of mine.

"I love you beyond reason, with all the persistence of revenge and all the violence of hate. I love you with the bones beneath my flesh and the blood in my veins. I love you into the deepest dark and under the harshest light. Let me be your Forever. You are already mine."

"Yes," Malec whispers, his eyes shining.

The High Priestess moves her palms to our foreheads, lifting her face to the suns. "With the truth of two hearts I bind this marriage, in words of power and ties of magic. May the joy of Eonnula live in you both and bless your union. A kiss will seal it, and the goddess shall sanctify it."

I lunge for Malec, and he wraps me up against him, his mouth searing mine with a heated promise, while the crowd erupts around us. I kiss him twice more, lavish and lingering. But my plan isn't complete... not yet.

"We're bound now," I murmur into Malec's ear. "The Conduit of Caennith, bound to a powerful Fae. Such a thing has never happened."

I sense it—the moment when he understands. He stiffens, grips my shoulders, pushes me back slightly so he can look into my eyes. "Oh shit. You beautiful, brilliant, magnificent woman. Why didn't I think of it?"

"Oh, I'm not done being brilliant yet." I snap my fingers at the Caennith Priest. "You there. Stand with the High Priestess and lead these people in worship. Let it be the loudest, wildest song you ever sang. We need a Surge bigger than any in our history, and you're going to lead us into it."

He hesitates, pouting a little—but as I suspected, the prospect of such glory is irresistible, and he bounds forward, shucking off his robe and shouting for music.

The royal musicians heed the Priest's call, beginning a glorious swell of song. At first the Daenalla look very uncomfortable, cringing and staring as the Caennith Fae and humans begin to dance and sing and leap.

But the High Priestess steps forward, beginning a low chant that resonates beneath the wild music, strengthening and deepening it. The Daenalla join her, one after another, street after street, until the city and the countryside tremble with the rolling bass notes and the hectic rhythm of dancing feet.

The crowd's emotions are running high already, fueled by the dramatic awakening of the Void King and by the surprise wedding. Their fervor is reaching manic intensity, and despite the sheer numbers and the presence of divergent faiths, the harmony they produce is so beautiful I can barely inhale. I feel as if my heart might swell right out of my chest, shattering my ribcage. I'm fairly sure I'm crying without meaning to—my cheeks feel hot and wet.

I pull Malec close and speak low, beneath the surging music. "I don't know exactly what will happen. If my theory is correct, you and I should both be Conduits now, because the spouse of the Conduit becomes one too. But there's never been a Fae Conduit before, so I don't know how it will work, or how it will feel. When the Surge occurs, if you receive it, don't release it outward to the crowd. Channel it upward, to the sky. We're going to punch a hole in the ceiling of this realm and let the Void in."

He winces, hesitation and fear in his eyes. The Void tore him apart last time. It makes sense that he wouldn't want to face it again.

But I touch his cheek, willing him to have courage. "I couldn't convince everyone to congregate near the Edge. I needed to bring them somewhere safe, somewhere they would agree to gather. But there's no Void here, so we have to summon it from the nearest access point." I point upward.

"You want to try my barrier spell?"

"Something like it, yes. Since you're a Conduit now, you won't need a Spindle to channel and gather the Void. All you need is yourself. There's enough life here to entice the Void, and when it comes, you're going to gather it and create something new. You had the right idea—making the Void work against Itself. But you've spent so long playing the defensive side, you didn't go far enough."

I slide my hand down to his chest, clasping a fistful of his robes. "For me, an effective defense has always meant a quick, merciless offense. Instead of making a barrier out of the dark, you have to create something bigger—a monster formed from the Void that will devour the Void. The largest Endling you've ever conjured, laced with the light of the goddess Herself. Do you understand? Can you see it? Because I can't do this without you."

He nods. "I see it. I understand."

"Good. We may have to adjust the plan depending on what happens."

312

"We'll keep talking to each other, communicating what we feel." His eyes sparkle with determination. "This just might work. If it does, I'll be your slave endlessly."

"I thought you already were." I give him a small smile.

He laughs and takes my face in his hand, pulling me in for a kiss.

The people scream for us, for the goddess, for the Light—a fever pitch of explosive praise.

I feel it coming—a cosmic wave of magic, shaking the city with the force of its power.

"Now!" I scream to Malec, to the High Priestess. "Now, now!"

I grab Malec's hand, lift it high. With my other hand I seize the Caennith Priest's fingers, while the High Priestess holds onto both him and Malec.

We raise our hands as the titanic force of the magic hits us. My head snaps back, power rushing through me until I think I might shatter.

"Up!" I gasp. "Send it up!"

The Caennith Priest has no choice—his hands are locked with ours, he's part of the chain—and as the four of us face the sky, a column of pure light roars through the circle of our joined hands, screaming upward like a bolt of white fire. It sears straight through the arch of the sky, incinerating the layers of air.

Our hands separate, falling to our sides. The light vanishes, and at the apex of the sky's arch I see a hole, blacker than shadow.

The crowd's song fades as the people realize there's no Surge rolling back through them, no blissful moment of peace or thrilling replenishment of magic. Everything we gathered was shot upward, into the distant Void.

No, not everything.

Green light envelops Malec, licking across his scarred features, gloving his hands, glimmering on his feathers. I can't see his eyes anymore—just green orbs of flame.

There's something different about him, though—a glitter of golden magic sprinkled through the emerald fire, threads of pale yellow light twining around his fingers.

"Aura," he says, in a voice deep, pure, and divine. "Look at yourself."

I glance down—and my whole skin is alight with a golden glow, threaded with sparking green. I can feel magic inside me— and it's not borrowed or channeled. It is mine. Because I am a Conduit, married to a Fae King. Our natures, our magic, are shared and augmented by our union before the goddess.

I look up at Malec, grinning. "Fuck, yes."

He laughs, wild and wicked, emerald flames licking between his teeth.

The Edge-Knights close in around the dais, dozens and dozens of them. Over the past month Fitzell called them in from every border garrison and distant watchtower, and they're here now, ready to make a last stand for the realm. Each knight produces a shining blade, slices their palm, and lifts the bleeding wound toward the heavens.

The hole in the sky is beginning to close. We have to act quickly.

"Now, Malec," I prompt him.

He begins to chant. He needs no herald—his voice carries all the power of something eldritch, something divine. I join him, echoing every word.

"Mastery of the arcane, confinement of the abyss. Let me be blind to the light, deaf to the world. Come to me, father of destruction. My bones shall house your infinity, and my mouth will bleed your shadows. I tether you, bind you, pour you into me."

Screams erupt from the crowd as serpentine coils of darkness poke through the hole in the sky, writhing in, twisting and coiling down toward the city. The High Priestess lifts her hands, and with a voice buoyed by the herald's magic, she speaks words of explanation, of calm. Throughout the city I've sent trusted servants who know my purpose, messengers to explain what we're doing. The remaining guards of the city move through the crowd as well, calming the panic of the people.

I can't fret about the city right now—can't worry about a mob or a frenzied stampede. That responsibility belongs to Fitzell and her soldiers, and to the High Priestess. My role is to be with Malec, to join him in this great work. I can't let terror overcome me, not even when ice crystallizes my bones at the sight of the darkness descending to feed upon us.

"Your violence shall be mine to tame, and your monsters shall answer my call," I chant with Malec. "Because I have need of you, Formless One, Endless Depravity. Glorious Abyss, inhabit me. Spill into my soul, split my veins, fracture my heart. Submit to me, reside in me, yield to me. I am the residence of the tempest, the cup of endless wine, the guardian of your greed."

Malec reaches up, as if to embrace the Void and accept it into himself. I do the same, forcing myself to breathe, breathe, breathe as the darkness rushes in, colliding with the magic of Eonnula inside me.

"You are in charge of it," Malec shouts to me. "Force it to submit. Shape it, absorb it." He reaches for me, laces his fingers with mine so our hands are palm to palm.

A jolt of energy passes over me, and suddenly I can see through him, into him—his will and mine are one, his power and mine are one, and we have but one mighty purpose.

Malec has decades of experience creating Endlings. His will dominates the Void, commands it, and shapes it—but I provide the vision of the creature we need—a monster with smoky scales and golden wings, with a maw like an endless chasm and teeth of glittering light.

The creature forms above us, birthed from our minds, tethered to the darkness we've channeled—and we keep pulling more of the Void through that hole in the sky, swelling the great dragon larger and larger, until it seems to fill the whole realm.

Malec and I speak together, our voices entwined and echoing with cosmic sovereignty. "Consume the Void. Devour the darkness that craves the absence of life. Protect this realm until the end of time."

The dragon rears up, wings spread across the world—and then it streaks away, blazing toward the horizon.

Vaguely I hear the roar of the crowd, Malec's shout of triumph. Dimly I see the hole in the sky sealing itself. Faintly I smile, flushed with the hope that we've done it at last. We've created not a wall, but a guardian for our world.

I can still feel magic in my bones, in my heart—but it's faint now. I've spent nearly all of it—and whatever my new powers may be, I'm still human.

I struggle to stay on my feet, but my legs wobble, and I fall. Malec catches me before I hit the floor.

32

THREE DAYS LATER

I've never been so desperate for anyone to wake up. The healer assures me Aura will wake—her human body just needs time to adapt to the changes wrought by our union.

I can't believe I never thought about the combination of a Conduit and a powerful Fae, married before Eonnula, sharing their powers. I'd even researched the transference of power between the Conduit Heir and their spouse, and investigated the magical reasons why humans who marry Fae usually end up with longer lifespans, though they don't gain their partner's powers. I should have seen the correlation, the potential.

As for Aura's vision for the guardian Endling, the great dragon—I am in awe. I've been in a constant state of awe since I woke from my cursed sleep a few days ago. With Aura's kiss, a weight inside me lifted. The destiny of the realm is a burden we share now, with each other and with both kingdoms. No longer do I feel as if I must shoulder it alone.

I lift my cup of wine from the nightstand nearby and sip, savoring the full-bodied richness. Wine was becoming increasingly expensive due to the Edge swallowing vineyards. In the future, that shouldn't be an issue.

As I take another swallow, Aura stirs, flouncing over in bed. Her brows pinch together, and then she sits up abruptly, rosy and defiant, looking ready to stab someone.

"No," she says firmly.

I grin, amused. "No?"

She frowns deeper, still caught in the throes of the dream she was having. "Malec?"

"Little viper."

The blur of sleep clears from her expression, and her eyes widen, asking me a silent question.

I let a smile of triumph spread on my face, and she presses a hand to her mouth, her eyes widening.

"So it worked," she whispers.

Tears gather in my eyes, even though I'm still smiling. "Yes, love. It worked."

She reaches out. "Tell me."

I scoot a little closer to her, taking her hand in mine and stroking her knuckles. "The dragon flew to the Edge and began to devour the Void, just as we commanded it to. It's incredible, Aura—it ate back the dark so far, it uncovered parts of this realm that haven't existed in living memory. It's as if they were there all along, only obscured. There's nothing alive in those places, of course, but we can reclaim and resettle them now."

"Once we're sure the realm is stable." Her eyebrows pull together in a frown, so I bend down to kiss her puckered forehead.

"Yes, we'll wait until we're sure. But it seems the Guardian is taking its role very seriously. We've had reports of the Void's shadows writhing nearer in some places, but the dragon always flies to that spot immediately and swallows the darkness, leaving our lands untouched."

"How long will the dragon last?"

"There's no way to know. My Endlings used to last until my energy ran out, but this Guardian seems to be self-sustaining—it lives on the darkness it consumes. People have seen it basking in the light of the suns as well."

"And will it be a threat? Might it turn on us someday?"

"I doubt it." I caress her cheek. "And if it ever should, you and I have the power to dispel it, since we are its creators."

"Its creators. I still can't believe it." She touches the center of her chest. "I feel—different. I can sense the potential for magic inside me, but I don't have any energy left."

"We'll go to worship tonight and remedy that. How do you feel otherwise?"

She tilts her neck to one side, then the other, a contemplative expression crossing her face. "Good, I think. Hungry. For food, and for—" Her gaze flashes to mine, a suggestive heat in her blue eyes.

My body weakens with delight—and a shadow of apprehension. "I'm at your service, Your Majesty."

"Good to know, husband." She touches my nose lightly. "But first, tell me of my—family." Her lip curls as if the very word tastes bitter.

"After you fell asleep, some of my knights loaded your parents and the Three Faeries into carts, still in their charmed chairs," I tell her. "The Three Faeries were furious, of course, but empty of magic, since you siphoned it all and they got nothing from the Surge. Fitzell and my knights left the Regents and your parents just beyond the border. According to my ravens, they were eventually freed by their servants and they returned to the summer palace—though I'm not sure how long they'll retain any of their holdings."

"Why is that?"

"It seems that the Regents and Royals have fallen out of favor. The people of both Caennith and Daenalla are calling for a unified realm, under your rule and mine. After the Guardian's work began, humans and Fae from both kingdoms went to the border wall and began tearing it down, by muscle and by magic. It's all but demolished now."

A cautious joy lights her face. "So—have we done it, you and I? Have we saved our realm and united our kingdoms?"

My answering grin is so wide my face hurts. "I think maybe we have."

"Thank the goddess." Her smile turns quizzical. "Does that mean the prophecy was true after all? Are we Eonnula's promised saviors?"

"Does it matter?" I slide off the bed onto the floor. Kneeling there, I grip her thighs and pull her to the edge of the mattress. My hands cup her knees, then glide upward, pushing the nightdress out of my way. "You're my savior, my goddess. Allow me to worship you, little viper. I will eat this beautiful pussy, and then you will eat dinner."

I lean forward, my mouth close to her center. I breathe in her scent through the thin panties she's wearing, and my mouth waters. She's been tended and cleaned by magic during her sleep, and her fragrance is as delicious as ever.

Aura pushes my head away gently. "I love your mouth, but I want your cock."

"I'm scarred there," I tell her. "It's not painful for me anymore, but it might feel different to you. It's no longer the flawless piece you remember." I attempt a wry smirk, but I suspect it's more of a pathetic grimace.

A flash of gentle pain in her eyes—and then her gaze turns molten and commanding.

She rises from the bed, holding her head high. "Get up."

"Aura—"

She slaps my cheek lightly, then takes my throat in her hand. I let her pull me to my feet, my dick hardening at her dominance.

I'm as fearful as I am aroused. I wanted to give her some pleasure first, to soften the blow of what she's about to see—the ugly scar along the side of my once-perfect cock.

But she's determined to have her way.

"Lie down," she orders.

I obey, spreading out my wings, centering myself between them on the bed, and propping my head on the pillows. My heart is pounding. A tumult of anxious thoughts crowd my brain as Aura releases the buttons of my pants, one by one, and reaches inside.

My fists curl tight as I wait for her reaction.

Silence.

"Malec, look at me."

Shit, I didn't realize I had closed my eyes. I couldn't bear to watch her expression when she saw the ruin of me.

With a bracing breath, I force my lashes to part.

When I look down, she's leaning forward, her rosy mouth hovering just above my cock head. My dick bobs in response to what I'm seeing—her perfect lips opening, sliding over the pink head, taking me in—all the way in—gods-fucking-shit.

She runs me as far into her mouth and throat as she can, then slides her lips off me again. Her wet tongue trails a long, slow lick right up my shaft, over the thick white scar that snakes along the side of my dick. This scar is lumpier than most of the others—just my luck.

"You told me it was beautiful, once," I grit out. "And now—"

"Now it bears a mark I cherish. A sign of your sacrifice." Aura sows little kisses along the scar, and I let my head fall back with a groan, tears leaking warm from the corners of my eyes.

"I love you." She bathes my cock head with her tongue, lavishes it over and over until I can hardly breathe. "I love you, Malec—all of you, no matter how you change. You are mine. You alone. You always."

She sucks on me earnestly then, her golden head bobbing in glorious rhythm. I'm stricken with desire, panting, writhing, desperate.

Just before I come, she slips off her panties, moves astride my hips, and sinks onto me, embracing me into her warm, wet heat.

I reach forward, jiggling her clit with the tip of one claw, then sending a little pulse of magic to swirl over that spot. With the Void so far away, I don't anticipate using its power again, but there are plenty of other tricks I can employ for her benefit.

My wife reaches for my hands, and we lace our fingers together as she rides me, faster, harder, her golden hair spilling forward, brushing against my scarred chest, over my heart.

"By the goddess, Malec, you feel so good—shit—ah, ah, ah—" Aura shrills, clutching me tighter—and then she gives a breathless shriek, while her pussy convulses around me. I come immediately, helpless to the divine sensation of those blissful spasms, prey to the sight of my gorgeous Queen gasping, shuddering, wild with pleasure. My body arches, and I let loose a throaty roar as the climax explodes through me, continuing in waves so exquisitely violent I can barely see.

When the pulses of bliss ease into a soft afterglow, we both go limp, and Aura falls forward on top of me, panting.

"I've never had one so long," she whispers. "Fuck."

"We're married," I manage breathlessly, stroking her back. "Fae partners can give their spouses more powerful pleasure than before the bonding."

"What?" She stares. "They never told us that in Caennith."

"Well, they wouldn't, would they? The Priesthood didn't want humans and Fae bonding for life."

"Bastards."

I laugh. "Indeed."

We lie still for a moment in the quiet, simply breathing and existing together. It's a respite we deserve after all we've endured.

I am loved. *Me.* Loved exactly as I am, with all my mistakes and my darkness. I am forgiven, desired, and cherished by the person who once viewed me as her greatest enemy. When I sink into gloom again, she will be there, loving me through it. And when I want to soar for joy, I can carry her with me.

She and I may have saved the realm together, but she alone has rescued my soul.

Buoyed by these thoughts I rise, still holding Aura close to my heart, and I ring the bell for a servant. "I'll order our dinner, my love," I tell her. "Then you can dress, and we'll go to worship."

33

AURA

I sit with Malec on lush green grass, under a star-flecked sky. The faraway coils of the Void still pass across the suns in their regular rhythm, causing nightfall, but another shape crosses our skies too—the winged dragon Malec and I created together. As long as it roams the borders of Midunnel, we do not need to fear the writhing dark.

With the curse past and the threat of doom lifted, my heart is lighter than it has ever been in my life. My parents and my false mothers are gone, dealing with the citizens of their own kingdom. Malec and I have decided we won't make any move to rule Caennith at present, unless its people come to us and plead for governance. As my parents age and decline, the rulership of Caennith will pass to me anyway, as the true heir. Right now, we are waiting. Which means I don't have to encounter my family again until I'm ready. And that, too, is an immense comfort.

Malec's relief shows in the lightness of his laugh, the easy set of his shoulders, and the sparkle of his eyes. It rings through the merry, taunting words he exchanged with his Edge-Knights this evening as we filed into the grassy, starlit arena, Kartiya's place of worship.

The Void has been driven far away, and he can no longer access its magic. But he assured me that his natural power is enough. It's a power I possess now, too, even though I'm human. We share his magic, and the light of Eonnula, and the abilities of the Conduit. And within us both lies the latent capacity to channel and shape the Void, if we should ever need to do so.

A rustle of silk on grass heralds Dawn's arrival. She settles in on my left side, giving me a quick smile. Having her here all the time is a blessing from Eonnula. It makes me feel more settled inside, knowing that one relationship from my old life is real and lasting.

Vandel takes the spot beside Dawn. I spot the two of them exchanging a glance, and when Dawn looks my way again I raise my eyebrows, smirking. She nudges me, a bashful smile on her face.

Beyond Dawn and Vandel are Kyan and Andras, sitting close together, and Ember beyond them. I spot Fitzell with a broad-shouldered man and three children. Near her family is the High Priestess of Hellevan, not a leader this time, but a worshiper as well.

The High Priestess's eyes meet mine, and when I give her a grateful nod, she smiles.

The Kartiyan Priest, a slender, white-haired man with dark brown skin and kind eyes, presides over the gathering from his seat on a flat circle of pale paving stones. Malec and I, along with those most precious to us, have gathered near him. Tiers of grassy ledges radiate from the round lawn where we sit, climbing upward and outward, each circle wider than the last. The outdoor chapel is like a great ridged bowl set into the ground, designed to provide seating for hundreds.

There is no blaze of sun, no manic roar of frenzied cheers, no strident voice urging the crowd along to greater heights of hectic desire.

The grass glimmers in the starlight, and the rows of worshipers speak quietly to each other, their murmurs interspersed by the occasional laugh or the cry of an infant. Peace governs the night, breathes in the light wind, and whispers to the space inside me, the new pathway reserved for magic.

The Priest is singing. I'm not sure when he began the melody, but it wreathes through the worshipers, quieting the conversation, soothing the children. More voices take up the song, some in words and some without, a harmony building naturally into something greater.

Just as in Hellevan Chapel, some people mourn aloud. There have been many lives lost to the war, after all. But even in the mourning there is hope, and relief. I hear it in the gliding melody, sense it in the reverberation of low voices.

I don't sing. But I hum along to the music of the man beside me.

Malec hears me and reaches over to clasp my hand, his dark eyes alight with love and joy.

We don't need to speak elaborate words to each other. We did that on our wedding day, and those vows still echo in my mind.

I love you beyond reason, with all the persistence of revenge and all the violence of hate. I love you into the deepest dark and under the harshest light.

I bled, and the blood reminded me that I was alive, that I was more than the dark hope to which I clung. I want to stay awake, for you. Alive, for you.

As I think the last words, a delicious flush of power surges through my body, rolling outward from my heart to my fingertips.

I inhale, startled and blissful. When I look down at my hand, clasped with Malec's, my skin has a golden glow, and his fingers are bathed in green light.

Never have I felt more alive, or more perfectly whole. I laugh aloud, and Malec does too, before leaning in to kiss me softly.

As we kiss, waves of light pulse outward from the two of us, rolling up through the tiers of worshipers, illuminating every Fae with an instant burst of magical energy, bathing the humans in a surge of peace and hope.

The song falters as the worshipers gasp and exclaim. But they don't leave. They stay, resuming the song, more joyfully this time.

Blissful and overwhelmed, I turn to Malec. And I'm shocked to find that tears are trailing down his cheeks.

"Aura," he whispers. "I have never felt such hope."

I lace my fingers with his, relishing the sensation of magic refilled, watching our friends glow and smile and sing.

I can hardly believe I'm here. Liberated from the curse, without fear of the realm's imminent collapse, sitting beside the Void King—my husband—my fellow Conduit, my partner in magic, lover and friend. I have no mothers to please, no Royals to revere, no Princess to guard.

I'm free. I think I could fly... and maybe someday, with the help of my new magic, I will.

A winged shape blots out some of the stars overhead, and at first I think it's the Guardian, soaring in the distance. But it's a raven, who descends to perch on my knee, surveying me with one round black eye. When I reach out, the bird lets me pet its ebony feathers. A link quivers between my mind and its consciousness, and though the tenuous connection slips away before I can grasp it, I know that with time and training I'll be able to summon and speak with ravens as Malec does.

I grin at my husband, and he winks before pulling me close, wrapping his wing around me.

After a moment's hesitation, I let my head tilt against his shoulder.

We rest there, my maleficent lord and I, while the stars glisten in the Void and the song awakens the goddess in the hearts of our people.

MORE BY
REBECCA F. KENNEY

The IMMORTAL WARRIORS adult fantasy romance series

Jack Frost
The Gargoyle Prince

Wendy, Darling (Neverland Fae Book 1)
Captain Pan (Neverland Fae Book 2)

Hades: God of the Dead
Apollo: God of the Sun

Related Content: *The Horseman of Sleepy Hollow*

The PANDEMIC MONSTERS trilogy

The Vampires Will Save You
The Chimera Will Claim You
The Monster Will Rescue You

For the Love of the Villain series

The Sea Witch (Little Mermaid retelling with male Sea Witch)
The Maleficent Faerie (Sleeping Beauty retelling with male Maleficent)

The SAVAGE SEAS books

The Teeth in the Tide
The Demons in the Deep

These Wretched Wings (A Savage Seas Universe novel)

The DARK RULERS adult fantasy romance series

Bride to the Fiend Prince
Captive of the Pirate King
Prize of the Warlord
The Warlord's Treasure
Healer to the Ash King
Pawn of the Cruel Princess
Jailer to the Death God
Slayer of the Pirate Lord

The INFERNAL CONTESTS adult fantasy romance series

Interior Design for Demons
Infernal Trials for Humans

MORE BOOKS

Lair of Thieves and Foxes (medieval French romantic fantasy/folklore retelling)

Her Dreadful Will (contemporary witchy villain romance)

Of Beasts and Bruises (A Beauty & two Beasts retelling)

Printed in Great Britain
by Amazon

23541500R00185